Alien

Efrain Palermo

Printed by CreateSpace, an Amazon.com company

Look for the second book in the *ALIEN CARTEL* series
- ***TIDES OF RETRIBUTION*** -
by Efrain Palermo

Dedicated to Mac Tonnies
a fellow traveler who left too soon

Published by Exoplanetary Press • Copyright © 2013 by Efrain Palermo
Second edition printed March 2014 • Cover design by Efrain Palermo

All of the characters and events in this book are fictitious, and any
resemblance to actual persons, living or dead, is purely coincidental.
No part of this book may be reproduced, stored in a retrieval system, or
transmitted in any form or by any means, electronic, mechanical, photocopying,
recording, or otherwise, without the prior permission of Efrain Palermo.
All Rights Reserved. ISBN-13: 978-1494409081

"Nothing is so firmly believed as that which is least known."
- *Michel de Montaigne, 1580 A.D.*

Prologue

The old man lay helpless, unable to move. Cold sweat matted his sparse, gray hair. Fear oozed from his sleeping body and condensed on the floor of his small hut. The shaman was knee deep in a nightmare. His dream paralysis nailed him to his bed as he was attacked and overwhelmed by large, blue insects. Their gaping mouths spewed forth a toxic dark blue smoke. His skinny, veined arms jerked in his sleep as his eyelids fluttered.

Despite his old and frail body he had a warrior spirit. He fought valiantly but he was losing this dream-battle. A cockroach the size of a chair gnawed on his arm. His other hand was crushed in the mouth of a man-sized praying mantis. Its large, angled eyes looked at him with an otherworldly intelligence. The shaman struggled to get away. His body thrashed about in his sleep and his struggles finally woke him up. He opened his eyes, relieved that he was awake, but he was not in his room.

Instead of the simple furnishings of his hut, he was in a dark cave with a floor of molten lead. The stench of sulfur singed his nostrils and burned his eyes. Hot bubbles of lead burped an eerie, dark blue powder that settled on his skin. The particles morphed into microscopic insects, which then burrowed into his body. Horrified, he frantically looked around for a way out, but there were no exits on the cave walls. With a superhuman effort of will, he awoke from the second nightmare and opened his eyes again. This time, the bare walls of his hut greeted his half opened eyes. The late-morning sun was burning a hole through his small, dirty window. He was usually an early riser, but this morning his dream had kept him under longer than usual. The shaman was not a stranger to unusual dreams, but this one had shaken him.

Unconsciously, he rubbed his arm, half expecting to find it chewed off and his blood crawling with insects. The shaman reached for a drink from the bowl he kept by his bed, but it was not there. It was on the other side of the room, upside down in a pool of water. He had knocked it over there in his sleep.

Whenever he took his Ayahuasca brew, his soul was transported into realms beyond his wildest imagination. In his trances there were symbols to interpret or future events to unravel. His dreams, good or bad, were prophetic. This time, the shaman was at a loss on how to interpret his grotesque dream.

He stood up from his straw bed, staggered and almost fell. He started to go outside but changed his mind and sat down in his chair instead. His body trembled and his breathing was fast and shallow. He took a deep breath and held it for a minute before he exhaled. A prayer escaped his lips to ward off evil spirits. The ancient invocation, which predated the Incas, was very powerful and he rarely used it. The shaman repeated it ten more times until he felt safe enough to relax. When he regained his composure he rewound the dream and looked at it again. This time he was able to read the portents in the nightmare. What he saw unnerved him.

A dog barked in the distance followed by the laughter of village children. Life was going on outside of the walls of his hut, uninfluenced by his horrific dream. People were going through their morning routines. They were oblivious to the future he had foreseen. As a prophet, he was always faced with the responsibility of telling the truth about the future. Should he tell someone that they were going to die a gruesome death in six months, or let them go on living ignorant and content until that time came? Outside of his window he saw children happily chasing a dog. He smiled and decided to let people enjoy what little time they had left. The shaman closed his eyes and settled into his chair. '*It may not be too late to change the future if I can understand the past.*' The shaman left his body and traveled the rivers of time to uncover the beginning of the end of human civilization.

Chapter One

Deep in a Colombian jungle, a group of peasants worked silently as they processed tons of coca leaves into cocaine. The workers included men, women, and young kids. A pregnant mother was working alongside her children. They needed to feed their families and it made no difference whether they picked coffee berries or stuffed gasoline filled drums with coca leaves. In the dark hours after midnight, the warm rain made the plastic wrapped cocaine bricks as slick as giant jungle slugs.

Ten cartel guards surrounded the workers and supervised the operation. The men on watch had AK-47s, Israeli IMI Galil assault rifles and sawed-off shotguns. On the perimeter of the clearing were two men with rocket-propelled grenade launchers perched on their shoulders. On a small hill, a bunker was manned with two .50 caliber machine guns. The excessive armament was not for the workers, who could easily be cowed with a harsh look or a swift kick. The heavy security was for the rival gangs and the Colombian police, who wanted large busts to give them the illusion that they were winning the war on drugs.

Under a mildewed tarp, a long table was being used to make bricks of cocaine. A carefully measured amount was packaged in layers of plastic wrap. A drawing of the cartel's logo, a golden poison dart frog, was inserted before it was tightly wound with clear packing tape. The completed products were then hauled over to a Russian built submarine moored in the river fifty yards away. The loaders had to wade through thick, sticky mud to get to it. The cartel men were in a rush, twenty tons of cocaine had to be loaded before the high tide. The submarine cost the cartel five million dollars, but with it they made over one hundred million dollars profit. It was an investment worth the small army that protected it.

The guards were uneasy and on high alert for the *policia*.

The dense canopy of the jungle choked out any ambient light. Dark clouds and a misty rain gave the operation added cover. A helicopter could hover right above them and would not be able to see what was going on. However, it only took one informant with a GPS unit tracked by the Drug Enforcement Administration, to make the jungle cover meaningless.

The sound of a military helicopter filtered faintly through the verdant forest. The guards froze and signaled the workers to stand still and be quiet. The echoes of spinning blades came closer and then slowly faded as it moved away from their location. The guard's fingers relaxed on well-worn triggers and the workers nervously continued to load the submarine. Slowly the tide came in and lifted the heavily laden sub off the muck of the riverbank. Hurriedly, the last of the bricks were loaded and the workers were sent away with the few pesos they had made for their night's work. A sealed envelope was given to the submarine captain. He keyed the secret coordinates into his iPad marine navigation app for a rendezvous with a container ship off the coast of Puerto Rico. The guards were breaking camp when a distant light glimmered through the canopy. It was below the tree line and moved silently. Instantly the leader gave hand signals to set up defensive positions. In the war against drugs, any form of surveillance could be used against them, including muffled drones.

The illumination in the distance moved slowly and erratically, as if searching for something. The light blinked on and off from yellow-white to a dark blue. The guards were not tech savvy, but they knew the federales used advanced, American supplied electronics to find them in the thick jungle.

The light faded as the aircraft lost its scent and started to move away from them. It dimmed and then suddenly disappeared. The men's pupils had adjusted to the luminous source and its sudden departure made the darkness thicker. The singsong coqui of mating frogs started up again. The guards were on high alert. Their breathing was quick and shallow, the thump-thump of their heartbeats drowned out the ambient jungle sounds. Just as they began to relax, a bright light flooded them from above the river. Blinded by the sudden illumination, they fired in its general direction. Assault rifles went on full automatic and sent a cloud of bullets. The .50 caliber machine guns spat out forty rounds a minute. Bullets ricocheted off the hull of the unknown craft with high-pitched pings. Rocket propelled grenades hit the ship and the jungle lit up like an illegal fireworks display.

There was a loud boom from the unidentified flying object that eclipsed the small arms fire. An intense purple flash and black smoke filled the air. Something in the vehicle had exploded. The sound of tortured metal cut the air as it flew by overhead. It was low enough to snap off the topmost tree branches. A gust of wind sent shredded leaves and twigs to the men below. The craft angled downward into the jungle and disappeared. A tremor shook the ground beneath the men's feet followed by a concussive blast of air.

The raucous firefight had deafened the men and left their ears ringing. In the abrupt silence, the men's heavy breathing filled the air as they tried to regain their composure. No one moved. The guards were tense and looked for another target. Surveillance aircraft never flew alone and the men were ready to attack or flee. The click-click sound of replaced magazines filled the air for a few seconds and then it was quiet again. After five minutes of holding still, the men's nerves settled down. The urgency of getting the sub launched took over. The tide was fully in and the sub was afloat. The captain had hidden behind some trees with his crew when the fighting started. As one, they ran into the sub and started up the diesel engines. With a puff of black smoke, the mini-sub slowly churned its way down river. The guards stood watch until it turned a bend of the river and disappeared from view.

Their job done, they turned to investigate what they had shot down. A downed US military drone was worth a lot of money to the Russian mafia. The prospect of making a few extra pesos on the side spurred the guards to make their way to the wreckage hidden somewhere ahead in the jungle. The coming dawn exposed the debris trail and damaged trees, which led directly to the crash site. The men followed the trail in single file cautiously, with the safeties off their weapons.

An opening of broken trees revealed the ship straight ahead. Dull gray metal contrasted coldly against the dark green foliage. Surprisingly, there were no wings or propellers on the craft. It was unlike any drone they had ever seen. The guard leader, Alejandro 'Chimbo' Muñoz, radioed the base dispatcher. To his surprise, the head of the cartel, Raul "Cojones" Melendez, was on the other end of the line.

"*Jefe*, a drone came up on us just as we finished loading the sub." Alejandro explained breathlessly.

"What the fuck! How did you let that happen?" The anger in Raul's voice sent cold shivers down Alejandro's neck.

"I don't know, *jefe*. It snuck up on us, but we shot the shit out of it and it crashed. We are coming up on it now" Alejandro tried to sound calm, but it was not working.

"*Pendejo*, secure any of its electronics and equipment. I'm sending a helicopter over to bring it to the compound. Hurry up before it gets too light!" Alejandro acknowledged his boss with a heavy sigh and clipped the phone back on his belt.

The guards approached the craft and surrounded it. Close up it was larger than expected and too big to be a drone. The craft did not have any visible means of propulsion. There were no propeller blades, jet engines or wings. The men figured the trees must have ripped off the wings. The nose of the ship was stuck in the jungle floor but it still looked imposing. It was twenty feet wide and thirty-five feet long. It was shaped like an oval plantain. It was thicker around the middle and all of its edges were smooth curves. Alejandro walked up to the ship and his nose twitched at the scent of ozone. He tentatively touched the hull. The metal looked cold but it was warm to his touch. A tingling sensation traveled through his fingers and made the hairs on his arm stand up. When he pulled his hand away, static electricity snapped back with an audible crack.

"The gringos must be desperate to build something like this just to track us," snickered one of the guards. The other men laughed nervously.

The craft was upside down. Alejandro ordered the guards to help him turn it over. Part of the ship lay across a broken tree stump and they used that as a fulcrum to flip it over. As it upended, a mangled hatch swung open and out fell a pilot, face down and unconscious. He was wearing a gray metallic suit with red stripes down the sides that gleamed in the early dawn light.

The man closest to the hatch pulled out his gun and climbed down. He turned the pilot over and screamed. He dropped his weapon and ran headlong into the woods, tripping on tree roots and looking back over his shoulder. The guards who were on the other side of the ship came over to investigate.

"¿!Carlito, que paso!?" One of them yelled after the man who had taken flight. But Carlito was already out of earshot. The guards reached the side where the pilot lay and froze with shock.

"Ay Madre!" Someone gasped out loud. Alejandro came up and pushed the men aside to see what was going on.

"¡Hijueputa!" Alejandro exclaimed.

The face was not human. The head was unnaturally bulged at the top and tapered down to a narrow chin. Its eyes were closed but it was evident that they were larger than normal. The strange pilot did not have a nose and had a small, lipless hole where the mouth should have been. Those initial impressions were bad enough but what was worse and set some of the men to mumbling prayers under their breath was its skin color. The skin was blue, but not the blue of the sky or a flower. It was the color of someone who had died from asphyxiation. It was a splotchy, organic blue that signaled death. Its chest moved rhythmically, it was breathing. The pilot was still alive.

One of the men who felt brave walked up to it and went down on one knee. He leaned in closer to get a better look. Above its closed eyes, the strange pilot had bulging, dark blue veins that reminded the guard of his grandmother's varicose legs. He sniffed and grimaced at the fetid mixture of methane and sulfur rising from the pilot's body. He hurriedly turned away and vomited.

"*¡Dios mio!*" Alejandro said aloud, his voice was tremulous. He fumbled for the phone on his belt and it fell to the ground from his shaking hand. He picked it up and called his boss.

"*Jefe*, there's a pilot and he's alive, I think. But ... " He hesitated to say what he saw.

"*¿Que?* Keep him alive until the helicopter gets there!" The cartel boss was already counting the US dollars he could get as ransom. Americans paid dearly for its downed pilots.

"But...but..." Alejandro's tone was subdued, "He's not a gringo, or *federales*. I don't know what the fuck it is, but it is not human."

Raul "Cojones" Melendez did not get to the top of a vicious drug cartel by being afraid or stupid. The fear he heard in his hardened underling's voice made him think twice before yelling a string of curses at the man.

"Ok, listen carefully. Tie him up. Remove anything from his pockets that can send a rescue signal. Do not kill him. If he needs killing, I want to be the one to do it." Raul tried to contain his temper, but it was difficult.

"The helicopter will be there in three minutes. Tie the aircraft to the helicopter straps. Then I want you and your men to come down here and report directly to me. Tell no one what happened or what you saw. Your men did well this morning. I received a text from the sub. It's safe and in open waters with no sign of pursuit. Make sure you get everything from the crash site. Before you leave cover your tracks and hurry the fuck up!"

"*Si, jefe.*" Alejandro ended the call and gave his instructions to his men. In the distance, the whoosh-whoosh of the approaching helicopter was a welcome sound.

Chapter Two

The base of the Melendez cartel was three miles south of Cali, Colombia. A narrow, unmarked road snaked through the jungle to the compound. The estate was a fenced-in expanse of one hundred cultivated acres. It had a palace built in the Spanish style that Louis the XIV, in the height of his decadence, would have envied. In the war between the cartels, Raul "Cojones" Melendez found a vacuum in the center where he could prosper.

With the help of a few million US dollars, Melendez had convinced the government in Bogotá to let him have his own zip code and police force. Like the Vatican, his estate was filled with exquisite, imported paintings and sculptures as well as the gaudy art of the locals. On one wall, track lighting on the ceiling lit up Raul's prize possession; a piece of an ancient cave wall painting. It had been illegally pried from a wall in the Lascaux Caves in France.

The compound had its own airfield and a hangar full of high performance private planes. There was a small zoo filled with exotic animals and birds. Raul was not an animal lover, but he enjoyed owning illegal and endangered species.

What did Raul "Cojones" Melendez do with millions of tax-free dollars? He did whatever the hell he wanted to. But Raul was also a student of history and he knew that holding power all to oneself was a recipe for disaster. Unlike Julius Caesar, he delegated power among his subordinates and gave back to the local community.

Raul sat on the balcony outside his bedroom sipping a cup of coffee. It was made from his own arabica coffee beans, which he grew and legally exported around the world. He opened up the El País newspaper and started browsing through the news. Raul did not get much sleep last night and woke up way too early. He lost track of what day it was. He flipped to the front page of the newspaper to check the day. It was Saturday, April 26. He thought it was Friday, he did not realize that April was almost over. Raul poured another cup of coffee and reminisced about his life.

Raul was born to a mother lying unconscious from a meth overdose. She died in the hospital the next day. With no other relatives, Raul became a ward of the state. At the age of three, a loving couple from Arizona adopted him. A year later, they realized they had made a terrible mistake. Raul was not a cute and cuddly kid. His eyes were squinted as if he were planning a heist. Raul was mean and a bully. He was kicked out of one daycare center after another. Out of desperation, the mom hired a nanny to take care of him at home. The nanny only lasted two days before she quit.

One morning while making coffee, the mother looked out the window and was shocked to see her cat by the kitchen door. It was dead and bloody. They had a security cam outside and reviewed and played back the recording. It showed Raul squeezing out through the dog door with a kitchen knife in his hand. They watched the video horrified as Raul coaxed the cat to him. He stabbed it six times and then calmly crawled back into the house.

They were mortified and realized they had adopted a devil child. The couple had adopted Raul to make a difference in a child's life. They came to the sad conclusion that he could not be brought up to be a good and productive person. He was damaged goods, they did not want to raise and harbor a criminal. Raul was bad even before he was born; his birth had only exposed the world to his evil.

With a heavy heart, they took a trip to Mexico with little Raul. In a small, dirty Mexican town, they left him on a church doorstep with a note pinned to his shirt. It stated in broken Spanish that his parents had died and to please take care of him. Attached to the note was an envelope with five hundred US dollars. They sat him on the steps of the church and gave him some tamarindo candy. The dad told him to stay there and they would be right back. They never returned. After a few hours, a group of teenage kids came upon Raul sitting by himself on the church steps. The teenagers found his note with the money attached. They beat him up, took the money and threw away the note. They laughed at him and kicked him a few more times. Thus began Raul's life on the streets. It had been a long, hard road from there to a cartel kingpin.

Raul heard the incoming helicopter before he saw it. It merged with the sounds of breakfast being cooked and the morning activities of the compound. It grew louder as it neared. He finally saw the whirling blades, a golden halo of reflected sunlight.

The sun warmed his tanned face. His deep dark eyes, dark hair and light skin were typical of the people of South America. He was not as fit as he used to be. He had put on a few extra pounds courtesy of his rich, pampered lifestyle. He was handsome, but his line of work and the viciousness with which he conducted his business, had tainted his good looks with cruelty. Raul's world was filled with kidnapping, murder, informants, and revenge killings. But what had happened earlier this morning had unnerved him. Raul changed from his sandals into his Italian shoes and prepared to go out to the helipad. He instructed his lieutenants to ready the interrogation room and ordered another crew to pull out his private Pilatus PC-21 plane so they could use the hangar to store the remains of the crashed craft.

From the balcony he saw his twelve-year-old daughter, Juanita, playing in the courtyard. She was dancing around her nanny, flapping her arms and singing. She wore a brightly colored layered dress, with yellow, green and black stripes. To complete her outfit, she had on a long red sash with white fringes. Red Mexican Tithonia flowers were pinned to her chest and hair. As gaudy as the outfit was, it looked sweet on her.

Raul had been in love only once in his life. His mistress Eliana became the love of his life and bore them a child, Juanita. Raul loved his little girl. Cruel as Raul was, this woman and child had found a tiny place in his heart. One day, while Eliana was shopping in Bogotá with Juanita, a rival gang member recognized them. Kidnapping the mother and child and demanding money from Raul in exchange for their lives, seemed like a good idea at the time. They were wrong. When Raul received the ransom note he flew into a rage. He rounded up a platoon of his hit men and found the kidnapper's hideout. In the gun battle, three of the kidnappers were killed and two were wounded. Eliana was killed in the hail of bullets. Juanita was unhurt, but she was traumatized. The wounded kidnappers lasted four days before their tortured bodies finally gave out. That was the last time Raul had fallen in love.

Raul leant over the balcony balustrade and yelled to the nanny, "Sofia, take Juanita into the house right now!"

"Hola Papi!" Juanita waved to him as she was being pulled away. Raul smiled and waved back. He did not want her to see what the helicopter was bringing in.

*

Raul and ten of his men were armed and ready on the helipad. They shielded their faces from the helicopter's downwash as it gently lowered the alien craft hanging from its straps near the hangar door. After the ground crew undid the cargo straps, the helicopter landed on the helipad nearby. The blades were still spinning as Raul rushed to the craft. He peered through the door at the unconscious pilot strapped to its seat. In the back of the helicopter were two guards who wanted to be as far away as possible from the blue abomination.

Raul nodded silently. *The men were right, this is not a gringo or anything human, but what is it?* Two men brought a gurney up to the side of the helicopter. The unconscious pilot was laid out and tied to the stretcher. In the morning sun its blue color looked natural. Raul looked closer. It was not make-up or tattoos. Raul had only seen that skin color on decayed corpses. To see that sick, blue hue on a living creature disturbed him and raised the hackles of his humanity.

The alien's craft was moved into the hangar, away from the eyes of any federales or US drones. The huge hangar doors were closed and locked. A heavily armed guard was posted at the door. Raul followed his men and the litter into the house and then down to the sub-basement. Inside the soundproofed interrogation room, the guards and Raul surrounded their prisoner whom they had propped up limply in a chair.

"What is it?" Raul asked out loud. One of his deputies, José 'Papo' Morales, raised a hand diffidently.

"*Jefe*, I know what it is." José was a frequent listener to Coast-to-Coast AM and a firm believer in UFOs and extraterrestrials. He wore his hair unnaturally combed and styled like his favorite 'Ancient Aliens' show host. Everyone in the room turned to him.

"It's an alien from outer space." He said matter-of-factly. One of the men snickered in the background, but it was more out of fear than derision. The strangeness of the downed craft and the face of the alien were proof enough. Raul's first thought was the loss of any US ransom money. He pulled up a chair and sat closer to the alien. The rest of the men, though they were armed and deadly, kept their distance. Many of them crossed themselves and muttered prayers to Santa Muerte, the Mexican Saint of Death. Raul was as scared as the rest of them, but like a wolf, he did not show fear in front of his pack. Raul swallowed down the bile that rose in his throat, soured with the coffee he had drunk earlier.

Up close, Raul noticed more differences between the alien and humans. He had seen people deformed through birth or accidents. No matter what the deformity was, he could still tell they were human. This creature was different. It had a head, two arms, two legs, and hands but any resemblance to humanity ended there. The closed eyes were unnaturally large and spaced too far apart. It didn't have a nose or ears. It looked very strange, missing those everyday, human features. The small lipless mouth could not open very wide to eat much of anything. Its bulging head and narrow chin accentuated the differences that could only happen if a species was spawned on another planet.

Raul noticed something that he had not seen earlier. The

alien did not have any genitals. It was wearing a skin-tight suit made of a very light, metallic fabric. There was no bulge of a scrotum between its legs. Even a tiny cock would have been noticeable through that thin fabric. There was only a smooth flat area between its legs. It reminded Raul of a Ken doll with its politically correct lack of genitalia. The creature looked male, except for that part.

"¡Mira, no tienes verga!" Raul laughed as he pointed between the alien's legs. The men in the room chuckled. If there was one thing that defined *un hombre*, it was his manhood. The status of the alien went down a few notches in that room full of macho men. If Raul ever got into a fight with the alien, he would be sure not to kick it between its legs.

The Vatican had recently made a statement that God in his infinite glory, had created all life in the Universe and therefore, they were all subject to his love. If the Pope could see this blue monstrosity, he would retract that statement and live the rest of his life sealed in his glass cage. Raul thought wryly. The alien's hands seemed normal enough. Evolution had clearly determined that fingered hands were the best way to grasp things. The fingers were of equal length and had no fingernails. The fingertips were wider and fleshier than a human's. After a few minutes of silently scrutinizing the alien, Raul relaxed a little. Even the men in the room came closer to look at it. They had unconsciously held their breath. As they breathed in, the alien's pungent odor filled their nostrils.

Raul poked the alien's chest with his extended finger. Without warning, the creature sat bolt upright and opened its eyes. The sudden movement sent Raul reeling back in his chair. It tipped over, spilling him to the floor and taking down a man who was right behind him. One of the men, who had his finger on the trigger and the safety off on his .40 caliber Glock 27, jerked and fired a round accidently. The gunshot added to the surreal horror of the moment. Time slowed down to a standstill and then continued its normal pace. Everyone in the room looked at the alien to see what it was going to do next.

After it had moved the alien stood still. The loud sound did not seem to affect it. Its eyes were wide open as if it was afraid. Fear was a universal emotion and a language the men knew very well. They had seen it countless times in the people they had tortured and killed. Despite its inhuman strangeness, the face of fear was something the men could relate to.

Its opened eyes revealed large pupils, bluish-black in color. The sclera was charcoal black, unlike the white of human eyes. It was very unnerving to look at. Raul sent a scathing glance at the man who had fired the shot. Raul then noticed his favorite bird was dead in its cage. It was a beautiful and endangered green and blue Motmot bird. It must have died from the shock of the gunshot. Raul looked back at the errant shooter with an icy look that said, 'You will not be alive by day's end!'

Raul got up from the floor, picked up his chair and positioned it again in front of the alien. The fear in the alien's eyes emboldened Raul. This was familiar territory, Raul and his men with guns drawn and their victims cowering. The rest of the men relaxed too.

Now what? Raul did not care that science and humanity could benefit from the technology of this grotesque, but advanced being. He was not thinking of the scientists around the world who would have given anything to study its make up and civilization. Raul did not give a shit about the myriad questions philosophers and astronomers had pondered for millennia about life out in the universe. Raul's mind was focused on how to make millions selling his drugs without getting busted.

"Who are you?" Raul asked, as he stared directly into its eyes. No response. Maybe it didn't know Spanish. He repeated his question again in English. Again, there was no response. Raul had a man ask it the same question in Portuguese and French. Still, there was no reaction, not even a blink. It sat unmoving. A slight movement of its chest was the only sign that it was alive and not a wax museum monstrosity. Raul noticed that it did not have any ears. Perhaps it might not be able to hear me.

An idea occurred to Raul. He told one of his men to bring in

Eduardo, a prisoner who was locked up in another room. Eduardo had been found with a DEA issued GPS unit. After being interrogated for three days he confessed to his duplicity. He had been kept alive and tortured. Eduardo was brought in, barely conscious and held up by two men. Raul motioned the guards to bring the prisoner closer. His eyes were barely open but he saw the alien sitting there, looking intently back at him. He had hoped that his long days of torture and torment would finally be over. Instead, Eduardo was face to face with a demon. He let out a sigh that sounded like a death rattle. Without a word, Raul put his .50 caliber, customized Desert Eagle gun against Eduardo's head and fired. His head disappeared in a red and pink misty splash. The echo of the shot was still reverberating in the room as Raul pointed the gun between the alien's weirdly spaced eyes.

Its reaction was immediate. The alien's large eyes opened even wider. The waves of fear that emanated from it were so strong that one of the men peed his pants. The force of its emotion stuck to them like thick mud. It emitted emotional wavelengths no human being could possibly experience without dying first. The men shuddered and their knees buckled.

"No me mates." The alien said in Spanish. Some of the men heard it in English... "Don't kill me."

Now, we're getting somewhere Raul thought to himself as he lowered his gun and smiled.

Chapter Three

Raul ordered food and a case of Tecate beer for himself and his men. This was going to be a long day. A cleanup crew took away what was left of Eduardo's body. Raul's mind was racing with endless possibilities. What were the chances of a UFO coming within gunshot of his operation in the jungle and then crashing with its pilot still alive? If the government had found it, they would have kept the crash a secret and hogged the alien and any technological treasures for themselves.

Many Mexicans and South Americans believed in UFOs but Raul had never seen one himself. He was wholly preoccupied with the cartel's business and did not give a crap about what was flying overhead unless it was a DEA drone or a Colombian Special Forces helicopter. The stars above were mere points of light, too far away to care about.

The various cartels throughout South America and Mexico were always vying for the next best way to get drugs across the border into the US and abroad. As soon as the DEA busted one smuggling operation, two new ones opened up. Still, it cost the cartels a lot of money and time to keep one step ahead of the DEA. Then there were the smaller, local cartels to worry about. They were constantly trying to take over his operation rather than build their own. *"Maricones!"* He cursed out loud at them as he thought it through.

Raul realized that the alien craft had come upon his men quietly and unseen. If not for the lights, it would have been undetectable. He wondered if the Alfonso Bonilla Aragón International Airport in Cali had picked up the craft on their radars.

"!Oiga! Juan," Raul addressed the man in charge of booking flights for him and his men. "Call the airport and find out if they noticed anything unusual on their radar this morning. Bribe or threaten them, I don't care which, but find someone who will

talk!" Juan hurried off to run his errand.

Meanwhile, the alien had stopped broadcasting its fear. It had sensed that something had changed and it was not going to be killed outright. The alien sat still, barely breathing. Its large eyes, which never blinked, looked at Raul the way a respectful but fearful dog looks at the master who beats it. It had not said another word since its first utterance. Raul knew he must choose his next words carefully. Time was on his side. Raul glanced at the clear, warm skies outside the only window in the room. He was relieved there was not a horde of UFO's in the skies above his compound.

If the alien had a backup or an extraction team, they would have been all over his compound by now. Raul relaxed and continued his train of thought. *This alien came from a far away place and its technology is clearly far superior to anything on Earth. What if I could use their technology to get my drugs delivered undetected? They must have weapons that are more effective and less messy than that Desert Eagle pistol.*

Raul used the one thing he knew he had over the alien, its fear. He went over to a nearby table strewn with interrogation tools. He chose a pair of pruning shears that were stained and rusted with the blood of fingers it had lopped off. Raul sat down next to the alien and picked up a pencil that was on the table nearby. He held it up to the alien's face and clipped it cleanly through the middle with the shears. Looking directly into the alien's eyes, Raul picked up its right hand with his left. The alien's hand had no warmth to it. It looked like normal, smooth skin but it had the scaly feel of a reptile. Raul grabbed a finger, extended it and made a movement to cut it off. The alien hurriedly retracted its hand as waves of fear emanated from it. Raul smiled to himself. It did know fear.

"Who ... " Raul rephrased his question and spoke louder, "what are you?"

"I am a being from a distant planet." The alien answered quickly. Its hands shook visibly.

"What are you doing here?" Raul asked it brusquely.

"We are in need of a metal which is rare on our world, but is plentiful on yours. I came to your planet to establish a trade agreement. I did not want to cause any alarm and I carefully followed your river until I could make contact. My life detectors indicated that your men were nearby. I came over to introduce myself and that's when they shot me down." There was a hint of indignity in its voice.

The alien had talked without moving its lipless mouth. Raul had not realized it at first but the alien had communicated telepathically. It sounded as if it had spoken directly into his ear. If Raul did not look at its mouth, he could have sworn it was speaking normally. The UFO aficionado, José 'Papo' Morales was in the room. His eyes were as wide as the alien's as he listened to it 'talk' into his mind.

"¡*Oye* Papo!" Raul's voice broke José out of his reverie.

"Come over here." José went over and sat next to his boss.

"Papo, you know all about this UFO shit. What do you think about what it said?" Raul asked him.

"I think it's legit. I've seen a lot of shows about aliens and I can tell you, this one is for real." José nodded vigorously. He was very proud of his esoteric knowledge. Raul faced the alien again.

"I am one of the most powerful men on this planet. I can get you anything you want, if you have something that I want." Raul was as cunning as he was deadly. He waited patiently for its answer.

"When planets form around a star, they inherit the metals and minerals of the star that seeded it. Some planetary systems are richer in some elements and poorer in others. In our star system, the heavy elements are plentiful, but not the lighter ones." Raul heard it in his mind in perfect Spanish.

Raul understood every word it said but he had no idea what the hell it was talking about. He turned back to José 'Papo' Morales, his expert in 'all things not of this world.'

"Papo, do you know what the hell it is talking about?"

"*Si jefe*, I have heard of this and I understand what it is saying. What is abundant on our world, may be scarce on theirs." José said with an air of someone who was finally important. He had spent countless hours listening to podcasts and surfing the web and he was well versed in the subject. Raul nodded his thanks to José and motioned him away.

"So, what is it that you lack on your world that we have plenty of?" Raul asked the extraterrestrial.

"*Aluminum,*" it said without hesitation. Raul was taken aback. Maybe its telepathic, no-mouth-moving way of talking isn't working right. The alien said it needed aluminum, one of the least expensive and plentiful metals around, could this be for real? Raul's devious mind went into high gear.

"That is a very difficult metal to get. It is true that it is abundant, but it is very hard to extract. It will not be easy to collect and transport it. So tell me, what do you have that would be as valuable to me, as this metal is to you?"
The alien cocked its head and appeared to be thinking.

"*What do humans want but is difficult to get?*" The alien was clearly trying to find a point to negotiate from.

Raul pondered its question. He thought of all the things he supplied and what people wanted. He replied with the one thing that truly answered its question.

"People want the powder that my business produces, but it is very difficult to make enough of it to handle the demand." Raul managed to say that with a straight face. The alien appeared thoughtful.

"*In my ship there is a small, hand held device with three blinking red lights. It is my communication link to the mother ship that is in orbit around your planet. I will need it to confer with my superiors. I think we may be able to help you with your problem.*"

One of Raul's men retrieved the communicator. It was slightly larger than an iPhone but much denser. It had intricate, electronic circuit type patterns on its surface and three blinking red lights. As soon as the device was handed over to the alien, two of the lights pulsated with a dull, green color. The alien held the communicator up to where its ears should have been and seemed to go into a trance. It was obviously in touch with the mother ship above. After five minutes of this silent conference, the alien came out of its trance.

"My superiors have gone over everything that we could offer as trade which would match your needs. Our race is very advanced in technology and biological engineering." It paused, as if for dramatic effect. *"Our scientists can create an additive which can be mixed with your product. It would make your powder more potent and increase the users desire for it."* The alien's aspect went from fear to the practiced air of a trade negotiator.

Raul could not believe his luck. This could make his brand of cocaine better than the competition and it would only cost him a couple of aluminum beer cans. He could rule the entire drug trade with the alien's additive. But Raul was not done yet. He was going to squeeze this alien sucker for all it was worth.

"This thing you can add to my powder is good. But by itself, it is meaningless unless I solve two other problems." Raul moved closer to emphasize what he was saying.

"One of the problems of my business is distribution. Our planet is rugged and full of many obstacles. We have a difficult time getting our powder quickly to the people who need it. If you could supply us with a few of your space vehicles, that would be worth a lot of aluminum to me."

The man Raul had sent to the airport had reported what he found out. At the time the alien craft was shot down, only scheduled planes had shown up on the airport's radar. Every drug trafficker in Mexico and South America wanted a mode of drug transportation that was undetectable. The constant police surveillance forced cartels to build elaborate underground tunnels and pay small fortunes for sophisticated mini-submarines. An alien space ship that was undetectable to radar would give him a huge advantage.

The alien pondered Raul's request. The emotional level in the room turned a dark shade of greed.

'How much aluminum can you exchange for these items?'
"Thousands of pounds." Raul answered quickly.

"I believe we can work something out." It did not show any reaction to how much aluminum Raul had offered.

"We only have two shuttle ships and your men destroyed one of them. However we do have spare space drives and cloaking fields, enough to modify ten of your vehicles. What is this other problem?" It asked carefully.

"Our men better weapons to protect our goods from those who want to take them away from us." Raul almost pouted. He was putting on the act of the small businessman who was being bullied by larger competitors.

"We are not a warlike race. We are bio-engineers and traders. All we have to offer in the way of weapons are portable lasers." The alien radiated impatience. It sensed that it was being taken advantage of.

Raul realized he was getting way more than he had hoped for. Haggling too far could ruin everything.

"Ok, it's a deal." Raul's avarice seeped out of him like a dirty, wet mop. He rushed to ratify the negotiation before the alien caught on to him. He pulled a table over and surreptitiously put the shears away. He grabbed paper and a pen from a drawer and began to firm up the details.

Raul did not know what the alien was thinking or feeling. Its small round mouth did not have the muscles to make a smile and it never changed its expression. Its large dark eyes were like a hologram. From one direction Raul saw a helpless alien desperate to make a profitable trade agreement. From another angle, its black pupils reflected Raul as a small roach about to be stepped on by an ancient monster. Despite his misgivings, Raul wrapped up the deal.

Chapter Four

Raul allowed the alien to stay in contact with its mother ship, but had insisted it remained captive until after the drug ingredient was proven effective. Raul was no fool. He knew that he had no leverage on the alien or the ship in orbit. If he let it go now, it could simply leave and never come back. There was no way that Raul's extensive assassination network could follow it out into space.

The orbiting ship sent robotic couriers back and forth to the compound in the dead of night. Raul wanted to keep any spies from neighboring cartels, the Colombian police or the DEA from getting wind of what was going on. The alien had requested a live human as a guinea pig in order to synthesize the drug additive in their bio laboratory. It had informed Raul the test subject would not survive. Raul immediately gave the order to his men to get someone. Within ten minutes, a farmer who was working by himself in a nearby field was grabbed, blind folded and stuffed into the alien courier craft. He was never seen again.

Two weeks later a robotic courier delivered the completed additive. The alien extracted a metal box from inside the courier ship and opened it. The box had twenty vials filled with a bluish liquid. He brought the small bottles inside the warehouse, which held stacks of plastic-wrapped cocaine bricks.

"I thought you were going to manufacture a powder I could mix in with my product?" Raul was perplexed. The alien held the vial up to the light.

"*Our scientists did an extensive study of the biological makeup of the subject you gave us and analyzed the different products you provided. They concluded that the drug you call cocaine would be the best carrier. The transformation virus has been engineered to multiply in your powder and make it one hundred times more potent. As a bonus, it will not debilitate or destroy the host.*"

The alien opened the vial, which had a very narrow opening. It went over to a nearby table where a kilo of coke was cut open. Everyone looked on intently as it put a drop of the liquid on the white powder. Immediately, the blue droplet grew in size and then burrowed into the brick. Moments later the coke changed color from white to blue. Vapors rose from it and then dissipated like exhaled tobacco smoke. The alien announced that the process was complete.

Raul had two test subjects ready. One was a hard-core meth addict, complete with missing teeth, open sores and scraggly hair. He was found passed out in an alley. He was abducted and woke to find himself strapped in a chair face to face with a Halloween monster. The other person was a tourist from Germany. He had thought walking alone through the hills surrounding Cali would be a good way to get off the beaten path and meet the locals. Three armed men with bandanas covering their faces confronted him and asked him roughly if he took drugs. The German, who was a vegan and completely drug free, was glad to answer that he did not. Relieved that he would not be a threat to anyone's drug business, he turned around to continue on his hike. The masked men hit him over the head with a sapper and knocked him unconscious. He was blindfolded, cuffed and taken to the compound.

Raul wanted to see what effect the enhanced drug would have on a hopeless addict and as a control, someone who was totally clean. The two men were tied to their chairs and nervously awaited their fate. Raul took a small pinch of the transformed powder between his fingers. He forced open the mouth of the toothless meth addict and rubbed the powder inside his cheek. In seconds, the addict sat up straight and smiled for the first time in months. He looked around the room and asked out loud where his mother was.

"Why do you want to know where your mother is?" Raul asked him, a little freaked out by his sudden transformation.

"I want to tell her that I'm ok. Oh, and please sir..." He took a deep breath. "Can I have a pinch more of what you gave me?"

The addict spoke with a stronger voice than he had in years.

Raul ignored his request. He was satisfied that the drug, even in such a small dose, could affect a hard-core addict. Raul took another pinch of the bluish powder and approached the other prisoner. The German had seen what happened and kept his jaws tightly clenched. Raul grabbed his chin, and tried to open his mouth. But the tourist's terror kept his mouth shut like a bear trap. Raul punched him in the face, wrenched his mouth open, and rubbed the powder inside his cheek. Then he sat back to see what would happen. The German's head slumped forward and his breathing noticeably slowed down. After a few minutes he straightened up and spoke in German-accented Spanish.

"I apologize for resisting. I will not cause you any more trouble or say anything to anyone. Please, let me go," he pleaded. "I have a wife, kids, grandchildren and..." he hesitated and asked embarrassingly, "Can I have a little bit more?" Raul had not heard him. He absentmindedly told his men to take the two test subjects outside and let them go.

"How much of this virus can your lab make?" Raul was amazed at the virus' efficacy.

"Our laboratory can replicate the virus at the rate of twenty vials a day. We can make as much as you like." The alien's intent was clear. How much could be made depended on how much aluminum Raul could procure.

After an hour of tough negotiating, they settled on thirty pounds of aluminum per vial. Raul went over to a corner of the room where a dirty sheet covered a large, lumpy pile. He pulled the cover off with a flourish, which revealed a stack of pure aluminum bars. Raul's men had buffed and polished each one with aircraft polish. The reflected brightness cascaded through the dingy warehouse making the men squint. Raul looked askance at the alien who was staring at the bullion. The cold, silvery light sank into the alien's black pupils without any reflection, as if swallowed by a black hole. The alien's inscrutable strangeness was bared for a second. Raul had a peek into an alien soul and it unnerved him. He swallowed his uneasiness and turned away.

The alien managed to smile without any lips. It was clearly pleased. Raul ordered the guards to take the pallet of aluminum to the alien's courier ship and the alien handed over the vials. Raul extended his hand to seal the deal with a handshake. The alien did not understand the gesture and kept its arms by its side. After an awkward moment, Raul retracted his hand.

*

Raul wanted a brand name for his new product. In the early days of marijuana cultivation, Acapulco Gold was the most sought after pot on the market. The product's name, its gold color, and the quality of its high made it valuable. He wanted to make his brand of blue cocaine as famous as "Acapulco Gold" and he named it "Melendez Blue." Raul had an artist design a logo in the shape of an alien's head and made labels out of them. They were inserted in cocaine bricks and replaced the poison frog emblem. Raul directed his dealer organization to only sell Melendez Blue. He dropped from his inventory pot, meth, ecstasy and even pharmaceuticals. Melendez Blue quickly spread into the United States and Europe. In just one week, millions of people were already hooked on Raul's enhanced cocaine. Users began to call it *"Alien Blue"* unaware of its true nature.

Chapter Five

Raul had bribed three large aluminum companies in Colombia to order and transport the bullion. Customs would have become suspicious if thousands of pounds of aluminum were bought by a cartel. A steady flow of aluminum found their way to the Melendez compound, which was picked up nightly by the alien's shuttle.

The tainted coke was mass-produced, packaged and distributed via the cartel's chain of middlemen and dealers. Immediately, the appetite for 'Blue' exceeded his wildest expectations. The high volume demand taxed his distribution network and Raul was anxious to get to the next step of their deal. He called the alien into his office and sat him down. Raul still did not know its name. He had asked it once what it called itself. The alien said that its name could not be translated, so Raul just called it "Mr. Alien" derisively.

"Hey Mr. Alien, your drug virus is working great and the demand for it is increasing. Now I am ready for the second part of our agreement. I've seen how fast and silent your courier ship is. Your space ships are very advanced." Raul smirked to himself... before we shot it down. "Do we need to build a flying saucer for your space engines?"

The alien's tone was thoughtful. *"Your planet is very preoccupied with what they call UFO's and that type of craft would cause a panic. I suggest you use one of your common, wheeled modes of transportation. Our engineers could then install our drive engines in them. When they are not airborne, the vehicles can be parked outdoors without causing any alarms."*

Raul liked that idea and pondered what type of vehicle to use. When he was a kid, Raul saw a dusty aluminum Airstream travel trailer being towed behind a dilapidated pick-up truck. He imagined that the trailer was really a space trooper's spaceship in disguise and that image had stuck with him. The aluminum-skin would also show off his extravagance to the alien. He had his secretary order ten of them from eBay.

The trailers arrived a week later and that same night, a shuttle ship came down with engineers, their tools and portable space-engines. The extraterrestrial mechanics were short in stature, only about three feet high. They looked similar to the captured alien except for their skin, which was a dusty gray color and bumpy like a toad's. In just two days they transformed the travel trailers into UFO narco transport ships. The anti-gravity generators and the radar absorbing fields took up a small portion in the interior, which left a lot of room for cargo.

Raul created a crew from his experienced small plane pilots who were trained by the alien to fly the new drug ships. After the training was completed, the cartel's alien air fleet began their undetectable drug runs.

*

Eduardo was the Melendez drug middleman for New York City. He had worked with Raul for many years before getting promoted to the field. Eduardo had received a shipment of Raul's new drug and had given out test samples and sold a few kilos. He was receiving calls for more of the product and had set up a drop with the Dragons. The Black M.F. Dragons were a Puerto Rican gang that controlled a sizable chunk of the South Bronx. They were the major coke dealer in the area and had bought a kilo of Melendez Blue to try it out. The results were startling and clients wanted more. The gang leader contacted Eduardo and placed an order for twenty more kilos.

A meeting place was set up for the buy at midnight on the rooftop of an abandoned building on Fox street. Eduardo went to the rooftop an hour before the meeting and activated a beacon. It had been hand delivered to him by a Melendez courier. The courier said it was an alien device and it would guide the ship to him. Eduardo turned on the beacon and placed it on top of an old chicken coop. He lit a cigarette and waited.

The cartel aircraft hovered silently above LaGuardia Airport. Through the windows the crew saw the lights of planes coming and going. The drug ship was invisible to the radar of the aircraft and the airport below. The trailer's aluminum skin was camouflaged with black velour flocking paint. The pilot had to be careful not to get in the flight path of any planes. A green light on the console lit up, indicating that the beacon was activated. A 3-D heads-up display appeared in front of the pilot. A purple line extended from the yellow dot of their position to a red dot on the ground below. The pilot ignored the strange upside down hieroglyphics attached to the image. As he oriented the ship to the new position, the purple line turned green. The pilot proceeded to the rendezvous to deliver the twenty kilos of coke in the cargo bay.

On the rooftop, Eduardo anxiously scanned the skies for the approaching ship. Eduardo had not been at the compound for a while and had not seen Raul's alien or the new airships. Eduardo was looking southwest toward Manhattan when he felt a gust of wind behind him. He turned around and nearly jumped out of his skin when he saw the black travel trailer hovering in the air eight feet above the roof. It had appeared silently out of the dark sky. This was the first time he had seen one. He had been told what to expect, but it still surprised him. It was unnerving to see a trailer floating soundlessly in mid-air.

The door opened and a man inside threw out several heavy duffle bags onto the sticky, tarred roof. The hatch closed and the ship left as suddenly and as quietly as it had appeared. Eduardo opened up a bag and took out a coke brick. There was not much light on the roof but he could make out the blue, packed powder through the clear packing tape that wrapped it. A drawing of an alien's head on the brick looked back eerily at him in the darkness. Eduardo returned the kilo back in the bag. He took out his Beretta 92A1 pistol, checked it and put it back in its holster. He sat and waited for the gang leader to arrive while marveling at the craft he had just seen.

*

In a gang infested neighborhood in Portland, Oregon, the

kingpin of the local Crip gang, Larmaine "Chompers" Maurice, was meeting with his drug connection from Colombia. The Colombian agent was listening to Larmaine's concern about the high price of the new drug.

"Yeah this is expensive shit Larmaine, but it is a far more superior and expensive shit. Whoever tries it will want it more than anything else." The cartel distributor pointed to the open brick of bluish powder on the desk between them.

"I will only deal with you so that once word gets around, you will be the only distributor in all of Portland." Larmaine gave it some thought. His customer base ran from the well-to-do in Lake Oswego, to the crack-heads in his neighborhood alley. But his profits had diminished. It was hard to make a buck when drugs got cheaper and every swinging dick was slangin. The opportunity to have the corner on a drug no one else had was very tempting. Larmaine took the sample and ordered a kilo of Blue to try out on his clients. The scenario played out coast-to-coast and in-between, as the Melendez distribution organization planted the seeds of their new network.

*

It had been three weeks since 'Operation Melendez Blue' started. The demand for Raul's brand of coke began to affect the sales of other cocaine dealers. In Austin, Texas, the 'Mi Familia' Mexican gang leader was edgy and in a pissed-off mood. What was once a booming coke business had suddenly dried up. People stopped buying his product and it was starting to affect the gang's finances. He needed to figure out why their coke sales had dropped so drastically. The gang leader sent a team to bring in one of their regular drug addicts who had stopped buying from them. They found him sitting in a park, eating a half-eaten sandwich he had picked out of a garbage can. They forced him into a car and brought him in to be interrogated. After a few questions punctuated with the repeated use of a rubber hose, the addict confessed that he was now addicted to a different cocaine, Melendez Blue.

The gang chief asked around and found the source of the

new drug. He traced the blue bricks with the alien logo to a cartel in Cali, Colombia. 'Don't those pendejos know only Mi Familia's coke can be sold in Austin?' He was fuming when he made an encrypted call to Los Zetas, his Mexican coke supplier. It was time to set things straight.

Raul was having his lunch of lobster and champagne outside in the courtyard when one of his lieutenants rushed up to his table and asked to speak to him.

"¡Jefe!" Gasped the lieutenant, out of breath from running. "One of our informants just called me. A platoon of Los Zetas just crossed the border into Colombia and they are coming here for us!"

Raul had expected retaliation from the rival cartels, but not this soon. The Los Zetas were the most criminal, brutal, and militant group in all of Mexico. They were a band of rogue Mexican Special Forces soldiers trained in the weapons and tactics of that elite military group. Raul was not concerned. He had a storeroom in a secure basement filled with hundreds of the alien's blue vials. His new drug distribution network had been operating smoothly, unimpeded by drug enforcement agencies. Now was the time for the final part of his deal with the creature from outer space.

The alien was kept on a tight leash and it was not allowed to go outside the compound. During the day, it was kept under guard in a windowless room. Raul wanted to keep prying eyes from noticing a strange inhuman creature walking around his estate. At night, three henchmen closely shadowed the alien with orders to blow off its very large head if it made any move to escape. Raul ordered his lieutenant to bring the alien to him.

The alien was escorted to Raul's table and sat quietly while Raul kept eating. He finished off a large Maine lobster tail dipped in garlic butter and washed it down with chilled Chateau Neuf de Pape brut.

"Mr. Alien, my business is moving along very nicely with the help you have given me. I hope that the thousands of pounds of aluminum we provided was to your satisfaction?" Raul raised an eyebrow to emphasize his rhetorical question. The alien was impassive as Raul continued.

"Our drug is taking over the market and we are starting to attract the unwanted attention of my competitors. My men need superior weapons to protect our business. I will give you one thousand pounds of pure aluminum in exchange for your alien weapons. After this our agreement is fulfilled and I'll let you go."

The alien became animated, relieved at the prospect of finally leaving its prison. It used its communicator and after a silent minute, it responded in its telepathic voice.

"As I have stated before, we are not a warlike race. However, we do have small lasers we use for protection against wild animals on the planets we trade with. The technicians on our ship can modify thirty laser weapons for human use. My superior will give his approval on the condition we can take my crashed ship back with us. You will be allowed to keep the anti-gravity drives in your vehicles and the weapons. Our storage rooms are filled with enough aluminum to make us the richest clan on our planet." It gave a mental sigh, *'I want to get off this planet and go back home."* A hint of impatience seeped through its demeanor that Raul attributed to it being homesick.

Raul had enough vials to transform hundreds of tons of cocaine. The pure, blue cocaine was too potent in its raw form. At the processing plant, they had to cut the transformed drug down seventy-five percent with white, regular cocaine. Further on down the distribution chain, dealers would cut it again with baking soda, crushed sleeping pills or Levamisole, a drug used to de-worm animals. Even diluted that much, Melendez Blue was still more potent than anything else on the market. Raul already had enough of the transformed drug to make addicts out of entire countries for many years to come. With the alien's weapons, his conquest of the $400 billion drug market would be complete.

"It's a deal, I will have your ship and the final payment ready." This time, Raul did not bother to shake its hand. The alien put its communicator beside its head and after a few minutes, it said that a ship would land that night with the weapons.

The alien's damaged ship was on the tarmac along with a pallet of aluminum bullion. Raul had five heavily armed guards with him. One of the men pointed to a light in the sky that began to move side to side. A black triangular shape blocked out the stars as it loomed closer. It descended until it hovered silently a few feet above the heli pad. A hatch opened and a blue-purple glow came from inside the ship. The lint on the men's clothes lit up and their teeth glowed eerily. A ramp extended to the ground and an alien engineer in a red metallic outfit emerged with a large bundle. It laid the package down on the ground and went back into the ship. Raul's alien bent down, opened the package and pulled out a weapon. The gun looked like a geek's wet dream. It had semi-transparent coils and tubes wrapped around the muzzle. Overall, it was about the size of a Colt .45, but it looked more like a Hollywood prop than a real gun. The alien showed the weapon to Raul.

"This is a portable gamma ray laser. The beam it emits is invisible. To help with your aim, there are tracers imbedded in the gamma ray's beam." The alien reached out and flipped a toggle on the side of the laser gun.

"When you turn this switch, it takes it off safe-mode. This rapid blinking light on the aiming sight indicates that it is operational. The vibration you feel in the pistol grip will also let you know that it is ready to fire." The alien explained as if talking to a child.

Raul hefted the pistol. It vibrated in his hand and reminded him of his cell phone's buzz. He looked around for a target. Raul's guards flinched as the weapon swept over them. He settled on a herd of goats grazing alongside the edge of the airstrip. A dot of red light illuminated his target when he pulled the trigger. The goat yelped and looked up, its eyes wide with fear and pain. The goat leaped into the air and fell thrashing to the ground. Raul motioned one of his men to bring it over. The dead goat was retrieved and dropped at Raul's feet, it still twitched and smelled of seared flesh. It had a ten-inch hole right through its chest. There was no blood and the inside of the opening was neatly cauterized. There was a gaping hole in the goat's chest where the heart used to be.

Satisfied, Raul motioned the men to load the pallet of aluminum into the alien's ship. Two aliens exited the space shuttle and fastened the crashed ship to it with metallic straps. The now freed alien turned his back to Raul and without a word, boarded the ship. The other aliens followed and within minutes the craft rose silently with the damaged craft gently swaying underneath. It angled out across the ocean for a few miles and then zoomed straight up until it was swallowed by the black sky.

*

A sleek powerboat left a contrail of foam behind as it disturbed the Caribbean Sea's midnight calm. The 46-foot, 1,350 horsepower Mercedes-Benz cigarette boat was coming in from Puerto Rico. It had been a cartel workhorse transporting drugs from Colombia to Puerto Rico. The ever-increasing sophistication and patrols of the Coast Guard had kept it mothballed in a boat slip in San Juan. Raul had ordered the boat back for his own use. His small fleet of alien airships made drug-running boats obsolete.

The boat's pilot could see the lights of Cali on the horizon. He was happy to finally be coming home. He was looking for the beacon on shore to guide him in when a dark shadow caught his eye. He turned toward it and saw a black triangular shape rising slowly above the compound. It rose higher and then flew toward the boat at an incredible speed. The pilot was right underneath the craft's flight path. He had a clear view of it as it flew overhead. The underbelly suddenly opened and ejected a large, wooden crate. The portal closed and the craft flew straight up and left a donut shaped hole through the clouds. The package hit the water hard and barely missed the boat. The pilot clutched the gunnel as the boat rocked on the waves kicked up by the splashdown. The impact had ripped apart the wooden crate and revealed the aluminum bars it had inside. The sea greedily swallowed them in a maelstrom of gray foam and bubbles.

Chapter Six

Raul looked inside the weapons bag and found a sheet of instructions written in Spanish. Underneath the guns was a portable charging station. It was solar powered and was to be placed on a rooftop with clear access to the sun. It had docking stations for five weapons at a time. The sheet explained how a row of lights on the side of the gun indicated how much power it had. Raul checked and saw that the weapons were fully charged. One of his lieutenants, who had been keeping track of the Los Zetas' trek through the jungles of Colombia, came up to Raul and reported their location. The Los Zetas were in a part of the jungle Raul was familiar with. He was looking forward to trying out his new, alien arsenal. Raul called his hit team together and they boarded five of the trailer ships. He handed out the alien weapons and then boarded the lead ship. As one, they took off silently into the night and headed toward the oncoming enemy.

In minutes, they were over the Los Zetas trail. The ships hovered at three hundred feet, silent and invisible like giant bats. Gunners armed with their laser pistols and night vision goggles peered out of open doors into the jungle below. In the lead ship, Raul leaned out precariously from the ship's door. He scanned the openings through the jungle canopy with his military-grade night goggles. The elaborate headgear made him look like a mechanical alien. The ship's pilots and gunners were in communication with each other via wireless headsets. A pilot quietly whispered in his mic, there was a heat source to the north of him. Silently they floated to that location. Raul saw them first.

The Zetas' body heat glowed spectrally through his glasses. He quietly ordered two of his ships above the center of their column and he spread the others in front and back. On his command he ordered the firing to commence. It was eerie for the men who were used to the recoil of a normal gun. The laser weapons did not have any kickback when the trigger was pulled. It was like shooting a fake gun in a video game. The beam itself was invisible but tiny pulses of light acted as tracers sending a flurry of red dots through the leaves. The rays impacted silently. At first, the shooters didn't think they were hitting anyone. But the screams of men in agony from the jungle floor proved otherwise.

Raul had one of the Zeta men in his sights. He fired and the man's arm fell bloodless to the ground. The man was in shock and wondered why his arm was no longer attached to his body. The finger of his severed arm spasmodically pulled the rifle's trigger, which added to the confusion of the battle. Raul cut the man's leg off at the hip, toppling him over. Raul found another target and proceeded to slice that man up too. The battle was over in three minutes. The Los Zeta men had fired back into the jungle in vain. They were unaware that their death was coming from above.

Raul grinned wolfishly. That was fun! He landed his ship in a nearby clearing and walked up to the bodies and dismembered limbs scattered on the trail. Raul found a body with its head still intact and used his gun to cleanly cut it off. Raul was going to send the head to the Los Zetas headquarters with the Melendez logo pasted on its forehead.

After landing back at the compound, Raul was approached by Juanito, his second-in-command. The man who had been driving the cigarette boat was by his side.

"*Jefe*, this guy said he saw something strange on his way into port."

The boat driver explained what he had seen and that he thought it looked like bars of aluminum had splashed into the sea. Raul didn't say anything. He acknowledged the boat driver and sent him away.

Why would they toss their aluminum payment into the ocean? Raul frowned at the thought. It just didn't make any sense to him. Who knew how alien minds worked? Raul really didn't care. Though it was a strange occurrence, it was of no concern to him. Their deal was concluded. He paid them, they delivered the goods and now they were gone. Raul was left with a potential of untold wealth. Armed with superior alien technology, he was a force to contend with. Raul shrugged to himself and put aside the alien's strange behavior. His attention shifted to the reorganization of his drug network. He had big plans for taking down the other cartels and absorbing them into his empire.

The taste of his recent victory with the Los Zetas was still in his mouth. He called up the largest brothel in Cali and told them to bring all the women they had to the compound. It was time to reward himself and his men for a job well done.

Chapter Seven

Special Agent Paul Brittany was fidgeting in his chair. He was waiting to be briefed by the head of the Special Operations Division of the DEA, John Holcomb. A chart in the front of the room had pictures of the major Mexican and South American narco-traffickers. Scores of photos were labeled with DEA code words. The codes were confidential passwords, which opened encrypted computer files on each individual and group. Paul noted some of the pictures had a red X on them. Paul sipped his coffee and let his mind wander as his boss got things in order.

The drug bust yesterday went well. He had been tracking a dealer who was making a lot of money selling bad ecstasy pills to the party crowd in Ybor City, outside of Tampa. The dealer was getting the drug from a Mexican cartel that shipped it across the Gulf of Mexico into Tampa Bay. The Mexican jungle lab did not have good quality control and some of the pills had been killing teens at rave parties. It had been a tedious investigation but in the end, Paul got his man. He felt a glow of satisfaction, one less kid-killing drug dealer loose on the streets.

"Hello, Paul." John Holcomb sat down to start the briefing. Paul's mind snapped to attention.

"There is something very wrong going on in Mexico and South America. Drug bosses are being killed and the splintered cartels are being corralled under an organization based in Colombia run by the Melendez cartel. Many of the smaller drug gangs and even the bigger ones like the Los Zetas have been disbanded. Their leaders were killed and their cocaine distribution network was taken over by Melendez." He frowned as he continued.

"This isn't business as usual. When cartels fight each other for territory or they want to make a statement, they go around cutting off heads and dismembering people. The bodies go through the local coroner's office with a cursory inspection. But a corpse's strange wounds caught the eye of the coroner who then contacted the chief of the local police. He forwarded this picture to one of our agents in the field." John handed over a photo of a dismembered torso that was laid out on a stainless steel autopsy table. At first it looked like any other cartel killing. Paul's eyes squinted as he leaned forward to get a better look. The torso's stumps were less as if they had been cauterized. Stranger still, were the three large holes that went right through the body. The steel of the exam table was visible underneath. There was not any blood there either. John nodded slowly and sat back.

"They found a new way to torture, kill and intimidate their enemies. Our analysts discovered one particular gang, the Melendez cartel in Colombia, was consolidating all the cartels in South America and Mexico. Normally they hate each other and never work together. Cartels see their own gang as familia and the others as enemies." John shook his head. "I don't have to spell it out for you, this could be a big problem for the US, let alone Canada and Europe."

Paul nodded solemnly. It reminded him of how Genghis Khan ruthlessly forced warring tribes to unite under his banner and nearly took over the world.

"There's more, Paul." John sounded like a doctor telling his favorite patient that he only had three months to live. "We've uncovered a new, more potent form of cocaine out in the streets. It's a tinted brand known as Melendez Blue or Alien Blue. It's been cut with the usual crap, but we don't know anything about the color additive. The few cocaine bricks we confiscated had a label with the outline of an alien head. This could be a sly reference to 'aliens' crossing the border or someone's marketing idea to capitalize on the popularity of UFOs. In either case their product stands out and it's becoming popular." John handed over the pictures of the confiscated drug to Paul.

"The word on the street is that blue coke is better than any other drug around. It makes meth look like a high from eating chocolate. This drug is more potent than meth or crack but without any of the side effects." He sighed deeply. "We're getting reports of hard core addicts who switched to 'Blue' and actually got their shit together. They found jobs, brushed their hair, got dental work and started acting like citizens. The only thing is, they still had to have it. The upside is that instead of stealing their grandma's TV and pawning it for meth, they got responsible and found jobs."

Paul considered this statement. In all his years of busting crack heads and drug gangs, the only people he had seen who tried to be intelligent about taking drugs were the dealers themselves, most of whom did not even touch their own products. A crack head working at a job to buy drugs instead of stealing, that was unbelievable.

"There is one more piece to this puzzle." John opened another folder that was marked "CLASSIFIED" in red letters across the top, he pulled out another photo paper-clipped to a field report and slid it in front of Paul. "This is a picture taken at a small town on the coast, south of Ponce, Puerto Rico."

In the picture, the dilapidated houses of the poor were clustered among shuttered warehouses. A hundred years ago, it was a gorgeous tropical bay. Now, it was just an industrial dump. All of the beaches were gone, either paved over or turned into filthy concrete docks. Even the palm trees looked sick and scraggly. It was not the Puerto Rico you saw in the travel brochures. In the bottom of the picture a mini-cocaine sub lay beached against a sea wall. It stuck out of the water like a wart.

"Paul, this mini-sub was found abandoned. When the DEA office in San Juan sent agents down there, they found the sub in good working order. Two weeks after this picture was taken, another mini-submarine was beached in Miami in the same condition. The Texas border patrol has reported a decrease in mule traffic. Several drug tunnels have been found abandoned. All along the Mexican border and coast to coast, the number of drug seizures has decreased dramatically. At the same time the incidence of drug use, especially this Melendez Blue cocaine, has spiked. This indicates that the drug traffickers have found a new method of getting their drugs across the border. It has to be an awfully good system for them to abandon multi-million dollar mini-subs, tunnels, and their usual mules."

Paul's eyes narrowed, reflecting his consternation. When all of the pieces were put together, it spelled big trouble.

"Paul you are now the head of the investigation team tasked to this problem." His boss stood up. "The code name is 'Alien Cartel.' Your team needs to find out who is consolidating the rival cartels and how they are doing it. Tied to this problem is the blue cocaine. Find out what makes it so special and how it is being distributed."

"Oh, is that all?" Paul rolled his eyes. They both smiled, but only for a fleeting moment. The situation was serious. They had a gut feeling that there was something else going on behind the scenes.

*

The fifth floor in the DEA headquarters building was assigned to 'Operation Alien Cartel.' Paul met with the two other department heads of the task force in a room set up for briefings, meetings, and general head banging.

Paul sat down with his team in the briefing room. Heading up the investigation into drug transportation and distribution was Special Agent Carlos Martinez, an ex-SEAL Team Six member who was also fluent in Spanish. He had worked many undercover ops in South America and knew the ins-and-outs of cartel and militant factions. At 210 pounds, with smoldering dark eyes and close-cropped dark hair, he was not someone you wanted to mess with or try to rob in a dark alley.

Paul was glad to have him on his team. He and Carlos had investigated a drug tunnel that ran under the US-Mexico border. He leaned back in his desk chair, as he remembered that incident. They had entered the tunnel on the American side and were deep underground when a hidden door opened just twenty feet ahead of them on the Mexican side. Three drug runners stepped into the tunnel and instantly spotted them. They'd tried to raise their AK-47s, but the tunnel was too narrow.

"¡Alto, deje las armas!" Carlos yelled as he and Paul drew their guns. The three men ignored him and tried to swing their weapons up.

Paul and Carlos fired round after round into the group. The two men in front went down and died instantly. The man behind them finally got his weapon up and blindly fired on full automatic. The sound of the gunfire in the tight tunnel was deafening. The third man finally went down. A flashlight that was dropped by one of the drug-runners lit the scene. Paul could make out the bodies of the three dead men. A black pool of blood was expanding like an oil slick underneath them.

"Holy Shit!" Carlos's voice came from behind him, "Paul, are you ok?"

"Yeah, I'm OK I think. Damn, where the fuck did they come from?"

"There must have been another tunnel that merged into this one." Carlos' flashlight played over Paul's body. "Paul, you're bleeding on the right side of your face."

Paul felt his face and his hand came away wet and warm with fresh blood. He probed his body for any other bullet wounds. His bulletproof vest had stopped four bullets, but otherwise, he was ok.

"It's alright, just a scalp wound." Paul turned his light on Carlos.

"Carlos, there's blood on your left arm." Carlos reached over with his right hand and followed the blood to his shoulder. Two bullets had hit him just outside his ballistic vest.

"Fuck!" Carlos said under his breath.

They heard the echo of footsteps of the Mexican police running and shouting from the other end of the tunnel. Paul's walkie-talkie crackled to life with demands from their team on the US side. Their back up was also running toward them. Paul and Carlos looked at each other and smiled. They had survived. Paul felt for his lucky charm underneath his shirt. It was a flat pyramid in white enamel with a twenty-four carat gold cap. The day after he'd started wearing it, he was involved in a raid at a crack house. The drug dealer pulled out a gun and pointed it point-blank at Paul. He pulled the trigger, but the gun jammed and Paul had disarmed him without incident. He had worn the amulet ever since. He touched the pendant under his bloodied shirt and silently thanked it.

Carlos was his own good luck charm. Two months after the tunnel incident, Carlos was back on the job. While working as back up for a DEA agent who was talking to an informant, he was jumped from behind by two gangbangers. Carlos used his black-belt skills in kajukenbo to put both of them in the hospital while his arm was still in a sling.

Paul exchanged a nod and brief smile with Carlos. Besides his street savvy skills, he was also a great organizer and a good man to have in the office. Sitting next to Carlos was Dr. Joy Anderson, PhD. She was in charge of analyzing the chemistry of Melendez Blue and what made it so addictive. Her librarian eyeglasses made her look like the scientist nerd that she was. Her smooth black skin wrapped an athlete's body. She ran marathons for fun and partied hard. She had been in Portland, Oregon, the day before, participating in the Warrior Dash. She was uncomfortable and shifted in her chair. Her thighs were still sore from running through the mud at that event.

When it came to analyzing a DNA sequence or cracking an unknown substance, Dr. Anderson was second-to-none. Paul had worked with her before and she was the first person who had come to mind to head up the analysis section of "Operation Alien Cartel." He had to pull some serious strings to get her out of her top position at the FBI's crime lab - DNA forensics division. They exchanged professional smiles; he caught a gleam in her eye and felt a warm flush he hoped was not noticeable.

Paul had been divorced for ten years. His wife had told him to choose between his job with the DEA or their marriage. It was a hard choice. Paul loved his wife but he also had devoted his career to putting away major drug criminals. She wanted him to leave the DEA and take a desk job with her father's company. He could not do it. Since their divorce, Paul had shied away from serious relationships. He did not want to put anyone else through the pain his wife went through. Paul lost himself in his work, until he met Joy.

Paul remembered the last time he had worked with her. On an especially tough case Paul had worked long hours alongside Joy. Night after night, standing or sitting next to Joy, made it hard to focus on the job at hand. The way her strong athletic flesh stretched her tight dress drove him to distraction. A few times their eyes would make contact and then quickly dart away. One night while working late, their eyes lingered on each other longer than usual. The look they exchanged spoke volumes. It was unspoken, silent, but as loud as a heart beating after a downhill run. The act was sealed in that brief instant. A few nights later, their mutual daydream became a reality.

Joy also remembered that night and morning of passion. When she was in her twenties, Joy had been married once. In that same year, she was divorced. She had dated here and there since then, but no one had touched her inner being and her body the way Paul had. There were many nights when she wanted to pick up the phone to call him but the timing never worked out. Joy had put all that out of her mind, until now. The memories of that moment flooded back to her. She maintained her composure and hoped Paul did not see the hardened nipples under her tight blouse.

Paul nodded to both of them, satisfied with the competence of his team. He started the meeting and relayed the data from his briefing with John Holcomb.

"Ok guys, this is a serious situation." He leaned forward, his arms on the table. "There is something going on with the cartels that is different and deadly. The threat to our country and the world is real. We have been fighting the good fight against the distribution of illegal drugs. The Border Patrol, the Coast Guard and other agencies have kept drug imports in a precarious balance. That is about to change with this new, super-addictive drug and their secret distribution network. If Melendez consolidates all of the South American cartels under his umbrella it would spell disaster for the US and the world. We've got to stop this situation before it gets out of hand." Paul's team nodded quietly. They got it.

"I am leaving tomorrow for Mexico. I'm meeting with the *federales* there to get their Intel and then I am going to Colombia. We have the President's full backing on this." He looked from one to the other. "If anyone gives you any shit, or gets in the way of you doing your job, wave that Presidential Order in their face. Okay? Let's get it done." He stood, his expression as somber as theirs, and headed to his office to prepare for his trip to Mexico. He had to shake the feeling that he might not survive this mission.

Chapter Eight

DEA Special Agent Carlos Martinez was into the third hour of his stake out. It was almost 3:00 a.m. and there was no sign of the drug drop his well-paid informant had told him was going to occur tonight. He was staking out a dilapidated tenement building in the slums of Richmond, Virginia. Carlos was sprawled out on a piece of dirty cardboard. The sidewalk around him was littered with garbage and chicken bones. An empty bottle of Mad Dog 2020 wine was held loosely in his outstretched hand. He had spilled most of it on himself. Any casual passerby would mistake him for one of the many passed-out drunks who made a piece of sidewalk next to a dumpster their home.

Carlos had been acting the part of a homeless drunk in the same spot for three days. From his vantage point he had a clear view of the entrance to the building. Twenty blocks away, two of his men kept watch with high-resolution telescopes with attached digital cameras. They were on a rooftop, which was higher than the one under surveillance. Four blocks away in an unmarked van, a SWAT team waited as backup. They were not there to bust the drug exchange, but to observe how the drugs were being transported. The dealers could be busted at any time, but doing so now would give away their informant. Any leads on the mystery of their drug distribution and transportation network would be lost.

Finally at 3:30 a.m., a black Escalade drove slowly up to the entrance. It parked and three burly men climbed out. As they walked toward the building, they looked suspiciously up and down the street. The lead man noticed the bum passed out next to the dumpster but took him in as a natural part of the landscape. He continued his visual sweep of the area, and then nodded his head to a passenger in the car. The man got out of the car and walked into the building with three of his guards. One heavily armed man stood guard at the entrance.

"Heads up everyone. A black Escalade has parked in the front of the building. Three men entered, one is standing guard at the door." Carlos whispered into the microphone hidden in his collar.

The rest of his team went on high alert. After a half hour the three men emerged. Two of the guards carried heavy duffle bags.

"Shit!" Carlos cursed silently. *How did they get the damn drugs into the building without me seeing it? Had it already been planted there? No, the informant was very clear that it was being delivered tonight.* As the Escalade drove away he whispered into his microphone.

"Rooftop team, Rooftop team, did you guys get anything? Over."

"Oh yeah, we got it!" The surveillance man's voice sounded incredulous. "But you are not going to believe this shit, sir! Over."

"Ok, copy" Carlos whispered back, "Meet at the hotel in half an hour."

Back at the hotel, Carlos cleaned up and showered off the reek of old sticky wine. Clean and dressed in his everyday clothes, he walked into the living room that served as a temporary mission area. The two men from the roof top surveillance team and a member of the Richmond Police Drug and Gangs Unit were quietly waiting for him. Carlos grabbed a cold beer from the fridge and sat down on the sofa. On the coffee table in front of him were spread out the green tinted photos from the long-range night scope. Carlos picked one up by the edges. It was freshly printed and still warm. It took him a few seconds to orient to the green and black image. He made out a black, rectangular shape with rounded corners, hovering over the rooftop. It looked strangely enough like a travel trailer. There were no visible means of locomotion and it had been totally silent. If it were a small helicopter, he would have heard it. At 3 a.m. in the morning, the streets were deathly quiet.

"What the hell" Carlos flung the photo back on the table. "Are fucking UFOs working as mules for the cartel?"

The roof top team leader shook his head. "At first we thought so too. We didn't even see the craft until it was right over the roof. Then the hatch opened and we took a pic of this."

He laid a photograph on the table. A brighter, green light illuminated the inside of the floating vehicle. Carlos could clearly make out a man silhouetted in the open hatch. The man had a bandana wrapped around his head and baggy pants hanging off his hips. A black rifle was slung over his shoulders. The surveillance tech spread out more time-stamped photos, taken in rapid sequence. The man in the ship grabbed duffle bags from inside and threw them onto the rooftop. It was over in three minutes. This time the surveillance camera team was ready and kept the telescope trained on the craft as it started to rise. It rose to about twenty feet then accelerated skyward. It was too fast and the telescope lost it.

"So that's how they've been getting away with this for so long." Carlos looked at the men in the room, "They are using a propulsion system that is silent and doesn't have any exhaust. They can deliver their drugs anywhere they want to. It's no fucking wonder we haven't been able to catch them in the act." Carlos shook his head. What the fuck?

He asked one of his men to check with the air traffic controller at the Richmond International Airport. He wanted to know if they had recorded any mysterious blips on their screens. Carlos had a sinking feeling that the airport would not have spotted anything. He wrapped everything up and booked a flight back to DEA headquarters to report his findings to Paul Brittany.

Back at DEA headquarters, Joy was in the Forensics section analyzing a sample of the Melendez coke. Under a high magnification microscope, Joy saw clumps of bluish material but could not resolve what they were. She took the sample into the next room that housed her new toy, the Titan3 S/TEM, a scanning transmission electron microscope. She had first seen it when she did an apprenticeship at Penn State. She never dreamt that she would get to play with one. Paul's team had unlimited funding for their operation. She got whatever she needed to get the job done. Under its super-high magnification she was able to see what gave the cocaine its color – blue pyramidal structures with rounded corners. Their entire surface was covered with hair-like cilia. It was not a chemical additive at all. It was a virus.

"That is a very odd additive," she muttered out loud. Joy took a picture of it through the electron microscope and uploaded it to her computer. She put the image into the program's search engine for virus and bacterial matches. After a few seconds the computer flashed a dialog box on the screen: NO MATCHES FOUND. Joy meticulously collected enough of the organisms for a DNA analysis. She put the sample in a bio-bag, attached an orange 'Top Priority' tag on it and sent it to the DNA lab.

While Joy was waiting for the lab results, she opened up a refrigerated vial containing the blood of a Melendez Blue addict who was admitted to a local hospital. She prepared the sample and put it in the electron microscope. Dwarfed by platelets and red blood cells were bluish, round crystals with corkscrew tails trailing behind them. Joy increased the magnification. What she had first thought was a crystal was a clear membrane that covered a mass of globules. It reminded her of something. Then it came to her, it looked like the gelatinous cluster of frog eggs. She zoomed in through the membrane and saw dozens of paramecium-shaped organisms inside. She had never seen anything like that before. Her fingers trembled at the controls. She realized she had stopped breathing until her body forced her to take a shallow breath.

She zoomed back out and looked around the blood sample. She found another round pathogen, its tail was slowly moving, and it was still alive. Joy was intently studying it when it erupted. Joy jumped back from the microscope in shock. Mustering her courage she looked at it again. The crystalline shell had ruptured and the paramecium shaped particles it ejected were slowly moving away. The pyramid shaped virus had replicated itself into a new form. It had incubated a new virus which it then let loose in the bloodstream.

Shit! This was far beyond an ordinary drug additive. A sudden knock on her office door startled her. It was the courier from the DNA lab. She grabbed the envelope from him and rushed to her desk. She ripped open the sealed envelope. The cover sheet was titled: "SAMPLE UNKNOWN." The attached graphs had the dark columns of the chemicals that make up DNA, but there were gaps.

The computer had found an unknown nucleotide that it could not synthesize or replicate. The DNA of that pathogen was unknown and it was spreading inside human hosts. Joy tore the phone off its base. Before the receptionist could answer Joy yelled, "Get me the head of the CDC NOW!"

Chapter Nine

Paul looked out of the dirty window onto the desolate streets of Juarez, Mexico. He was at the coroner's office waiting for an assistant to pull a corpse out of refrigeration. There were so many drug killings in Juarez, that the police investigated only the most heinous of murders. The majority of the innocent people caught in the crossfire were transferred to burial without any official investigation or autopsy. But the recent series of corpses had the local coroner baffled.

The attendant came in and silently opened a refrigerator door and pulled a drawer out with a covered body. He pulled back the sheet and revealed a partially dismembered corpse. The body parts were not hacked off with a dull rusty machete, as was usually the case. The exposed ends of the limbs were neatly cut and cauterized. But it was the holes that had alarmed the coroner. They were three inches in diameter and went completely through the body. Paul stuck his finger inside one of the cavities and felt the sides. It was dry and rough like cauterized scar tissue. A laser could make a wound like that. But a laser powerful enough to make a hole that big, would fill an entire building. It was not something machete wielding, gun-crazy gangsters carried around in the bush. Paul was not a techno geek, but he knew enough about weapons to know that portable laser pistols were not available at your local gun store. It must be some type of secret, military-grade weapon.

Paul asked the coroner a few more questions and copied his photographs of corpses with similar wounds. Then Paul hurried off to a meeting with an ex-Melendez cartel member. He got into his rental car and immediately turned the air conditioner on high. He wanted to cool himself off and blow away the stink of the morgue.

He pulled into traffic followed by three cars. The lead vehicle had a SEAL team in civilian clothes, followed by a van with DEA security agents. Trailing behind them in an armored Humvee were the elite Mexican terrorist tactical team - GAFE; the Grupo Aeromóvil de Fuerzas Especiales. An American manned black-ops Apache helicopter was on standby at a local military base. Ten miles above Paul's position, a thirty-six foot long MQ-9 Reaper drone followed him closely. Its four shark finned, baseball-bat sized AGM-114 Hellfire missiles were primed and ready to fire at a moments notice.

Paul had insisted that he personally investigated this arm of Operation Alien Cartel. His boss had been reluctant to put his best agent in the middle of that mess, but he knew Paul was the only man for the job. Wielding the power of his Presidential Order, he had sent in as much backup as he could to protect him.

Using the GPS in the rental car, Paul found the seedy hotel bar where the meeting was set up. His informant said he would be wearing a red shirt and a white hat. Paul spotted him in a dark corner drinking a beer. Paul nodded in his direction, got an acknowledgement and walked over. On his way he stopped by the bar and ordered a double Bacardi rum and coke.

Carlito Gonzales Paredes used to be a shooter with the Melendez cartel. Family issues brought him back to Juarez and he was on a leave of absence from the cartel. He got drunk one night in a local strip club. In a drunken bravado he had boasted about shooting down outer space aliens for Melendez. A DEA informant, who had been told to report anything about Melendez, overheard it and forwarded the information to his DEA handler. With the help of a few pesos, the meeting had been set up. Paul sat down and took a sip of his drink. The informant was fidgety; his eyes darted around the room. Paul addressed the informant in his fluent Spanish.

"*Tranquilo*, Carlito, I just want to know anything you can tell me about the Melendez compound. I am not going to ask you to wear a wire, or put you in any danger. What you tell me will stay with me. I need information, that's all." Paul took out an envelope and slid it under the table. The thick wad of cash in

Carlito's hand put him at ease. He took a swig of his drink and started talking.

Carlito was one of the guards that had shot down the UFO. Carlito embellished the battle and capture of the alien. He painted in grim detail his hand-to-hand combat to subdue the creature. What he neglected to say was that he was the one who ran for his life when they first discovered it. Carlito talked about the deal with the alien to supply drugs, weapons and aircraft for Melendez. Paul did not say a word. The informant was getting drunk and Paul could tell he was adding a little extra to the story. He listened politely, but his first reaction was incredulous. *What a crock of shit...Aliens?* Then he remembered what he had seen back at the morgue. Maybe there was some truth to the snitch's story. Paul finished his drink and headed back to his hotel.

Once he was in his room, Paul ordered some burritos and beer from room service and then took a tepid shower. The hotel's hot water heater barely warmed the water. After he was dressed he sat down and read his encrypted e-mail. He read the report from Carlos about the strange aircraft that was used to deliver drugs. Attached to the e-mail was a ghostly green image of a vehicle floating in the air. It was unlike any aircraft he had seen. As he was reading through the e-mail, a red blinking icon appeared on his laptop. It was an emergency e-mail from Joy. She had detailed what she had found about the additive. Attached were photos from an electron microscopy and her conclusion that this was an unknown and potentially deadly virus. Paul was very disturbed. This investigation was going in an unexpected direction. The informant's tale did not look like bullshit anymore and it validated his team's reports.

Paul felt his sanity slipping. It was so unreal. Melendez had captured an outer space alien and coerced it to provide him with its advanced technology. *It all made sense, but now what?* Paul had to stay focused. He put down a phobia he did not even know he had, an ancestral fear of extraterrestrials.

There was only one thing Paul could do; go to the Melendez

compound and arrest or kill that turncoat to the human race. That mission was real to him. *The aliens are NASA's problem, or whatever agency deals with that kind of shit.* With his decision made, he called his superior to set up the trip and the back-up he would need. Once that was done, he arranged a three-way video chat with Carlos and Joy on a secured CIA line.

After his administrative duties, Paul pulled out the Mexican rum he had bought earlier. The corner liquor store did not have his favorite Puerto Rican rum so he had to settle on a dubious brand. He turned on the TV and a Spanish dubbed version of the movie *Alien* was on. Hurriedly he switched the channel and watched a replay of a soccer match instead. That night he slept uneasily while nightmarish creatures stalked the subterranean recesses of his soul.

Chapter Ten

Juan Carlos Alberto's life never had a chance. He was born in a slum in Oaxaca, Mexico to a prostitute mother strung out on crack. She abandoned him in a brothel when he was three years old and she was never heard of again. By thirteen he was a male prostitute and was hooked on meth before his fourteenth birthday. He had been a homeless addict until six months ago. That was when he was kidnapped and taken to the Melendez compound.

After he was forced to take that strange new drug, his life changed drastically. He began to take better care of himself. For the first time in his life he thought about working a real job instead of selling his scrawny body to the lowest bidder. Juan had an urge to take better care of himself. He took showers, got his hair cut and looked for work. He found a job collecting food scraps from garbage cans and hauling them to a small pig farm. When Melendez blue was available in Cali, he bought as much as his budget allowed. He made sure he had enough money to eat and a place to sleep. After six months of snorting blue coke he gained weight, the open sores went away and his hair grew back.

Juan Carlos was surprised when he woke up in the morning with a headache and nauseated. His eyeballs ached and his intestines growled. He got dressed and drank some coffee. The flu is not going to stop me from going to work! He went on the long walk to get the wheelbarrow at the pig farm.

He was in the middle of town when a wave of nausea hit him. He stumbled to his knees, embarrassed that he was going to throw up in the middle of the sidewalk. He heaved twice and threw up. Instead of the eggs and coffee he had that morning, a blue gelatinous mass with dark specks stained the sidewalk. The pain behind his eyes was more than he could bear. His stomach swelled tight like a pregnant belly. Juan fell onto his back and began to howl in pain. He coughed and a cloud of blue dust erupted from his mouth. His eyes bulged, swelled out of their sockets and exploded releasing a cloud of blue powder. People walking nearby stopped and stared aghast at the grisly scene. They screamed and ran in fear and disgust brushing off the blue dust that settled on them.

*

In Frankfurt, Germany, Jonas Neumann was having tea and a piece of Apfel-streusel pastry at his favorite outside cafe. The afternoon sun and the hustle and bustle of people and tourists gave him a sense of peace. Every day was a battle that he barely won. His body wanted the drug that was forcibly rubbed in his mouth six months ago in Colombia.

Jonas took great pride in the fact that he had not succumbed to that insidious urge. His only vice was eating too many pastries and he wanted to keep it that way. That morning, Jonas awoke with a fever. He wondered if he had gotten the flu and took some aspirin. Jonas went on his morning walk and the sick feeling subsided. He felt well enough to go to the pastry shop. He sat outside and had his pastry with some hot tea.

After a bite and a sip of his tea, the nausea came again. A sudden spasm bent Jonas over and he took off his hat to catch any vomit that might come out. After a few harsh, dry heaves his stomach settled down. He sheepishly looked around, but no one had noticed his discomfort. He shivered and then internal warmth enveloped him. He felt better now than he had for a while. He realized that his constant craving was gone. What a relief. That gnawing wantingness was gone! Jonas was proud of himself for never giving in to that urge.

Smiling inwardly, he ate the rest of his Apfel-streusel. When he picked up the pastry he noticed his hand had a blue tinge to it. His buoyant mood changed to one of dread. What was wrong now? The odd thing was he felt fine. Jonas went home and Googled 'blue skin.' He learned about argyria, a condition where skin turns blue from toxic exposure to silver. Sifting through the usual hits on cyanosis and other strange disorders, he came across a question asked in a drug rehab forum. A Melendez blue drug addict posted how he got sick one night and then the next morning he was not addicted any longer. The addict was concerned however because his skin color had turned blue. Jonas was relieved that he wasn't the only one with the strange symptom. He went to bed and slept uneasily.

At 3:31 a.m., he was jerked wide-awake from a deep sleep. He listened for the noise that had disturbed his slumber, but it was deathly quiet. Jonas concluded that his own snores must have roused him. He turned his pillow over and prepared to go back to sleep. As he started to drift off, a bright light lit up his room from outside his window.

"Damn headlights" he mumbled to himself half asleep. He turned away and pulled the blanket over his head to block out the sudden brightness. That's the problem with living in the city, car lights in the middle of the night. Even with his head covered, the light was still bright. He could see the red of his capillaries in his closed eyelids. Restless, Jonas pulled the pillow over his head and tried to sleep through it. He suddenly realized he lived on the thirtieth floor of his apartment building. Car headlights don't reach this far up! He got out of bed to investigate. As he walked toward the window, an intense purple beam hit him in the solar plexus. His body stiffened as if he had been hit with a taser. Before he hit the floor, his body hung suspended in mid-air. Before he went unconscious, to his horror, he was floated out of the window and into a spaceship hovering outside.

Chapter Eleven

It had been a little over six months since Raul Melendez made the deal of his life with the alien he had captured. His new enhanced drug was in high demand all over the world. Raul's superior airships and laser weapons gave him an edge over his rivals. He was building a vast empire of wealth and power. He had eliminated all the major cartel heads and taken the leaderless groups under his wing. The smaller drug organizations dissolved when demand for their products vanished.

Melendez Blue was the drug everyone wanted and Raul had the monopoly on it. The other cartels had no choice but to merge with him. They were losing money anyway. No one wanted regular coke anymore, 'If it wasn't Blue, it wasn't cool.'

Raul was having a late night coffee on his balcony, watching the night's drug shipments being loaded. Two spotlights on the airfield lit up the stacks of cocaine bricks on the tarmac. Another beacon was pointed upward; it illuminated one of the cartel's alien drug ships coming in for a landing. The aircraft was three hundred feet in the air when it suddenly lost power and plummeted. It landed on the pile of coke with a loud crash. A plume of powder mushroomed up over the wreckage. Raul ran down the stairs and out to the crash scene. The trailer had pancaked on impact. The pilot was still alive, but the co-pilot's head was at an unnatural angle. The red blood of a dead crewmember soaked into a pile of blue powder.

"¿Que paso!" Raul shouted. The pilot had an open compound fracture of the femur. The splintered end of a bone had ripped through his pants.

"I don't know. I was coming in for a landing and everything just stopped working and we lost power. *Aiiii jefe,* I'm hurting. Please, help me!" His eyes rolled back in his head and he passed out. Raul ordered a man nearby to get the pilot out of the ship and take him to the infirmary.

Seven of the alien-modified vehicles were parked on the air-strip, all prepped for the night's drug run. Raul went inside the nearest one and pushed the buttons that started up the anti-gravitational field. Nothing happened. He tried again but the trailer's alien engines were dead. He went to each ship in turn and the result was the same. Frustrated, he pulled out his la-ser pistol. Raul had customized and blinged out his weapon. The grips were gold plated and inset with diamonds. The helix shaped muzzle was chromed-out to a blinding shine. He fired at a chicken that was pecking nearby, but nothing happened. He aimed point blank at a rooster and pulled the trigger, but it continued pecking with its head intact. Raul grabbed the laser pistol from one of his henchman who wore it in an expensive custom-made leather holster and fired at the rooster. The gun was also malfunctioning.

Maybe the pistols needed to be re-charged? Raul was try-ing to find a reasonable explanation. He jogged to the building where the recharging units were mounted on the roof. When he reached the charging unit, the indicator lights were dark and the hum of super-charged energy was absent.

Raul went to the operations center and had the radio operator contact the two airships that were en-route to Russia on a drug delivery. The electronic hiss coming from the speakers indicat-ed that they too were lost. This is not good. Raul didn't let his thoughts show as he marched back to the trailer airships.

Raul's mechanics had spent all night working on the inop-erable vehicles, but it was useless. They knew nothing of the alien's technology. The mechanics were like monkeys trying to fix a Ferrari's V12 engine. Raul only got an hour of sleep and had a hard time waking up in the morning. He got dressed and was drinking a strong cup of coffee when his cell phone vibrated. The caller ID displayed the name José Colon, the mayor of Cali.

"Raul!" The mayor's voice was trembling with fear, "People are exploding in the streets! Blue dust is coming out of their bodies. It's that *diablo* drug you have been selling! I am going to call the ... " Raul abruptly hung up on him and smirked. *The mayor must be snorting my coke.* He was reaching for a pastry to have with his coffee when he heard someone shouting his name outside. Raul went to the window to see what was going on. Juanita's nanny was running toward him from her house.

"Raul! Raul! It's your daughter!" The nanny could hardly talk, she was panting so hard. "She was sick this morning, she threw up and, then ... *aiii Dios Mio!*"

"*¿Que paso?*" Raul yelled down at her.

"She threw up and then her eyes, her mouth ... Raul ... she ... she exploded ... blue dust burst out of her!" The nanny fell to her knees, sobbing hysterically. He ran down the stairs and sped toward the nanny's house. She tried to grab his hand as he ran by but he slapped her aside. He burst through the door and went to his daughter's room. Juanita was lying on the floor by her bed. Her mouth was open unnaturally wide; her eyes were large, empty sockets. She was dead. Raul was too stunned to react, time stood still. Sunlight through the partially opened curtains illuminated the blue specks that floated in the still air. Raul was used to seeing dead people, but not his own daughter.

Raul heard a scream from the courtyard. He went to the front door and saw the groundskeeper writhing on the ground a few feet away from him. The man screamed as his body erupted a blue mist through his eyes. Raul ran away as fast as he could back to his house.

Raul was alone in his office as the day slowly moved from light to dark. The overcast clouds in the sky closed over the sun like a coffin lid. Raul had tried all day to get the airships and pistols working but it was useless. The day dragged on, fraught with impending doom. Each hour passed like the footsteps of a coroner pushing a casket into a crematorium. Calls were coming in from everywhere. Addicts hooked on his drug were dying and spreading the infection to non-drug users. People who never used coke were getting affected, like his daughter. A teardrop found its way out of Raul's rarely used tear ducts. Juanita was the only person he cared about and now she was gone. The tear was not halfway down his cheek when his mood changed from momentary grief to rage.

Why the fuck did the aliens sell him faulty ships and bad drugs? Raul was not concerned about an alien plague on Earth. He was angry because he had been made a fool of. It took a few minutes for Raul to realize that he had been scammed. He recalled the boat driver's report. The aliens never needed the aluminum. It had all been a ploy. But to what end? Raul had heard that genetically modified foods have unknown side effects. That must be what had happened with the alien additive, it was a genetic mismatch. That was a business risk he had taken. He had already made over a billion dollars profit. What concerned Raul more were the alien ships and weapons. They had malfunctioned at the same time. The aliens had sold him damaged goods and left him with a drug he could no longer sell. They had a hidden agenda and had used him. Raul was ruthless and manipulative, but the aliens had beaten him at his own game.

Raul clenched his fists helplessly as his rage built up. He felt like he was going to throw up and a migraine headache burned behind his eyes. I must be getting sick from being so pissed off! He had no way to get back at them. Normally, he would send his assassins to handle deal-breakers. But these aliens were too powerful and were out in space beyond his reach. He pondered on a way to get back at those pendejos. After a few minutes he smiled, relishing the plan he had come up with. Raul was going to snitch on the aliens to the Americans. The alien's activities were secret and he was going to blow the whistle on them. *'That will teach those hijos de puta to fuck with me!'*

His private cell phone buzzed again. He looked at the phone screen, 'Caller Unknown.' That was curious, only a few trusted people had his private number. Raul reached for the phone and wondered what the bad news was going to be this time.

Chapter Twelve

Paul arrived in Cali without incident. He took a taxi from the airport to the Cali Plaza Hotel. On the way, the city looked like a ghost town. Garbage lay everywhere and hungry dogs roamed the streets. Even Cali's renowned party street Sixth Avenue, was deserted.

After he settled in his room, Paul called his security support leader. The same team that had covered him in Juarez was with him in Cali. He also had a unit of the Colombian Special Forces helicopters on standby. Paul was going head-to-head with a ruthless cartel and he wanted as much backup as he could get. It was late morning by the time he finished checking his emails and made some calls. The package of peanuts he had eaten on his flight had left him hungry. There was still time to catch a late breakfast. He went across the street to a restaurant that advertised all day breakfasts. A disheveled and nervous waitress came over to his table. She took his order perfunctorily and scurried away. While he was waiting, Paul casually looked out the window.

On the street corner, he saw a pack of scrawny dogs eating a pig or a goat that lay dead on the sidewalk. Paul took a second look. It wasn't an animal they were gnawing at it was a man. His eyes were empty sockets and there was a blue colored mess around his body. A man stumbled down the middle of the street. He bumped into a parked car, fell over backwards and screamed in agony. His eyes popped out of his head and exploded, sending a blue mist into the air. The man's stomach burst open and more of the bluish powder issued forth. The man twitched and stopped moving, he was obviously dead. Paul jumped to his feet and knocked over his chair. His mouth was dry and his stomach was in knots. Now he understood the fear he saw in the waitress' eyes and the deserted town. Joy's report came to his mind. He had just witnessed the alien virus at work.

Paul had no time to spare. He dialed the number given to him by a top-level informant to Raul Melendez's personal phone. It rang a few times before Raul answered.

"Who is this?" Raul answered brusquely.

"Hello, Raul Melendez? This is Paul Brittany, Special Agent DEA. I need to talk to you now!" Through the window Paul watched a girl as she ran screaming down the street before she fell behind a parked car.

"I have been expecting you Paul." Raul's voice sounded creamy with satisfaction, "I am sending a driver to pick you up at your hotel in five minutes. Don't worry, you will be safe." Paul thought he heard Raul laugh before he hung up.

A cloud of blue dust rose from behind the parked car and hung in the still, morning air. Paul tossed a ten-peso coin onto the table and left the restaurant. He had lost his appetite.

*

The cartel driver sped Paul through the winding streets of Cali, occasionally swerving to avoid a dead body on the road. Paul hung on as the car hit muddy potholes, straining the over-used shocks. They left the city limits and followed a dirt road into the jungle. Unknown to the cartel driver, the car was followed by Paul's back up. The MQ-9 Reaper drone was a few miles away with its missiles hot. The SEAL Team's armored vehicle was only a quarter-mile behind them. They were following the tracking signal emitted by a special CIA app in Paul's iPhone. A US Apache helicopter was minutes away, manned with soldiers from the seventy-fifth Ranger Regiment. Three helicopters of the Colombian Special Forces flanked them with door gunners at the ready. They were all tuned to the hidden microphone in Paul's collar.

They suddenly broke into a clearing revealing the vast Melendez estate. The driver drove under a rusted metal arch and up to the front gate. He gave a code word at the intercom and the heavy metal doors squeaked opened. The driver went to the front door of Raul's mansion. Paul had expected to see armed tattooed thugs filling the compound, but it was eerily vacant. A doorman came to the car, opened Paul's door and escorted him into the building. Paul heard the sound of squealing tires as the driver left in a big hurry.

Raul was sitting by himself in his spacious living room, sipping Courvoisier brandy. He looked very stylish in an expensive, custom-designed Miguel Caballero two-piece suit. The bullet-proofed Kevlar barely showed in the suit's elegant lines. Raul was not taking any chances. He stood up when Paul entered and crossed the room to shake his hand.

"*Hola*, Paul Brittany. Yes, I know who you are." Raul responded when he saw Paul's eyebrows rise. "We have been tracking you since you entered Mexico. Please, have a seat. Would you like some brandy, or a rum and coke?" Raul smirked. Paul wasn't at all surprised that he knew his drink of choice and ignored Raul's smugness.

"A rum and coke is fine." He took his drink from Raul, took a long sip and sat down. Paul was not worried; one code word spoken from him and all hell would break loose on this compound. But he didn't want to kill Raul, at least not until he got the information he needed.

"Mr. Paul Brittany, do I have a story to tell you. You may not believe me, it is fantástico!" Raul downed the rest of the brandy in his glass, and poured himself another one. He took a deep breath and his smirk faltered.

"I know you came here to arrest me and you are not alone. But hear me out first." For the next hour he told Paul how they had shot down a UFO and abducted the alien pilot. Raul talked about the drug additive and went into great detail on how the alien had duped him with defective weapons and inoperable space drives. The drug enhancer he had paid for with tons of aluminum was worthless and was ruining his business.

When Raul was done he sat back in his chair with a smile, satisfied with his story telling. Paul sat and stared at the rest of his rum and coke, the ice had melted and left a cloudy brew in his glass. Even though he had guessed much of it, Raul's tale still shocked him. The high-pitched mating call of the golden poison dart frog echoed in the silence. It became the soundtrack to Paul's fear of the unknown. It had gotten dark outside, but Paul felt even darker in his soul. The enormity of Raul's crimes stunned him. This one man had put the entire Earth in danger for his own greed. It was vital that Paul arrest him right away.

Raul was waiting impatiently for the DEA agent's response. Raul's demeanor looked smug on the outside, but it barely concealed the pain that racked his body. His eyes felt like they were ready to burst. He had not wanted to confront it, but he knew the alien virus had taken hold of him. He was going to die in a few seconds and there was nothing he could do about it. His tough, machismo persona melted away as the doors of death opened wide before him. He wanted to scream out defiantly, *"Fuck you, you fucking aliens!"* But it got stuck halfway up his throat. This was not going to be an easy death.

Raul made a gurgling sound and leaped to his feet, his eyes were unnaturally distended. He choked out a shriek and then his eyes exploded, filling the room with a fine blue powder. Paul covered his nose and mouth, turned around and sprinted from the room.

"Bravo Two Seven, I need an extraction, now!" Paul yelled into his hidden microphone. As he ran he brushed off the blue powder that had settled on the back of his neck. He burst through the door and saw the helicopter coming in fast over the treetops. Paul raced to the courtyard that was designated as the extraction point. The helicopter was directly overhead, kicking up dust with its downwash. The door gunner swung his machine gun back and forth looking for targets. But the compound was deserted except for the bloated corpses of the cartel's men.

The helicopter flared in hard and fast. Chickens caught up in the vortex squawked their displeasure. From the corner of his eye Paul saw an old, indigenous man on the other side of the fence. He wore the ceremonial outfit and headdress of a shaman or tribal chief. The old man swung a feathered staff around his head; he was trying to get Paul's attention. Time stood still when their eyes locked. The helicopter was hovering two feet off the ground and Paul jumped in before the landing gear touched down. As the helicopter took off, Paul looked for the shaman but he had disappeared back into the jungle.

The helicopter rose higher into the night sky and made for the military airport. The Melendez compound dwindled in the distance as they flew over the black jungle. Paul's insides were in a knot. A cold sweat sent shivers through him. The hot, humid air was heavy and difficult to breathe. A primal fear overcame him. It was the helpless horror of alien abduction. The landing beacons of the military airport loomed ahead. As soon as they landed Paul was transferred to a CIA owned Cessna and flown to the municipal airport for a connecting flight to the States. Paul was putting together his debrief. *How do you tell someone that aliens are real? Or break the news that humans are infected with a strange, alien germ?* Paul's thoughts followed each other in an endless circle the way a dog chased its tail.

The visuals of Raul's death played over and over in his mind, like a scratched record of reality. Paul compared the plight of humanity to the Aztecs. The measles and poliovirus killed more Aztecs than the conquistador's swords. Paul wondered if that was going to be the fate of humanity.

Chapter Thirteen

On the edge of the jungle where the mangrove roots met the sea, a native Indian eyed the spaceship as it flew overhead and saw it drop a large package into the water. The Indian saw the splash of its impact and how close it came to hitting a boat that was cruising underneath it. He melted back into the jungle and disappeared as if he had never been there. Finding his way through jungle footpaths in the dark, he returned to his village and reported what he saw to the tribal leader.

The chieftain took the news soberly. Some of his villagers had been recruited to work in the Melendez compound and they had reported everything that was going on. He knew about the alien and the strange ship from the sky that had been shot down by the cartel guards. Concerned about the mysterious events at the Melendez estate, he went to the shaman's hut on the outskirts of the village to consult him.

The shaman was a very old man. There was a rumor that he was 150 years old and he looked it. He was an old man when the chieftain's mother was born. No one really knew how old the shaman was, but he talked and moved like a man in his thirties. The shaman listened patiently to the chieftain's report. Through his visions, he already knew of the strange alien. He had been reluctant to investigate it any further. He was afraid he might stir something awake that needed to remain hidden from the eyes of man. The tribal leader relayed the villager's reports of the strange being that was held captive at the compound. The shaman was asked for his help and guidance. Despite his uneasiness, he had no choice but to look into the matter.

It was after midnight and the people of the village sat around the shaman. The elders looked on somberly as he prepared to take his spiritual journey. A large fire burned in a pit in the center of the circle. Occasionally, a pop like a firecracker would spit embers from the fire. The shaman meticulously prepared the Ayahuasca brew that would transform his being into an ecto-plasmic eagle. Mixed in with his concoction were powdered pey-ote buttons and a paste made from plants containing Dimethyl-tryptamine. The potent brew opened the doors between parallel dimensions and allowed the shaman access to them. After many magical chants, spells, and invocations to local spirits asking for a safe return, he drank half of the bitter brew. His eyes rolled back in his head and he fell back suddenly, as if from a heart attack. His quivering lips were the only signs that he was still alive.

The shaman left his body in the guise of a black and white Harpy Eagle. They were the largest and strongest raptor in the rainforest and their slate colored feathers appealed to the sha-man. He spiraled upward in his eagle avatar and saw his body lying prone by the fire. Above the jungle canopy he saw the car-tel estate in the distance and flew to it. As he flapped through the air, he transformed the eagle into a spiritual soldier. On its black head materialized a brass helmet with slits for the eyes. Copper chain mail covered its breast. The primary feathers on the wing tips became silver knives. The shaman was suiting up for war. He sensed a presence behind him and turned around and saw a blue hummingbird trying to catch up. It was one of the medicine man's spirit guides. It wanted to join this adventure. The shaman slowed down and welcomed it. The hummingbird's size was good for reconnaissance and if needed, it could use its body as a projectile.

As the two bird avatars flew over the compound, they saw a building with a column of black vapor rising from it. The smoke, invisible to mortal eyes, was thick and smelled like rot. The eagle followed the vaporous trail down through the top of the building. The shaman entered a room filled with black, vis-cous ectoplasm. It was difficult to fly through it, like swimming through thick mud. He managed to push deeper into the room and sitting in a dark corner he saw the alien.

The shaman had seen things in his spiritual state that had

tested his nerves, but never like this. A shadowy fear came over him. The old medicine man had exorcised many demons from his village, but this monster in front of him eclipsed them all. The alien seemed to sense his presence in the room. It turned its head and its large, black eyes looked right at him. For a brief moment, he caught a whiff of the alien's essence and it scared him. The dark, liquid smoke coalesced suddenly into giant claws tipped with sharp, obsidian talons. It slashed at his eagle-form and the shaman barely dodged it as he flew out of the room.

He had momentarily forgotten about his companion and saw the hummingbird trapped in a corner. A swipe of the ethereal claw smashed the tiny bird into the wall amidst a flurry of blue feathers. The spirit guide left its lifeless avatar and evaporated into nothingness. Before he escaped, the shaman caught a glimpse of the demon's mind and he saw the doom that was coming to Earth. The coming disaster had been set into motion thousands of years ago and it was too late to stop it now. On the periphery of his psychic consciousness, he perceived beings of white light that had tried to help mankind but were thwarted by evil aliens.

The shaman returned to his cold, limp body. The fire that had been hot and burning brightly when he had left was now a bed of dim, smoky embers. The elders had been waiting anxiously for his return. The shaman's eyes fluttered open as he sat bolt upright; his eyes were wide with fear. His hands trembled and the elders recoiled, frightened by his visage. The old man struggled to catch his breath. He calmed down and relaxed after some gulps of air.

"What did you see?" The village chief asked anxiously.
The shaman was silent for a minute, floundering in his attempt to translate into words the great vistas and horrors he had seen.

"There is more going on in this world than the eyes and heart can see," he finally said. "A great catastrophe is coming from the stars above. What is happening today is but a drop of water in a river stretching back thousands of years. We are small pebbles being pushed along by a black sea." The shaman shivered as he relived his narrow escape from the grip of that ancient, alien evil. "I looked into a black pit filled with poisonous snakes and scorpions. Beings of white light were trapped in there and were being bit and stung."

The elders looked confused and scratched their heads, but they knew the old man had his own way of explaining the things he saw in his visions. The shaman added more wood to the dying fire and took a sip of cool water. After taking a deep breath and letting out a long sigh, he proceeded to tell the story of the coming demise of the human race.

"Once upon a time, many thousands of years ago in the dawn of man, Earth was visited by people from outside our world," he began.

The elders listened with growing dread. They knew deep down inside that the world outside their village would be changed forever. The shaman drank down the other half of his brew and settled uneasily into another trance. The doors of his mind flew open as the Ayahuasca mix released his soul from his body. During his brief encounter with the evil alien spirit, the shaman caught a glimpse of an unknown, opposing force of good. His soul had contacted the time lines of both races. It had taken only a few seconds to download the psychic information, but it was going to take days to decipher it. The shaman did not understand everything that he recalled. The images were clear in his mind but they were beyond his earthly vocabulary. It was going to be difficult to translate such otherworldly visions for the village elders, but he was going to try.

Chapter Fourteen

An alien probe visited the Earth 14,869 years before the shaman was born. The extraterrestrial robotic ship had been on a mission to find intelligent life. It had visited forty different stars before it entered the Earth's solar system. The probe investigated each of the outer planets and Mars but only found lower life forms. When it reached the Earth it finally found what it was looking for. The probe sent a message to its home planet; it had finally found intelligent life.

The Earth was in the grip of an ice age. From space, it reflected so much sunlight that it looked like a small star. But it had vast equatorial regions free of ice. That was where the probe sent drones to study prehistoric humans. After three months surreptitiously studying early man, the extraterrestrial craft returned to the ship in orbit. All of the information was compressed and then transmitted on a tight beam faster than the speed of light. The data stream went to Alcyone, a giant blue star in the Pleiades star cluster nestled in the Constellation Taurus, and the home of the Cyn civilization.

*

The Pleiades was the most fertile stellar group in the galaxy. The supernova placenta that nourished the stars of that region was rich in precious metals and the building blocks of life. That area of space was a node of intersecting galactic ley lines left over from the creation of the universe. The confluence of positive and vibrant energies attracted life of a higher order. In the center of that convergence was Acyan, the fifth planet of Alcyone and the birthplace of the Cyn.

The evolution of the Cyn was rapid and free of the 'tooth and claw' upbringing of most intelligent species. After Acyan cooled down enough to allow life to exist, it only took two million years for the Cyn to fully evolve. In another twenty thousand years, they had a vibrant civilization. The Cyn's technology advanced by leaps and bounds and it was not long before they colonized the fifteen planets in their solar system. They developed faster than light space ships and traveled to their neighboring star where they found a planet that harbored an intelligent species. The Cyn helped them with technological know-how until they were able to traverse the far reaches of space. Thus began the Cyn Coalition, which expanded to include fifty star systems. However, planets with intelligent life diminished the further out they reached. They were rare outside of their region of space. Cyn scientists sent hundreds of robotic ships to distant stars to no avail, until a probe found the Earth

*

Cian Cy-M was in his office when he received an urgent dispatch from the Planetary Surveys Unit. He opened the message, it read, "INTELLIGENT LIFE FOUND BY PROBE C-N-16." That probe had been on a five hundred year mission to survey the one hundred stars that were assigned to it. There were sixty-five such probe-ships spread throughout their section of the galaxy. Over the last five thousand years, only three planets had been found with intelligent life. Cian was very excited about this news and wanted to personally relay it to the head of his department. He went to the balcony of his office and jumped into his speedster. Cian raced through the air at two hundred miles an hour to the Planetary Survey building thirty miles away.

Cian negotiated the crowded sky-highway with ease. To a human, the traffic would look as chaotic as the streets of Naples. But the Cyn's fast reaction time made two hundred miles an hour seem like a leisurely bicycle ride. Cian pushed his craft faster than usual until he saw the Planetary Survey building in the distance. He braked his vehicle hard as the landing platform acknowledged his approach. He timed his jump from the speedster perfectly before it came to a full stop. He ran up two flights and burst into the office of the Chief of Extra-Planetary Affairs.

"Sir, one of our probes has made contact!"

"I know." The chief smiled and waved his copy of the same

news. "The survey probe's downlink transfer is complete. It has been loaded into your computers. The planet looks like a good candidate." He said it verbally but the Cyn were also natural telepaths. Their mental exchange was much quicker and had greater volume than could be conveyed verbally. They used spoken words because they loved the sound of their language. The combination gave their speech great depth and meaning that could never be fully translated in a non-telepath culture.

Cian thanked his boss and rushed to his office. He sat down at his console and his computer screen materialized in front of him. Tendrils of energy snaked out from the screen and connected to his head. Once the interface was connected, the flat screen turned into a 3-D box that filled the room. His mind moved quicker than the computer's quantum circuits as he searched through the probe's data banks. Multiple sub-menus opened and closed. His mind-controlled cursor found the information for the new planet and expanded it. Cian brushed aside the geological data and found the section on the indigenous life. A kaleidoscope of images filled the screen with thumbnails of the major fauna of Earth. Each image was color coded with bars that showed the intelligence level. Most animals had a portion of the bar filled and an aquatic species was a quarter full. But one life form had theirs solidly filled in. Cian expanded the tab for that species and he saw a human for the first time.

Cian called up all of the images and videos the probe had collected and studied them. The intelligent life forms averaged around five feet high. They were much shorter than the Cyn's average height of six feet. Their eyes were smaller with pupils different from his. The Cyn had evolved eyes that could see in the ultraviolet, which gave their pupils a uniform purple coloration. He rotated a three dimensional image of the male and female of the species. Cian thought the humans resembled the Cyn, albeit hairier. They had unusual tufts of hair on their brows and their skin was a range of brown and pink hues compared to the Cyn's light gold color. But aside from the human's smaller eyes, the two species was similar in look and structure. Each of the species in the coalition had their own physical characteristics in response to their environments. But the animating life force was the same.

Cian rotated a man's image and zoomed in on a festering sore on his lower leg. The human's skin was obviously not as rugged as his own. Though the Cyn's skin was supple and soft to the touch, it was tough and able to withstand the extreme ultraviolet radiation from their sun. Cian studied the voluminous data files for eleven hours. He did not have to stop to eat or dispose of his body's waste. His body used the energy of his life force for its metabolism. The cells of a Cyn's body did not have to synthesize food for energy, but they needed the basic materials to build or repair cells as required. The Cyn evolved an organ that stored organic molecules. They ingested a biotic 'soup' that filled their reservoir, which lasted for three years.

Cian reviewed hundreds of hours of movies taken of the natives hunting and interacting with each other. After pouring through all of the data, he wrote his report and recommendations. The last form he had to submit was his approval for intervention. Cian looked at the map on a wall that showed the fifty planets that were members of the Cyn Coalition. The Cyn had seeded forty-five of those planets while they were still young. They only intervened and changed the social course of a species if they had the potential and resources to become a contributing, space faring civilization. In the beginning, they readily found planets with intelligent life that qualified. However, after hundreds of thousands of years, they became harder to find. The search widened to hundreds of light years with diminishing results. The last planet that qualified was two thousand years ago.

He looked out of his office window. Cian had been working all day and it was late at night. Acyan's three moons were in the sky. The largest moon, Ma-Cyan was five times larger than Earth's moon. It had a heavy metal core that gave it enough gravity to retain its atmosphere. Unlike Earth's moon, which was mostly gray in color, Ma-Cyan was a mini-world, a baby planet hanging in the sky. It had blue-green seas, purple land-masses and small ice caps. The second largest moon was covered with sulfur and iron. It was painted in varying shades of red and orange. The smallest moon had vast areas of dark green olivine surrounded by mile-wide ribbons of raw silver. The silver reflected the sun, sending streamers of light into space. The moons were aligned in a triangle in the night sky with the stars of the Pleiades wrapped around it. It was a beautiful sight and it took Cian's breath away.

Cian saw through the barbarism of early humans. He envisioned them evolving with some help, into a highly advanced and ethical society. In ten thousand years, they would be eligible to join the coalition to trade, exchange culture and prosper. With a flourish, Cian signed the recommendation form. A panel representing the fifty planets of the coalition approved it and Cian was elected to be in charge of the Earth Advancement Unit. He put a team together and organized the first phase of the program. It took twenty years to prepare for the mission. When it was ready, Cian went with the preliminary expedition to planet Earth to begin the process of transforming humanity.

Chapter Fifteen

The shaman took a pause in his storytelling to quench his thirst. His eyes had been closed during his trance. When he opened his eyes, he was surprised to see the entire village sitting in a circle around him. Only a few elders were sitting by the fire when he started. Two hours later, the entire village had joined them as word had spread of his extraterrestrial visions; children and even the dogs had sat in. Now and then, someone would throw wood on the fire to keep the shaman warm in his trance. Nighttime had fallen and outside of the light of the fire it was pitch black. The shaman took another drink. He quietly looked around as if trying to remember where he was. One of the children took advantage of the momentary break and diffidently raised his hand.

"What is it little man?" The shaman asked the boy brusquely in between swigs from his water bottle. The little boy stood up squirming, his hands between his legs.

"Can I go pee?" He said distressed. He was squirming and could not hold it much longer. The villagers were shocked at the crude interruption. They looked back and forth between the boy and the shaman to see what was going to happen next.

"No!" The shaman said loudly. The little boy almost wet himself. In the same breath, the shaman started laughing and sent the boy scurrying away. The elders laughed and everyone else joined in and the mood relaxed. The shaman was happy for the short interruption and the laughter of the people. They were going to need that feeling of joy as his story progressed. The child returned and sat down, chagrined. The shaman lit his pipe and puffed smoke into the still air. Smoke rings danced through each other, delighting the children.

Without warning, a crow fell out of the sky and landed in the fire. The flames engulfed its feathers and it flew away into the night like a Phoenix escaping from hell. Its raucous "caaw caaw" dwindled into the distance and then abruptly stopped.

The smell of burnt feathers filled the air. Everyone was in shock. The thin veneer of levity was gone and exposed the underlying fear of the unknown. There was nothing the Shaman could say to diminish the portent of what just happened. His story was a runaway train and could not be stopped. The villagers who were listening did not leave. They were too scared to stay but even more afraid to go home alone in the dark.

Chapter Sixteen

The expedition took three months to reach the Earth. Traveling at the speed of light would have taken them 640 years, but Cyn scientists had discovered a way to circumvent that barrier. After thousands of years of expansion, the limitation of Einstein's law hampered the growth of their galactic civilization. They found that telepathy in the physical universe was instantaneous. Cyn engineers invented a way to envelope their ships in a thought-field bubble and thereby cheated the laws of physics. The thought-wave bubble disconnected a spaceship from the physical universe. Engines that annihilated matter more efficiently than atomic fission propelled the ship faster than the speed of light. Traveling at the speed of thought was not instantaneous, but it was enough to make traveling across the galaxy a matter of months instead of hundreds or thousands of years.

They used a thought-wave transceiver. Without a way to communicate faster-than-light, the Cyn's galactic civilization would not have been possible. A Cyn scientist had discovered the super-light speed spectrum by accident. He had been monitoring the first Cyn astronaut to set foot on their neighbor planet, 220 million miles away. The mission scientist sent a radio message to the astronaut and waited for the twenty-minute response lag. He had also sent the message telepathically at the same time. The astronaut's telepathic response came back in less than a second. The radio response arrived twenty minutes later. That was when it was discovered that thought waves traveled faster than the speed of light. They had never tested the speed or range of their telepathy beyond the planet's surface.

After hundreds of years of research they were able to artificially create telepathic wavelengths. As the distances between their space colonies expanded, the Cyn engineers perfected a thought-laser communicator. This concentrated the data-rich spectrum into an intense, tight beam that traveled incredible distances at the speed of thought.

The Cyn arrived in the solar system in May of the year 14,665 B.C. On board the transport ships were volunteers from around the coalition. The planets of their origin defined the shapes of the different races. Some were short and squat, others tall and slender with bulbous heads. Others, like the Cyn, were more human-like and could blend into a human population. Despite their variations in outward appearances, they all shared the love of freedom and the pursuit of intellectual and technological advancement. A team was stationed on Venus to build a thought-wave transmitter relay base. They used robots to build domes in Venus' caustic atmosphere for a spaceport and communications center.

The Aroo were a coalition member who lived on a planet similar to Mars. Their bodies were slight of build, about three feet high with long arms and fingers. They were tasked with building a depository on Mars. The library would hold the technology and information the earthlings would need in the far future. When the ship entered the solar system, it dropped the Aroo off on Mars. On the Cydonia Plain, the Aroo found a large mesa that met their requirements. They sculpted the top surface to look like a human's face. The inside of the massive mesa was hollowed out. They built vast storerooms for the gifts the Cyn will leave for mankind's future. If humans ever traveled to Mars, they would see the sculpted landform from orbit. The face would be a beacon that would lead them to the repository. If the people of Earth could get there, they would have earned the right to use what was in the library.

The rest of the expedition arrived and parked in Earth's orbit. The Cyn sent drones to the surface to look for suitable human settlements. Cian and his survey crew took ten years to map the Earth and plot the locations of the major tribes. They then gently abducted hundreds of humans. A paralysis ray was played over their bodies as they lay asleep on their rough animal skins. They were taken aboard the shuttle and transported to the ship in orbit. Their brains were intricately and safely studied to find the best way to enhance their functions. The abductees were then returned unharmed, unaware that they were the first humans in space.

After the survey expedition finished their mission, Cian returned home to Acyan and left behind two crews on Earth to continue their work. They were tasked with motivating humans and nudging them toward a higher civilization. Deputy Commander M'yani led the group based in the area later to become ancient Egypt.

The other Cyn crew was embedded in ancient Anatolia, the birthplace of Turkey. There they built a complex of concentric, monolithic stones. They were carved with animals and people of the region and from the different planets of the coalition. The relief sculptures were painted with iridescent metallic paints that glowed in the dark. Floating metallic spheres hung magically in midair between the stone pillars. Colorful, moving pictures were mapped on their surfaces. The sphere's movies ran in an endless loop. One animation showed the transition from barbarism to an interplanetary civilization. It took years for the brains of ancient humans to interpret the video images. It prompted neural connections between the brain and eyes, which had not existed before.

The whole complex gave off gamma brain waves that stimulated the growth of new ideas. The natives who came there left feeling invigorated. Their minds were filled with strange new thoughts.

M'yani's approach was different. He had a team of twelve Cyn engineers and scientists. They built a secret underground base far outside the rudimentary village of Abydios. After twenty years of observing the locals and learning their language, M'yani worked out a plan to introduce the Cyn's program to the local earthlings. M'yani was going to use the priesthood to motivate the people to build a great pyramid. The Cyn would then use that structure as a rallying point and a symbol for humanity's future.

After searching throughout the area, M'yani discovered a group of priests who were honest and sincere in their desire to help their fellow man. M'yani studied them and in particular, a priest named Luap. M'yani read his thoughts; Luap had grandiose ideas and visions of a better life for his people. The only thing Luap lacked was the technology to bring his ideas to life. His drive and enthusiasm warmed M'yani to him. M'yani was like a parent who helps a child fulfill their goals.

M'yani found an opportunity to introduce himself when the local priests were together at one of their rituals. The priests met after midnight, deep in the woods. They were chanting around a large fire in the hours before dawn and then they went into a meditative prayer.

He was observing them from orbit and decided that was a good time to make his appearance. M'yani came down from the dark sky in a small shuttle. Three miles above the priests' position, he turned on the ship's landing lights. The group around the fire looked up and saw what appeared to be a bright star descending toward them. To ease any sense of fear or panic, M'yani telepathically sent the group emotional waves of peace and serenity.

The priests were transfixed as the craft finally landed just thirty feet away from them. M'yani's ship was encased in molecularly compressed osmium. The dark metal gleamed in the light of the altar fire. The priests had never seen such metal as this. Artificial light was unknown in that age. The landing beacons and the other colorful indicator lights around the ship's exterior were magical to them. The priests fell back in fear, murmuring prayers to their gods.

A seamless door irised open and a short ramp extruded out of the opening. M'yani exited the craft dressed in a blue, metallic fabric. He had on a long flowing cape made of the same material. The threads in the fabric reflected the light of the fire and the ship. White boots and a white hat completed his uniform. M'yani appeared as if he was clothed in a halo of light and color. The visual effect was powerful. The men bowed in supplication and offered M'yani a leg of lamb they had roasting by the fire. M'yani took the offering and set it inside his ship as if to indicate he would eat it later. He did not want to offend the priests by telling them he did not eat food.

M'yani spoke to the assemblage. His telepathy enhanced his verbal communication, spicing his words with visions and otherworldly thoughts.

"Priests of Abydios, I have come from the Heavens above to lead your people to great glory. Your entire world will be transformed for the better over many thousands of years. The great changes in the far future will start with the seeds we plant today. The children of your children times a hundred will reap the rewards of your labors."

The priests were overwhelmed with awe. They were familiar with the spirits of the woods, but they had never seen anything like this chariot-riding god. Goose bumps prickled the arms of the priests, their pupils dilated and their breathing was shallow. One of the priests fainted, overcome by the experience.

"To start you on this grand adventure, I will help your people build the greatest building in this entire world." As he spoke, M'yani transmitted to their minds an image of a great pyramid. The sides were faced with dazzling white marble and at the peak was a band of copper ten feet wide. It was topped off with a cap of pure gold. Their eyes rolled back in their head, ecstatic over the mental pictures.

"Tomorrow before noon, gather all of your people and assemble them at the Three Hills. At that time, I will present myself and tell of the wonders to come." His melodic voice was telepathically enhanced and penetrated their souls.

"I am designating the priest Luap, to act as my liaison." M'yani pointed at Luap, who was astonished about the pronouncement.

M'yani went back into his ship and the door silently closed behind him. With barely a whisper, the ship slowly rose into the air and gained altitude, rising faster and faster. The priests thought the whole incident was just an illusion until M'yani's ship broke the sound barrier. The loud boom shook the leaves in the trees and quivered the blades of grass on the ground. A gust of wind from the shock wave put out the fire. The loud boom woke the people in the nearby villages. They were frightened of the thunder with no clouds. The priests put water on the scattered embers of their fire and rushed to their village to tell the people of the strange visitor and his commandments.

*

By eight o'clock the next morning, hundreds of people were waiting at The Three Hills. The area was a circular series of large hills, which created a natural amphitheater. The floor of the bowl-shaped landscape was used to grow wheat in the summer. A large dais had been erected in the middle of the field, which the priests used for religious rituals. People from around the region anxiously crowded the gentle slopes.

When the priests arrived early that morning, they were met with a most wondrous and unusual sight. Below them, large intricate designs were stamped into the wheat. Interlocking rings were overlapped by triangles and around the entire design larger circles swirled into smaller ones like a Mandelbrot fractal. The design filled the entire floor of the basin. Magically it had appeared overnight, for the people it was a sign from the heavens. Unknown to the villagers, after his meeting with the priests, M'yani had flown there and used his ship's pressor beams to emboss the design into the field.

Throughout the morning, hundreds of people continued to stream in from far and near. News had spread of the god in his shiny black chariot. Right at noon, the sky exploded with a loud bang. The concussion flattened the wheat field and birds were knocked out of the sky. M'yani had arrived.

The Cyn were masters of extra-planetary psychology. They used their knowledge of the mind to further their goals of peace and mutual trade. The Cyn's social engineers would spend decades surveying a planet to find the best way to communicate with its inhabitants.

M'yani's ship slowed down and landed light as a feather in

the center of the wheat field design. The entire amphitheater was hushed. Not a sound could be heard in the entire space. It was as if breathing was a sacrilege that would dispel that magical moment. The beards of wheat were still, mirroring a calm lake. A door appeared on the side of the craft and a ramp extended to the ground. An audible gasp whispered through the valley as M'yani emerged into the light of the warm noon sun. M'yani was dressed as he had been the night before. But in the sunlight his cloak and outfit sparkled like jewels. The villagers were enthralled and afraid at the same time. It was not every day one saw a god descend from the Heavens. M'yani walked around his craft and climbed a series of recessed steps until he was on the spine of his ship. He slowly turned around and addressed the gathering.

"People of Abydios, I've come from a distant world beyond the night sky. I represent a society who wants to help your world grow into a great civilization. We invite you to join us in the stars." M'yani spoke in a normal tone of voice, but he was heard clearly by every person present, from the front row to the very top of the hills.

M'yani projected himself into the minds of the people around him. It appeared as if M'yani was facing them directly. It was not until days later when the villagers were talking about the event, did they realize that no one had ever seen his back. While M'yani spoke, people continued arriving at the site. Thousands of people surrounded the Three Hills. M'yani's voice grew louder as he continued.

"There is much work that needs to be done and sacrifices to be made. Much of what we start now will not be completed in your lifetime, or in many generations to come. Every great forest starts from small seeds. You ... " M'yani opened his hands to the crowd to emphasize his point " ... are the seeds of your planet's future." Images of the Earth from space filled their minds. "People of Abydios, do you wish to take part in this grand adventure?"

There was silence for three heartbeats and then the amphitheater exploded. The entire crowd shouted their promise to the future of mankind. They beat their chests and pulled their hair in a frenzy of religious fervor. The waves of passion and energy between the hills made the air glow and vibrate.

Their minds were filled with visions of humanity living in harmony in strange cities of shiny metal. Food was plentiful in this dream of the future. There was no sickness or poverty and the world was free of crime and chaos. M'yani let the crowd's cheers run for a few minutes then raised his hand in acknowledgement. The crowd became quiet, hungry for his next word.

"There are many skills to be learned. It will take thousands upon thousands of years to achieve these goals. Along the way, every generation will reap the benefits of each step of this journey. Your children's children times a hundred, will join us in the heavens." It seemed as if he spoke to them from only a few feet away. Such was the power of M'yani's telepathic communication.

"Our first step will be to build a magnificent building to serve as a beacon for all those who would venture onto this path. Your priests will be the conduit between my people and yours. I will return in three days to begin. Thank you."

M'yani ended his presentation, entered his ship and flew upwards toward the sun, leaving behind a stunned crowd. Many wondered if it had all been a dream, but the concussive shock wave from M'yani's ship dispelled any lingering doubts of their sanity.

Chapter Seventeen

Twenty-five years after M'yani's appearance at the Three Hills, the construction of the giant pyramid was completed. The pyramid's footprint was twice as large as the Great Pyramid of Giza that was built by the Egyptians thousands of years later. To facilitate its construction, the Cyn engineers used a nearby limestone quarry to pulverize thousands of tons of limestone with a molecular vibrator. The engineers scooped up the powdery dust and mixed it with water and a chemical catalyst. They then poured the slurry into colossal molds on the construction site. The geopolymer solidified which created a block stronger than the original limestone. The molded blocks served as the main internal support structure. Giant blocks of granite for the inside walls were precisely quarried and polished to exact specifications. The Cyn placed the blocks on floating pressor plates, which elevated the heavy blocks a few inches above the ground, making them weightless. However the blocks had the mass and inertia of hundreds of tons. It took a small army of workers pulling and pushing to get the blocks to the job site. The Cyn could have easily transported the blocks themselves, but they wanted humans to earn their gift of civilization.

The people took great pride in building the giant pyramid. They worked closely with the gods from the stars for the future of humanity. Even the barbarian hordes ceased their attacks, fearful of the chariots crisscrossing the skies. Their fear turned into curiosity as they felt the draw of civilization. The barbarians asked if they could help, and they were accepted.

The outer portion of the pyramid was faced with closely fitted slabs of veined, white marble that was burnished to a mirror finish. Close to the top of the pyramid, was a four-foot thick layer of copper. The copper weighed eleven tons and was put into place by a Cyn construction airship. The exposed surface was polished and protected with a clear diamond film. Above the copper tier was a layer of black obsidian topped by a capstone of pure gold. The effect was dazzling. During the day, the flanks of the pyramid could be seen for miles. The gold crown reflected the sun and lit the path to man's future. A megawatt laser emitted a beam into the sky from the apex. The ionized purple light reached far into the stratosphere, a beacon that could be seen for hundreds of miles. Beautiful gardens and intricately designed pools surrounded the structure. Schools, hospitals and administrative buildings dotted the landscape.

What started out as a small settlement of huts grew into the world's first city; Abydios. The Cyn's civil engineers installed copper pipes for plumbing for fresh running water. Homes were built of fire-kilned brick instead of sun-dried bricks. Cyn capacitors were housed in large, clear glass bottles and had enough electricity to power a village for years. A massive project was underway to power every dwelling in the area.

Pilgrimages were made to the pyramid to see that wonder of the prehistoric world. Travelers needed food and lodging, which enriched the locals. The first tourists flooded the region. Shops sold miniature pyramids and dolls that resembled M'yani in his flowing robes. Visitors were enthralled with the new foods grown from Cyn seeds and wanted more. Farmers exported exotic crops from their farms. For the first time, they produced more than they could eat. The smelting of copper was taught and copper coins took the place of barter. Immigrants swelled the city and those who went back home carried with them a new vision for mankind.

*

The pyramid was the centerpiece of the new world. A ramp led up into it through an enormous doorway and continued inside to a grand gallery. The stepped ceiling of the gallery rose to three hundred feet. Its polished granite walls were seamless and covered with intricate drawings inlaid with gold and lapis lazuli. Laser engraved pictures detailed the Cyn's coming to Earth and the building of the great pyramid. It depicted the path to the stars and was understandable in any language. The Cyn had installed synaptic resonators inside the pyramid, which vibrated at the same frequency as human brain cells and prompted their growth. Visitors to the pyramid left more intelligent than when they arrived.

The first floor of the grand gallery housed enormous libraries and schoolrooms that taught reading and writing. Paper and ink were new and wondrous and the classrooms were always full. The greatest wonder was the light bulb. Pyramid workers, natives and thousands of visitors were captivated by the lights-without-fire. The bottled sun was the magic of the gods. The natives had to be told that they did not have to pray to them. Once a month when the moon was new and the sky was at its darkest, enormous floodlights lit the outside of the pyramid. Thousands of people gathered for the light show while M'yani gave rousing talks that fired their imaginations.

*

Luap was in his office in the building of worship. Effigies of gods and demigods lined the walls in large niches. The Cyn had not tampered with local religions and did not impose their own beliefs. The Cyn had only insisted that they were not to be worshipped as deities. Ever since the Cyn's arrival, Luap's world had been turned upside down and sideways. However, the changes were gradual, positive and natural. Luap marveled at how normal the sight of ships going back and forth through the skies had become. At night, he no longer jumped when he turned on a switch and the bottled-sunlight came on.

Luap was fifteen when he had first encountered M'yani that dark night twenty-five years ago. He spent many hours talking with M'yani, who was interested in everything human. Despite the immense gulf between their species, they became close friends. Luap was forty years old and revered as an ancient one in a world where the average lifespan was only thirty years. Humans in that area lived longer and were healthier.

The Cyn brought seeds from their home world and grew crops with health-giving properties. They loved botany and excelled at it. Their genetic expertise was used to modify the region's scraggly vegetables, which fed the growing population. In the past, only two out of five children survived childbirth. Of those, only half lived to their teenage years. That changed when the Cyn gave them nutrients that strengthened their pregnancy. The women went to newly built hospitals to birth their babies in antiseptic rooms with soft beds. More babies survived childbirth and villages boomed with a growing, healthy populace. The Cyn dispensed medicines that protected people against disease and infections. Luap himself was cured of a strange lump that had been growing in his stomach; he had become accustomed to the pain and discomfort. Luap did not realize how sick he was until he was cured.

Life used to be hard. The gods were fickle and nature capricious. The constant raids from barbarian tribes did not make life any easier. Survival used to be a day-to-day struggle. The future went only as far as the next crop cycle. Now, Luap contemplated the fate of humanity thousands of years into the future. Ever since the Cyn's arrival, his mind had become sharper and clearer. The generation born into that new world was healthier, more energetic and looked far beyond the present. The youth were always talking about the distant future and of civilizations among the stars. Life was good and as far as Luap could see, it was only going to get better.

*

Luap was unusually tired after a long day of teaching at the school. When he got home, he went to bed exhausted. Sleep overcame him like a rogue wave and he fell headfirst into a nightmare. He dreamt that he was in the middle of the city and people lay crumpled in the streets. Birds and animals were chaotically strewn among the human rubble. He walked over to the nearest person and a stench assailed his nostrils from the bloated body, everybody was dead. Packages and goods were in disarray on the streets and sidewalks, dropped from lifeless hands. Puddles of decomposing bodily fluids soaked the ground. There were no flies sipping at it; they too were dead. Luap rose above the scene forty feet into the air and lost track of his body. He looked around for it frantically and finally found it. It had perished on the sides of a crater.

The sight of his own dead body shocked him awake. He sat up with a start and squinted at the early morning light. Outside of his window, the gold and orange rays of dawn bathed the pyramid in a warm glow. The sunlight hit the gold pyramid cap at just the right angle and flashed a shard of warm, yellow light into his room. The golden beam did not dispel the dark cloud from his dream. Luap could not shake the feeling that something dreadful was about to happen.

Chapter Eighteen

The other Cyn crew in Turkey was having success as well with the humans in their area. The large stone pillars and floating metal balls they had built attracted and inspired the local inhabitants. The structure was not as grandiose as the pyramid M'yani's crew helped build, but it created the same effect on the populace. The Cyn expedition had picked this mountainous region because the natives in the area were highly intelligent. Despite their harsh existence, they were artists and natural philosophers. Their spiritual leaders were adept at astronomy and had created an accurate calendar. After surveying the minds of the local populace, building the stone complex was chosen as the best way to attract their attention. The colorfully painted stone carvings were works of art and appealed to the native's aesthetic sensibility. The layout of the site aligned with key stars and astronomical events and was in tune with their calendar. Classes were held every night at the complex that taught advanced astronomy.

The main attractions were the floating metallic balls. They slowly spun between the stone columns in mid-air. 3-D images were mapped on their surfaces, which showed the Earth from space. The different planets and races of the coalition were displayed as well. Cyn music played from speakers hidden in the pillars and were synchronized with the ball's images. The Cyn communicated verbally and telepathically in their speech and with their music. Human listeners heard the ethereal melodies and at the same time, received telepathic images and feelings. Every day, hundreds of people would gather around the spheres enthralled at the display. The pillars had the same synaptic resonators that were inside M'yani's pyramid. The brain wave emanators subliminally enhanced the I.Q. of all who visited the site.

The Taurus Mountain's base was composed of six scientists and engineers. One of them was Cy'ja, the only female on the team and a specialist in extra-planetary botany and agriculture. She studied the plants the natives foraged and enhanced their nutritional values. She had plowed the first farms in history using seeds imported from the coalition's planets. She also genetically modified native plants to make them more productive. Cy'ja made many visits to Abydios and had helped M'yani plant the first farms there.

Cy'ja was young for a Cyn, the equivalent of a human teenager. She was one hundred and fifteen years old, a small portion of their four hundred year lifespan. Though her body was young by Cyn standards, her mind had a continuous memory that went back nine hundred thousand years.

Cy'ja was training a farmer in the valley that was below their mountain base. She was showing him how to make and use natural fertilizer. Despite their size and subtle physical differences, the Cyn women were exquisitely feminine. The females bore babies and had a voluptuous body with smooth hips. They did not have large breasts because they did not breast feed, but in shape and sensitivity they were human-like. Men were attracted to the female Cyn, but their arousal was also mixed with fear and awe. It was considered improper for a man to lust after a god, and to humans, the Cyn were gods.

A native man was looking at Cy'ja intently from across the fields. He stood still as his smoldering, dark eyes focused on her every move. He had the dark-stained skins and leather belt of a warrior. From a loop in his belt hung an axe, flaky with the dried blood of his enemies. He was known as Closar the Fearless and he commanded the army in his province. He had been walking along the dusty path to the farm when he caught sight of Cy'ja in the distance. He did not look at her as a god. He did not feel fear or awe toward her as the others did. In his eyes she was the woman he loved.

Closar had been away putting down a small barbarian attack. He had killed three of the attackers and his platoon had driven the rest back over the river border. After a few days, the barbarians did not return and Closar was given a furlough. He had just arrived in the village that morning when he received orders to return to the fort the next day. He had hoped he would get a longer break and spend more time with Cy'ja. Regretful that his stay would be so short, he went looking for her. He found her at the farm where she was indoctrinating a farmer.

His eyes roamed over her body; even from this distance he could see her every curve. Cy'ja turned around and looked directly at him. She had sensed Closar's hot stare. She waved at him and smiled. Her warmth and presence enveloped him. It felt as if she was in his mind, kissing his soul. He closed his eyes and he was lost in the moment.

"Cy'ja," Closar whispered. She was hundreds of feet away, yet when she was in his mind, it felt as if she was close enough to kiss. "I just arrived this morning and now I have orders to go back tomorrow. I want to be with you before I leave." Closar knew she heard his every word and felt his yearning for her.

"Yes Closar, I want that too. I have to finish helping this farmer and then I will come to your place." Cy'ja gave him a mental kiss. Closar waved, turned around and headed to his dwelling.

Cy'ja continued talking with the farmer, who had no idea of her telepathic exchange with Closar. She was distracted. She had not expected Closar back so soon from his campaign; it was an unexpected pleasure. The pang of having him leave so soon was tempered by her anticipation of the night they would have together. A woman had once asked Cy'ja if females from another planet could fall in love and have sex with humans. Cy'ja told her that it was permissible in Cyn society to be in love with beings of other worlds. The Cyn recognized that love was between souls even if the bodies were from another planet.

"Our females can have sex with humans, but they can only be impregnated by male Cyn." Cy'ja had informed her nonchalantly. The woman's eyes had opened wide.

"Do you have a qefen-t?" The woman asked diffidently.

"What's a qefen-t?" Cy'ja was almost afraid to ask. The woman blushed and pointed between her legs.

"Oh!" Cy'ja laughed out loud. "Yes, we do, as well as most of the females in the galaxy." She quickly changed the subject to the clothes and jewelry of different worlds.

Cy'ja enjoyed working with humans. They made her laugh. Once the local women had become used to her, the "god" label had worn off. They treated her like one of their own. She was an extraterrestrial, but she was also a woman in every sense of the word. She had met Closar at a meeting in his village. Two days later, when she could not stop thinking of him, she realized that she had fallen in love. It did not matter to her that he was from a different planet. What mattered was that their souls had connected like twin flames. She did not see an earthling when she looked at Closar; she saw the man she loved. Cy'ja hurried the farmer along, barely paying attention to his incessant questions.

As soon as Closar was out of sight of Cy'ja, he ran home as quickly as he could. There was a shower stall outside his home. It was heated by water that ran through tubes the Cyn had installed on the clay-tiled roof. Closar hurriedly washed himself with a coarse washing bar. Before the Cyn's arrival, the local populace had used wet clay and sand to cleanse their bodies. On special occasions the men would use a bone strigil to scrape their skin clean. The women lathered themselves with perfumed oils and wore pouches of potpourri around their waists. Cy'ja had taught the locals how to make soap by using a water-extract of burned plant ashes and cassia oil. Closar dried himself off. The strong cinnamon scent of the soap filled his nostrils. Cy'ja told him that on her planet, the men bathed daily. Since then, Closar washed himself with soap every day when he was in the city.

He combed his matted hair, which had not been brushed for three days. His one-room home was dusty and a lizard had moved in and made itself at home. Closar tidied himself and his room in preparation for his woman. The lizard went flying out the door amid a cloud of dust. Finally, after cleaning up the place, Closar relaxed and waited for Cy'ja. As soon as the thought of her entered his mind, he was filled with memories of their times together. Younger men chided him for having an affair with someone who was not human. The older men did not say anything, but they smiled knowingly.

There was a saying, "love is like a blindfold," but that was not the case. Instead of blinding him, his love for Cy'ja had opened his inner eye. She had given him color in a world of black and white. The first time they made love was like a drug-induced dance. His soul had orgasmed along with his body. Closar had lain shivering in bed afterwards, his body drained from pleasures he never knew existed.

Closar saw Cy'ja through his window approaching his house. The anticipation was almost too much to bear and he had to contain himself and not run out after her. Before she could step through the door he held her roughly to him and kissed her deeply. The first time they had kissed it had taken him aback. The Cyn did not use saliva for predigesting. Their mouths were kept moist with water mixed with a type of glucose. Her lips tasted sweet with an unusual but pleasant aftertaste. After a long and deep kiss Closar closed the door and took her to his bed and roughly took her clothes off. Cy'ja's skin felt warm and soft when they were naked in bed.

Her pubic region had shocked him at first; it was totally hairless and it took him a while to get used to it. He remembered the first time he had entered her. She had internal ridges and muscles that were different from human females and it had aroused him. Closar made love to her three times before he could relax enough to climax. At the peak of his first orgasm, his mind opened up to hers. He entered into a wide-open, two-way telepathic union with her soul. Their physical and emotional sensations merged together and sublimated his passion to a higher realm.

They made love for six hours without pausing, lost in themselves. Afterwards they talked quietly into the night, their eyes and souls glued to each other. She told him of the wonders of the universe and he entertained her with his tales of demons and the men he had killed. Closar shared the dreams he had of flying through space as an eagle and how certain stars drew him more than others. She savored his every word as if they were musical notes. After they talked for a while, they pleasured each other again and again until they passed into a blissful slumber.

It was early morning and still dark outside. Closar was awake and dressed in his warrior skins and sheathed swords. A messenger had gently knocked on his door just before dawn and whispered that it was time to leave. He dressed quietly and then leaned over her to kiss her forehead. His necklace came free of his shirt. The metal pieces gleamed in the candle's flickering light. Cy'ja had given him a dark-blue star sapphire the size of a ripe olive. He pulled out a smaller necklace from his pocket. A purple and lavender amethyst gem wrapped in strings of silver was attached to it. He had bought it from a traveling vendor. It was expensive but it had reminded him of Cy'ja's eyes. Closar laid the amethyst necklace gently on his still warm pillow. At the doorway he took one last look at her sleeping peacefully. Reluctantly, he turned away and silently closed the door behind him.

Cy'ja awoke a few hours later and reached over to touch Closar. The side of his bed was empty, but she found his necklace on the pillow. She picked it up and the morning sun kissed it and sent purple splashes of light around the room. She lay back in bed and held the necklace to her bosom. Cy'ja closed her eyes and fell back asleep amid Closar's lingering, cinnamon scent.

She dreamt of a planet she had visited thousands of years ago. She was trying to catch a walking plant. It ran into a cave and she chased after it. The plant had gone to the back of the cave and stood next to Closar. His eyes were filmed over and his jaw was slack.

"Closar, what are you doing in there?" She called out to him but he did not respond. Closar soundlessly moved further back into the cave. There was no up and down motion to his body, he appeared to float backwards and then he disappeared. She jumped after him and ran headlong into a wall as black as coal.

The impact woke her up. She put her arm over his side of

the bed. For a split second she thought the cave had actually swallowed him and then she remembered that he had left earlier that morning. Cy'ja could have slept longer but the dream had disquieted her

Chapter Nineteen

The Cyn's human advancement program was moving along and was ahead of schedule. Plans were drawn up to construct similar pyramids and stone complexes around the world. On their home planet Acyan, Cian was coordinating the efforts of the Earth crews. He was very pleased with their progress and had submitted a request to the Coalition Council to approve sending ten more teams there. The Cyn stationed on Earth received regular resupply missions from their home planet.

One day, the Taurus base received a ping from one of their Earth-orbiting satellites. The ground crew used the satellites to organize ships in orbit. The next scheduled re-supply drop was not due for another two months. The base went on alert as multiple images of spaceships showed up on their screens. They used their base computers to try and match the shapes of the unknown ships to their database. No matches were found. An emergency message was sent to their home planet. While the base personnel pondered what to do next, an explosion destroyed a part of their base and killed the Cyn who were there. Another blast hit the base again seconds later. The entire station and personnel were utterly destroyed.

*

M'yani was having his weekly teleconference with the leader of the Taurus base when the 3D screen abruptly cut off. He tried to reconnect the video feed but he was not getting a response. His personal communicator emitted an urgent telepathic alert. It was the Cyn he had been in conference with.

"M'yani! There are unidentified craft in orbit. They don't match any of the coalition spacecraft in our database." M'yani heard a loud explosion in the background.

"We are under attack! I am going to ... " The call was abruptly cut off. A static buzz was all he could hear from his handset.

M'yani ran to his computer screen and punched in the satellite video link. He saw the same ships in space the other base had reported. Unknown spacecraft were in orbit and they were not Cyn coalition ships.

M'yani flipped on the internal comm. He announced to the other Cyn working in the station to meet him at the shuttle in the underground hangar immediately. As M'yani ran down the tunnel to the shuttle, a shock wave buckled the ground beneath him, throwing his body hard to the floor. A cloud of dust and debris followed from the end of the tunnel he had just left. He hoped his other team members had made it to the hangar in time. M'yani got up and ran at a full gallop. As he turned the last corner to the shuttle bay, he saw his men yelling for him to hurry. Relieved that they were safe, he ran and jumped through the shuttle doors. Another cloud of hot dust followed him in as the doors closed. Once inside, he turned on the shuttle's remote viewers. What they saw stunned them.

The viewer showed a jagged hole at the entrance to their base. Pieces of machinery were everywhere. Rocks and dirt were still falling down from the explosion. M'yani had built their headquarters underground with a long, wide tunnel to the surface for their shuttle. The end of the shaft was caved in from the orbital attack, blocking them in. As they watched horrified, another beam from orbit destroyed the main base. A mushroom cloud rose hundreds of feet into the air as the power stations exploded, adding to the beam's destruction. The shock wave reverberated through the shuttle. Another monitor relayed video from a satellite that was aimed at the Taurus base. It was unrecognizable. The 3D image showed a smoking, gaping hole where the base used to be.

There was a monitor on top of the gold cap of the pyramid. On its screen, M'yani and his crew watched as an alien ship approached the pyramid. It attached large grapplers to the gold and copper layers and took off with them.

Dumbfounded, M'yani watched as a large metallic sphere burned a hole through the atmosphere and smashed into the pyramid. A microsecond later, the entire pyramid exploded outward. Broken chunks of limestone, granite and marble flew thousands of feet in all directions. Through the expanding dust cloud, M'yani saw that the pyramid was gone.

All of this had happened in seconds. M'yani's mind went into high gear. He was processing information at quantum speeds free of the analogue, synaptic method that human brains used. The orbital video feed showed the unknown ships were leaving in a hurry. Another alarm went off in the control room. It was from one of the communication relay buoys in orbit between Earth and Venus. Its sensors had picked up a deadly coronal mass ejection from the sun. The buoy was destroyed by the radiation but not before it showed a solar blast headed straight for Earth. It did not take long for M'yani to deduce what had occurred. The attacking ships had artificially triggered a Solar Proton Event. M'yani checked another monitor and saw the cloud of lethal solar particles coming their way. That explained why the attacking ships had left orbit so suddenly.

The shuttle was made for orbit-to-surface flight and was not shielded against such powerful solar radiations, but M'yani's shuttle bay was twenty feet underground and would provide adequate protection against the coming proton storm. M'yani's communicator came alive. He looked at its screen and was surprised; the call was coming from the Taurus base.

"Hello? Who is this?" M'yani asked, not masking the tension in his voice.

"M'yani, this is Cy'ja. Our base has been attacked! I was at a nearby village when it happened. I am at the base now but I cannot find any survivors!" Cy'ja was frantic.

"Cy'ja, a solar storm is about to hit us. Is there any place you can hide deep underground?" M'yani was relieved that there was at least one survivor, but the coming solar event could change that.

"No, there is just an open crater where our base used to be. There are caves lower on the mountain but it would take me five minutes to climb down to them." Cy'ja was worried about Closar and wanted to warn him about the coming storm, but there was not enough time. M'yani knew that Cy'ja did not have five minutes. He had to get to her in seconds in order to save her.

"Cy'ja, I am on my way. Activate your tracker right now and stay right where you are!" All of the Cyn communicators had trackers in case of emergencies. A light came on his console indicating the connection with Cy'ja's tracking signal.

There was no time to lose. M'yani had to pick up Cy'ja and then get his shuttle to the Earth's far side. There they would be protected from the lethal cosmic particles. The tunnel exit was blocked. There was twenty feet of rock and dirt over the shuttle bay, but the ship's hull was strong enough to punch through it. M'yani telepathically signaled his men to get harnessed into their seats. There was no time to talk verbally. The men received the full import of M'yani's mental communication. What would have taken humans minutes to explain verbally, the Cyn did in nanoseconds.

M'yani took the commander's seat, strapped himself in, and activated the shuttle's main engines. An orange light came on the console indicating that the engines were warming up. M'yani wanted to pound his fist on the console. The shuttle's main engines needed four minutes to warm up. Normally that was not a problem. M'yani looked at the computer screen tracking the incoming radiation storm. He only had fifty-five seconds to impact!

M'yani blasted another thought to his men. There was only one way to get out with enough time to save Cy'ja. They had to use the shuttle's powerful maneuvering thrusters. Once they were in the air he would force start the main engines. The sudden engine start would cause an explosion. In the confines of the hangar it would tear their ship apart. However, out in the open it would give the shuttle a high-powered boost.

M'yani activated the four thrusters and four red indicator lights came on. This time, the warm-up sequence was only going to take twenty seconds. That gave him thirty-five seconds to fly to Cy'ja and to the dark side of the planet away from the sun. He was going to use the bulk of the Earth to shield his craft from the deadly radiation storm. Red lights on his console turned green. M'yani ripped off the safety latch and pushed the ignite button down hard. The shuttle rocked as massive thrusters meant for the vacuum of outer space obliterated the hangar outside the ship. He pushed the power lever all the way forward and the shuttle blasted through the overlying rock. With a horrendous screech of metal against solid rock, the shuttle broke free.

The outside monitor showed Luap running toward the base. M'yani had no time to stop and save him and sent him a mental burst. In that brief exchange, he gave Luap a synopsis of what had happened. M'yani ordered him to jump into the hole the shuttle had created and hide in the tunnel. With no time to spare, M'yani force-started the main engines when the shuttle was only one hundred feet in the air. Two of the engines exploded, blasting away that section of the force thrusters, but the others held. Dust and small rocks flew off the shuttle as it ripped through the atmosphere.

M'yani's craft reached the Taurus Mountains in seconds. He followed Cy'ja's signal and spotted her. She was on a flat section of rock and was waving at his ship. The shuttle's doors opened in mid-air, letting in a sudden rush of cold air. M'yani slowed down the shuttle by reversing the forward thrusters. But he had been going too fast to stop completely. The ship had slowed down to thirty miles an hour as it approached Cy'ja. At just the right moment, she jumped into the open bay amid a swirl of dust. Cy'ja's legs were still dangling out the door when M'yani took off. The ship's crew pulled her in and closed the hatch. The craft blasted away at two hundred miles per second. Multiple shock waves followed the shuttle. Ionized air was left in its wake as the ship tore through the atmosphere. From the ground, the shuttle looked like a giant meteor streaking through the daytime sky. Fearful of this fiery omen, hundreds ran for cover, which saved them from the sun's fury.

M'yani pushed his ship faster. The extreme G-forces stressed the shuttle's gravity shield. M'yani and the others were pressed back into their seats as the ship accelerated. Through the forward port, M'yani finally saw the terminator, the line where day turned into night. His radiation detection instruments suddenly went red. The solar storm had arrived. Hundreds of gigantic flares, multi-colored sprites and auroras danced in the dark sky ahead of them. Bolts of lightning hundreds of feet thick smashed into the ground below. The concussive waves shook the ship like a leaf in a hurricane. M'yani crossed the terminator and sharply angled the shuttle toward the surface with only microseconds to spare. The planet's body protected his ship from the cosmic onslaught while they waited out the storm.

*

The Proton Solar Event only lasted sixty-five seconds, but that was enough time to fry every living creature exposed to it. The only survivors were those who were deep inside stone buildings or caves. All of the hard work of the Cyn had been destroyed in seconds. Of the hundreds of thousands of people who had been enlightened, fewer than a hundred had survived from both Cyn bases. Over the next thousands of years, this phase of Egyptian history became a legend, a myth and then was forgotten. The pyramids that were built later in Egypt were pale shadows of the great Cyn pyramid. The building blocks that survived were used, reused, and reshaped until they became unrecognizable. The inlaid gold and lapis lazuli and other precious metals, were ripped out and sold or melted down, their origin lost forever. Egypt's first unrecorded golden era turned into their Dark Ages and was forgotten in the sands of time.

After the solar flare struck the Earth, it continued onward through the solar system. When it was safe, M'yani flew to the base in the Taurus Mountains in the hopes of finding any survivors. M'yani felt Cy'ja's sadness at losing her fellow scientists and the humans she had worked with. Cy'ja was biting her lips and wringing her hands unconsciously. Her concern for Closar seeped out of her mind. M'yani had met the human and had liked him immediately. He hoped Closar had found cover and was safe.

M'yani reached the demolished mountain base. The destruction there had created a chaotic mess of rock and melted pieces of Cyn machinery. M'yani was surprised to see that the stone complex was gone. A large hill covered the spot where the stone pillars had stood. The whole complex had been buried under tons of sand. He had hoped for more survivors but it was evident that no one else had survived. Cy'ja searched for Closar's telepathic essence. No matter how far he went, she could always feel him. Now all she felt was a painful emptiness.

M'yani flew the shuttle back to Abydios. When he neared the city he saw immense plumes of black smoke staining the sky. Abydios had been leveled. The city had been blasted from space. Abydios and the great pyramid they had helped build were both destroyed. Thousands of dead bodies and animals littered the streets and fields. M'yani arrived at the smoldering ruins of the underground station and slowly hovered over the hole the shuttle had excavated on its exit. It was then that he saw Luap. His body was laying headfirst, halfway down the slope of the crater. The proton storm had overtaken Luap before he could reach the safety of the hangar tunnel. M'yani looked at the devastation around him and at Luap's lifeless body and could no longer hold back his tears.

M'yani landed and went into the ruins with his men to salvage what they could of their base. Cy'ja asked him if she could take the shuttle and look for Closar. M'yani consented and she flew the shuttle as fast as she could to the border where Closar was last stationed. She spotted the stronghold and slowly flew over it. From two hundred feet up, she could see that no one was left alive in the fort. On the bank of the nearby river she saw the bodies of the barbarians who had crossed the river. She landed in a clearing and ran a quarter mile to the river. When she came out of the forest she saw the bodies on the river's bank. It was there that she found Closar. The radiation had come upon them while they were engaged in battle. He was on his back lifeless, surrounded by three dead barbarians. Blood was everywhere, they had died under Closar's sword before the radiation hit. She knelt by Closar's body. His eyes were closed and his face was serene, as if he were merely asleep. A bloody sword was in his right hand and in his tightly clenched left hand were the strands of a broken necklace. She pried open his stiff cold fingers and found the jewel she had given him. He had died holding the two things he loved. Overcome with emotion, Cy'ja sat down on the ground next to him, too sorrowful to cry.

She was lost in her thoughts and memories and was startled by her communicator's chime. It was from M'yani, it was time to leave. Cy'ja stood up, slowly walked to the shuttle and flew back to the destroyed Abydios base. M'yani transferred the base recordings to the shuttle's computer memory banks and left Earth for Venus. The Cyn had an interstellar base there the attackers had overlooked. From Venus, M'yani and his crew took a spaceship back to Acyan; saddened that a new and unknown enemy had sabotaged their mission.

*

Twenty miles north of Abydios, two hundred and twenty-four men and one woman exited from deep inside a cave. Their eyes squinted from the sudden transition into light. The meadow outside the mouth of the cave was littered with dead animals, birds and insects. They prostrated themselves on the ground and gave praise to the God of Destruction and their Savior.

Chapter Twenty

The Cyn's attackers were known as the Xxonox and their civilization was millions of years old. The Xxonox evolved on a planet trapped in an orbit around the star known on human star charts as Algol A. The supernova that fed the star's formation was tainted with dark, negative energy. It burped out its distaste for its existence and from its ashes Algol A was born. Algol A was ninety-three light years away from Earth in the constellation Perseus. Perseus held the severed head of Medusa in one hand and a sword in the other. Algol A was the red star in Medusa's "eye." The orbit of its binary sun eclipsed it regularly, which made that baleful star appear to blink. Ancient astronomers named it the "Demon" star.

The Xxonox's home planet was dirty, dry and dusty. Only twenty percent of its surface was covered by water. The skies were thick with methane smog, which kept the planet perpetually overcast. Algol A and its two neighboring stars barely lit the planet during the day. The life forms that evolved on the planet came into existence pissed off at having to evolve there. It was a backwater world in a slum section of the galaxy. The perpetual overcast hid the wonderful view of the triple star system and the starry sky beyond. The planet had two continents separated by a fetid ocean that separated them like a moat. In the middle of each land mass lay a brown and slimy inland sea. The eroded detritus of the surrounding terrain flushed into it like a toilet. The inland seas were perpetually covered with slimy, black algae and the fish there were inedible.

The atmosphere had oxygen, but it was heavily tainted with methane and sulfur. The plant and animal life had no redeeming values. Colorful flowers were not a part of the landscape. The continents had scraggly forests with dark brown, nettle-like leaves. The plants drew energy from the methane in the air rather than the light of its dim sun. The early life forms had reluctantly evolved until each continent had its own intelligent species. They were physically different from each other but shared the same distaste for their existence.

The two races were war-like and rapacious. After they had bloodily settled their internal conquests, they eyed each other across the dank ocean. Driven by the desire to invade the other, both sides developed the technology to build ocean-going ships. After a war that lasted 300 years, one conquered the other. The race that prevailed was the Xxonox. They exterminated their enemy and burned their bodies to ensure none of their genetic material survived. In honor of their victory, they renamed their planet Sutox, their word for pain.

Over three thousand years, they developed a society that was technologically advanced and morally corrupt. Their government was ruled by force and graft. They built cities and vast bridges made out of aluminum, the most abundant metal on the planet. The improved access between the two continents gave them room to expand their population. On most planets, survival was of the fittest and most adaptable. On Sutox, only the meanest, the most cunning and deceitful survived. If a good soul were to land on that planet from outer space, it would not survive. Sutox did not tolerate any being that had any shred of goodness.

The Xxonox race had started out with male and female bodies and they reproduced sexually. However the men hated their weaker counterparts and conspired to do away with all of the females in their race. This program took the males a thousand years to secretly plan. The Xxonox had become advanced genetic engineers and found a way to clone their male cells. They grew the cloned cells in vats until the body was full grown. Once they no longer needed females for reproduction, they killed them all. Over thousands of years, their sexual organs atrophied. A smooth patch of scaly skin was all that remained of their genitals.

The demand for heavy metals drove the Xxonox to venture

out beyond their solar system. Seven other planets also orbited Algol A. The Xxonox developed an interplanetary space fleet and hopped from one planet to another. Their search for heavy metals and rare minerals was fruitless. The other planets were as devoid of those resources as their own.

Out of necessity, they looked out beyond their tri-star system. The next star was twenty-five light years away and the spectroscopic analysis revealed the presence of the metals they sought. After thousands of years of working with the materials they had available, they created a space drive that could traverse space at a fraction under the speed of light. They traveled to the first star outside of their own star system. The planets there were uninhabited but had the resources they needed. Once they had access to rare heavy metals, their technology jumped a hundredfold. Their engineers made faster and faster space engines until they finally sped past the speed of light. It was not long before the Xxonox had depleted the new star system of its resources. With their new space drive, they targeted the next closest star, which was forty light years away. When they arrived they found a planet that had plenty of the resources that they were looking for. It also had something else they did not need: inhabitants.

The dominant species were intelligent, ape-like creatures. Their square-shaped heads had a ring of hair around their skull, which made them look as if they were wearing a fedora hat. The native beings lived a nomadic life. It was a pre-industrial, medieval type society. They were blissfully unaware of the lead, platinum, iron and gold underneath their feet. This was the Xxonox's first exposure to an alien species. Not wanting to get their hands dirty digging out ores, they decided to coerce the natives to do the work for them. The Xxonox studied them from orbit. They sent small ships to the surface and abducted them at will. On board their mother ship, Xxonox scientists dissected their captives' living brains as they searched for their mental control centers. When they were done dissecting their captives alive, the bodies were dumped into low orbit to burn in the atmosphere.

They were masters of genetic manipulation and manufactured a virus that rendered the inhabitants controllable by mind waves. The virus spread and rendered the entire population of the planet mindless slaves. The Xxonox overran the planet like a plague of interplanetary locusts. They ravaged it like hungry dogs and made a mess out of what had once been a beautiful planet. The Xxonox wanted the conquered planet for their new home, and moved in. For the first time in their existence, they could see the stars at night from the surface of a planet. Aside from occasional clouds, the sky was blue-green during the day and at night the stars flooded the sky. They renamed the planet Zutox, their word for retribution. They released a lethal virus that interacted with the earlier infection and decimated the entire indigenous species.

The Xxonox gave a farewell gift to the planet that had given them birth; they destroyed it. Once all of the Xxonox had moved out, hundreds of remote viewers were put into orbit to transmit the vacated planet's demise. Three billion Xxonox watched its destruction. Stadiums were set up all over Zutox with gigantic 3-D screens. There was a festive atmosphere with bands playing and the imbibing of copious amounts of their alcoholic drink, carbonated methanol. They had moved a planetoid from the fringes of their system into Sutox's orbital path. They watched as their mother planet got disemboweled. Its molten core congealed and dispersed along its orbital plane; Sutox was no more.

The chunks of the broken planet eventually formed an asteroid belt. After thousands of years, the rest of the planets felt the absence of Sutox like a missing tooth. The delicate, gravitational dance of the planets was disturbed. The two outer planets were flung into space, forever orphaned. The inner planets slowly fell into their sun. The star, Algol A was planetless and became unbalanced, making it wobble like a drunk into the path of its companion star. The two stars danced in ever tightening circles until they collided and created a new, larger sun. Such was the long-term effect of the Xxonox's matricide.

The next planet they took over was inhabited by a species

that physically resembled the Xxonox. Instead of bluish skin, the native's skin was a dirty, cigarette ash gray color. The Xxonox called them the Elanin, their word for gray. The eyes and bulbous head were similar to the Xxonox but they only grew to three feet. When the Xxonox mined their planet dry, they gave them a choice. They could be exterminated or willingly become slaves. There were not enough Xxonox to do the thousands of menial tasks needed to run a technological society. The Xxonox were expanding their empire and they needed able-minded worker slaves. The Elanin had to choose between genocide and staying alive as slaves; they chose survival. After two hundred thousand years the Elanin were in a symbiotic relationship with the Xxonox and forgot that they were once slaves.

*

The Xxonox were intoxicated with the abundant material resources at their disposal. They expanded their population with thousands of new cloning vats. It was not long before their adopted planet became over-crowded. Their population explosion threatened to implode their civilization. The Xxonox began to eye each other hungrily like over-populated rats that had devoured all of their food. To prevent the implosion of their society, they looked outward for more conquests. Over a period of 35,000 years they conquered twenty-five star systems. The more they expanded, the more they wanted. They had to spread further out to find suitable solar systems, which were becoming rare. But finally they found a new victim worthy of their rapaciousness. The Xxonox embarked on a four-hundred program to conquer their next target: Earth.

Chapter Twenty-One

It was 1:30 a.m. and oppressively dark in the shaman's village. All of the children had gone back to their homes to sleep. Two of the oldest elders had fallen asleep and were gently snoring. Everyone else was awake and attentive. The older women were constantly crossing themselves and saying prayers. The evil aliens in the story had frightened them.

The medicine man had connected with the soul-lines of both alien races when he was in his avatar form. Under the influence of his hallucinogenic brew, his mind soaked up the alien history like a sponge. He squeezed out the story of the Cyn and Xxonox from his mind. He was not just telling a story, he was relating an experience. The images in his mind were beyond his comprehension, but he did his best to interpret them.

He looked around at the gathering and was relieved the children had all gone to bed. The next part of the tale was too grim for young ears. Sensing a change in his mood, the audience huddled closer together and drew nearer to the fire. The elderly women's hands were a blur as they repeated the sign of the cross. The shaman closed his eyes and with a shiver continued his story.

*

The Supreme Council wanted the most able and ruthless of their kind to be in charge of the Earth invasion. Abn Su, a veteran of two planetary takeovers was selected for that mission. When he saw the survey statistics for the star system's third planet, he lusted for its mineral wealth. The amount of gold, platinum and heavy radioactive elements made this a particularly juicy planet to plunder. He readily accepted the commission.

Abn needed a successful and profitable project. His last invasion mission did not go well. It only yielded a small fraction of the minerals the surveyors had reported. It had taken his team one hundred and fifty seven years to figure out how to manipulate the physiology of the planet's inhabitants. They abducted thousands of the natives and conducted numerous tests, but it finally paid off. The virus they had designed won awards back on his home planet. But despite all of his hard work, the planet fell short of its mineral wealth projections and the blame was put on Abn.

Earth was a sweet morsel of a planet. It was exactly what he needed to redeem his reputation and reap a healthy profit. After ten years, his planning committee put together a mission plan and submitted it. The Invasion Council approved it and Abn Su was given official control. To make sure the job was done right this time, he intended to do the fieldwork himself.

Abn recruited a space crew and went to Earth on a reconnaissance mission. He had the original drone survey results that were done 396 years previously. The survey data had depicted a species that was in a primitive stage of civilization. The inhabitants were soft of skin and spent most of their waking hours chasing animals with sharp stones. Abn was pleased; this was going to be an easy planet to take over. Nevertheless, he always went on those missions escorted by armed battleships. His convoy was provisioned, fueled and launched for Earth. Abn's fleet consisted of his command ship, two battle cruisers and a survey ship filled with scientists and technicians. During the trip, Abn studied the reports they had on the Earth system and worked on how to proceed once they arrived. Abn was relieved when they finally reached the Oort cloud, the outermost edge of the Earth's star system. He was tired of being cooped up in the ship and was growing impatient. After dodging through the Kuiper Belt, the convoy entered the solar system.

They went past the outer planets and the survey crew did a quick inventory of their metal and mineralogical makeup. When they arrived at Mars, Abn decided to give it a closer look. In Mars' orbit they encountered the two moons, Phobos and Deimos. Their instruments indicated that Phobos was hollow. He decided to investigate and blasted a hole through a deep crater that scarred one end of it. Inside they found that it was hollow with gigantic crystals growing on the underside like a geode.

The interior of Phobos had once been solid ice. Over hundreds of millions of years, the push and pull of Mars' gravity warmed and melted it through tidal friction. The hot, watery interior leached minerals from the underside of Phobos. Over the course of millions of years, the warm waters deposited crystals on the underside of the crust. When all of the water sublimated into the hungry vacuum of space, it left behind massive crystals of olivine and opal. Phobos' micro-gravity interior allowed the crystals to grow into massive, obelisk shapes over two hundred feet long. The olivine crystals were shades of iridescent green with amorphous opal wrapped around them like multicolored snakes.

The Xxonox survey ship eased its way into Phobos' interior and turned on its powerful, exterior landing lights. It lit up the massive crystals of opal and olivine. The reflected lights bounced from one crystal to another and lit up the interior of Phobos like a pulsating laser light show. The beauty was lost on the Xxonox. All they saw was an empty space that was usable as a base. They built a docking port three hundred feet high that was shaped like a monolith. It gave them access to Phobos' hollow center and was used as a military outpost.

Abn's survey unit took a mineralogical reading of Mars' surface and found an unusually high presence of iron. Abn decided to explore the red planet further. As he was maneuvering his ship into orbit, Abn received an urgent dispatch from the Planetary Survey unit. They had found something strange on the surface that needed his immediate attention. Abn left the control room and rushed down to the survey station. When he walked into the survey monitoring room, there was an image of a face carved on the surface of a mesa. The alien face resembled the inhabitants of the third planet they were going to invade. The visage had been sculpted and was not a natural feature. Abn checked the life-form monitors and there were no higher life forms. There were only extremophile fungi and microbes, which thrived on the dark wet streaks on the surface.

Who carved the face of an earthling on this planet? Abn was puzzled. According to the last drone survey report from one hundred years ago, the humans were still technological savages. Abn ordered a shuttlecraft and a small crew to go with him to investigate. On the way down he marveled at the craftsmanship of the mountaintop sculpture. The closer he got, the more intricate the details became. The shuttle slowly hovered over the mesa. Bright, colorfully painted lines crisscrossed the face and terminated at the base underneath the chin. Abn zoomed in to that spot and the video feed showed a massive metallic door.

The shuttlecraft landed within one hundred feet of the entrance, kicking up fine red powder. After the dust settled, Abn and his security detail suited up and made their way to the entrance. A bronze door ten feet high was in a recessed alcove. The surface of the door had panels etched with drawings and strange symbols. One panel depicted a small hairy animal reaching out to a human and the human was pointing at a spaceship. Another panel showed the solar system they were in next to an unknown star system. On the right wall were two large buttons. Abn pressed the top one. It lit up and vibrated under his fingertips. He pushed in the other button and the door slowly swung inward on frictionless bearings.

It was dusk and the reddish, feeble light only penetrated a few feet inside. Abn ordered one of the security men to walk in. The guard hoisted his weapon and gingerly stepped over the threshold. He had only taken a few steps when the lights suddenly came on. Inside was a cavernous room with intricate machines and electronics on display. Shelves stacked with thousands of multicolored books lined the interior walls. In the center of the room was an intricately carved pedestal with a large book on it. Abn opened it and it had an index of different languages with pictograms. It was clearly meant to teach the language of whoever built this repository. This was definitely not the work of humans. Abn took the large tome and looked around and took pictures. After an hour, he went back to his ship in orbit. He had his linguistic scientists translate the book he had confiscated. It was deciphered and the translated version was sent to Abn.

The book told of a race called the Cyn who came from another star system. Their purpose was to guide the backward humans to a space age civilization. Abn was concerned that the Cyn were competing for the resources of Earth. But on further reading, he realized they only wanted humans to join their coalition. Abn was going to put a stop to their meddling. From orbit, he ordered the destruction of the depository. His battle cruisers pounded the mesa with high explosive missiles until it was an unrecognizable mountain of rubble.

The alien force traveled slowly from Mars to Earth at a leisurely, sub-light speed. During the trip, Abn studied the translated material. When he saw the carved face, he was concerned that another civilization with superior weaponry had beaten them to this star's planetary resources. It was not that the Xxonox were cowardly, they were just cautious. They never took a planet by force of arms. They used microscopic, organic agents to manipulate the planet's population and put them under mind control. Like an anaconda, they slowly choked a planet to death.

The Cyn's book revealed how they built a large pyramid and a stone complex to nudge the barbaric human brain to a higher level. Abn carefully read the material and noted that the Cyn did not have weapons of war. He was also relieved that the Cyn's star system was hundreds of light years away.

When he arrived in Earth's orbit, Abn ordered the surveillance unit to find the Cyn bases that were referenced in the book from the Martian library. There were two stations; one was hidden away in a desert mountain range and the other was based on the outskirts of a pyramid city. After a quick search, they found and pinpointed the bases.

Abn reviewed the Planetary Survey's results. He compared the new findings with the robotic survey that was done 600 years ago. The results showed that the Cyn's interference had progressed the inhabitants significantly in a short period of time. If the earthlings continued on their course, they could interfere with the invasion. Abn called an emergency meeting to work out a plan to thwart the human's advancement. He wanted to send the Cyn a clear warning; *"Stay away from my planet!"*

Chapter Twenty-Two

The shaman's visions took a pause as the hallucinogens in his system wore off. He was in a comfortable black void as quiet as a womb. He dreamt he was being kissed. His lips were gently parted and a wet tongue found his. He could not see who it was in the darkness of his mind. He had given up the pleasures of the flesh years ago and had not kissed a woman in twenty years. He forced his eyes open to find a feral dog licking his mouth. Disgusted, he kicked the dog in its sunken belly. With a yelp it scurried off with its tail between its legs and a hurt expression on its face.

It was after 3:00 p.m. and the sun was on the other side of the village. Men were in their huts enjoying their siesta. No one had bothered to wake the shaman up for lunch and he was famished. There was a cold pot of stew in an open kitchen. He dipped a large ladle through the crust of congealed fat and spooned up a piece of chicken. He had not realized how hungry he was and slurped more of the broth. He refilled his water flask in the well and ambled back to his blanket. The world around him looked insubstantial. His dream journeys were far more vivid than the outside reality. He felt rested but an electric knot in his stomach reminded him that he was not done yet. He had unraveled a lot of the alien's history but there was more. He did not understand all of it. The threads of his visions seemed unrelated, but he knew they would all come together in the end.

The shaman made another Ayahuasca beverage and drank down the bitter brew. His body had long ago stopped vomiting after drinking the vile concoction, but it still turned his stomach. He went to his blankets and looked for the dog that had licked him. He found it resting by a bush panting with its tongue hanging out. The shaman picked up a rock by his feet and threw it. He was surprised when it hit the dog squarely on its head. The dog barked halfheartedly, got up and moved farther away. At least he would not be bothered by it again. He pulled the blanket over his head to block out the afternoon sun, closed his eyes and continued on his journey.

Chapter Twenty-Three

Abn and his team came up with a two-fold plan to reverse the progress of the human race. First, he would implant a group of humans with hatred toward their fellow man that would last for hundreds of generations. This would keep the planet in turmoil for thousands of years. Then he would destroy the Cyn, their structures and as many of their tainted humans as possible.

For the first part of his plan, Abn needed to recruit earthlings who had a propensity for criminality, mayhem and chaos. He baited a trap to catch them. He found a deep cave that was off the beaten path in between the two Cyn bases. Abn recorded images of the cave and its surroundings. He activated a telepathic transmitter and set it to the frequency of a human's lowest moral and ethical values. He inserted feelings of power, riches, and sex in the transmissions. Xxonox biologists found those buttons would cause humans to react. Along with the emotional signals he patched in images of the cave and its location with hypnotic commands to go there. Abn set his trap and waited.

Three days later, he checked in on the cave via the hidden video equipment he had set around it. It was nighttime on the surface and over two hundred natives had gathered around the cave area. This had exceeded Abn's expectations. It was time to go down and implement his plan. He boarded his shuttle and took it out into space. As he descended from orbit he activated the telepathic relay on board his ship. Abn aimed the telepathic beam toward the cave area. It amplified and projected his focused thoughts to the milling crowd hundreds of miles below him.

"God and the Devil are coming. Be very afraid. Killing sets one free. You are the chosen ones." Those thoughts were projected unknowingly into the men's minds. Abn smiled as he descended through the atmosphere. His video screen showed the men in a hypnotic stupor. As he descended, his craft emitted a wide-aperture, visible-light laser toward the cave area. From the ground, it looked as if a bright star had suddenly appeared in the dark sky. The humans were primed and ready.

*

Serhann awoke uneasily in the middle of the night from a strange dream. He dreamt he was wearing a gold crown and stood on top of a mound of writhing bodies. The people under his feet did not have mouths or lips, but he could hear them in his mind. They were telling him that he was their lord and master. A star erupted in the heavens and a fiery chariot came down from the sky and landed near him. A blue skinned demon emerged from the craft and handed him a scepter. It was heavy and made of pure gold. The demon pointed to the dark sky above, and told Serhann that the God of Chaos had selected him for a special mission. If he were successful, he would be spoiled forever with gold, wine and virgins of both sexes. He was only required to get others to bow to the God of Chaos and eliminate those who did not. Then the night turned into day and the sun exploded in the sky, jarring him awake.

Serhann opened his eyes and awoke disoriented. The dream had seemed so real. He put his hand on his head, feeling for the gold crown, but alas it was not there. Maybe he had that strange dream because of what he had done earlier that night. He had ambushed a merchant, stabbed him, and relieved him of his purse.

"Thief! Thief!" A passerby had seen what happened and blew a bone whistle that pierced the night. Serhann panicked and ran. He arrived at his hut, breathless and scared. He worried he had been recognized. The satchel he stole held only a few bone ornaments, small stones and a prayer doll. It was worthless. If he were caught, he would be stoned for nothing. He hid under a dirty blanket, crouched in the corner of the stone hut. Hours passed and no one came looking for him. Exhausted and emotionally drained, he fell into a deep sleep, until the dream woke him up.

Serhann had an urge to go someplace that was important, but he could not remember where he was supposed to go, or why. The feeling became stronger as the dream faded. An image of a cave came to his mind. It was in the side of a large, rocky hill in the shadow of a saddleback shaped mountain. There was a meadow in front of the cave opening, flanked by a meandering stream. Wait! He sat bolt upright. He knew that area. It was many hours away on horseback. Serhann felt compelled to go there. He would have left that instant, but he did not own a horse. The prospect of walking that far did not appeal to him. He lay back down on his straw bed, pulled up the covers and closed his eyes. Even with his eyes shut the image of the cave beckoned to him; it reminded him of the slack, open mouth of a drunken whore.

He was restless and could not go back to sleep. There was nothing worth stealing in this pitiful, poor village. It was time he moved on. With his decision made, Serhann went to a nearby inn and stole a horse from the stable. He quietly led the reluctant animal to the outskirts of town, jumped on it, and galloped away as fast as he could to his destiny.

After a wild, three-hour ride, he found the cave. He was not the only one there. Scores of men quietly huddled around small, smoky fires. They were all hardened criminals, drawn to that area like flies to excrement. He walked stealthily into the clearing. A few heads furtively turned toward him but quickly darted away. Everyone was scanning the skies above and paid him no attention. Serhann felt compelled to look up too. All he could see were the stars twinkling in the blackness of the night. He felt no threat from the throng of criminals around him. He tied his horse to a nearby tree and found a spot near one of the fires.

When he sat down he noticed a woman alone on the edge of the clearing standing by a fire. She was looking up exposing her beautifully sculpted neck. Her hair was jet black and tied in a ponytail that extended pass her buttocks. Her bodice was slightly open exposing her full, taut breasts. Her skin was smooth and as dark as roasted olives. Serhann licked his lips at the way her nipples pushed against the fabric of her undergarment. Her rough hemp skirt had a slit exposing her thigh almost to her hips. Unconsciously, he became aroused. His hardened member lifted the hem of his wrap around kilt. The flickering fire barely penetrated the soft crevasse of her cleavage. He wondered why she was not being brutally raped by the throng of sexual deviants around her. He was mesmerized. The fire ignited pitch in the wood and made it brighter for an instant and exposed what Serhann had missed before.

She wore a necklace that at first appeared to be a string of dried sausages. But to his horror, in the sudden light he saw it for what it was, desiccated penises. A dagger hung from her belt, its blade encrusted with dried blood. Then it dawned on him, she was Lejla the Unspeakable. She was a witch who used her beauty to lure men to their deaths. It was rumored that many men had penetrated her pleasure only to pull away a bloody stump. The discarded members adorned her lovely bosom in that grisly necklace. Her beauty was a trap and she used her body the way a spider used a web. She hated men and used her magic to weaken and infest them with horrible diseases and death.

Serhann looked away just as Lejla looked down from the sky. She had blue eyes, which was unheard of in a land of dark, browned-eye people. Those who had looked into her eyes and lived said they were the color of a diseased vein. Serhann looked away and prayed to his gods that she had not caught him looking at her. His erection deflated and tried to retract behind his pubic bone. Serhann nonchalantly turned away and pretended to look at the sky. He felt her eyes boring through the back of his skull. He resisted the urge to run headlong into the desert but it would advertise his guilt and he continued to act interested in the moonless sky.

*

Unlike the others, Lejla knew why she was there. It was not dreams or voices in her head that had made her come. She was a witch and a psychic. She read the minds of men as easily as seeing fish at the bottom of a clear lake. Her cocktail of blue lily plants and mandrake enhanced her clairvoyance. Lejla became aware of an evil power far greater than her own hovering far out in space. The demon she saw in her visions was not conceived in the depths of hell. Its home circled a faraway star and had no connection to the mythology of Man. Its evil was not of this Earth and she wanted to learn from it.

Lejla looked upward and sensed the otherworldly presence out in the darkness between the twinkling points of light. She felt one of the men staring at her. She turned toward him but he had already looked away. She eyed him for a moment, daring him to turn around. After a few moments, she smiled and continued searching the heavens for her master.

*

Over the course of the night, more men arrived. The gathering swelled to two hundred and twenty-five people. Each new arrival looked around at the huddled men, then up at the sky. Even though they did not know each other, an unspoken brotherhood bonded them. A feeling of his own greatness grew in Serhann. Sitting exposed in the dark, his feeling of power was tempered by his fear of the demons of the night. It had been some time since Serhann had sex and that was with a young boy he had forced himself upon. His loins were excited by the thoughts of virgins and the orgies of his dream. The feelings of arousal and fear made a strange mix, flavored with the sour taste of the unknown. He was getting aroused again and made sure he was out of sight of the witch.

Someone shouted and pointed to the sky. A light, brighter than a star, had suddenly appeared. It was strong enough to hurt their eyes. It was an unspoken signal. The men stood quietly and looked skyward.

Serhann saw the bright star move across the firmament. It grew larger as it loomed closer and then the light went out. He was able to make out a circular shape that eclipsed the stars behind it. When it was only a hundred feet above them, a purple beam of light erupted from it and lit up their faces. The men in the circle of light slunk away, blinded and scared. Serhann realized that his dream was becoming a reality. The craft landed gently as a feather without kicking up any dust. A seamless door slid open spilling out ultraviolet light. A blue skinned demon climbed out and stood on the lip of the craft. Serhann had a feeling of déjà vu before he passed out.

The shaman slowly opened his eyes. He was not sure if he had been dreaming or reliving real events. It was early morning and the sun was trying to break through the low fog. What was left of his audience were huddled together asleep. His buttocks were sore and his limbs stiff from sitting in the same position for hours. He tried to convey the images from the memories of his encounter with the evil alien. The villagers had listened attentively, even if most of it was incomprehensible to them. One by one they had fallen asleep, many to uneasy nightmares. The fire became more smoke than flame. The red coals danced with images like a Rorschach test. A charred log popped and sent flaming embers into the dirt. A sudden release of smoke took on the face of an alien before it dissipated.

'That is not a good omen.' The shaman lay down on the cold damp ground, pulled the blanket over his head and closed his eyes. The Ayahuasca trance hugged him in its embrace and the alien saga took over the center stage of his mind.

Chapter Twenty-Four

When Abn was five hundred feet from the ground he activated a broadcast that rendered the throng around the ship unconscious. He landed as close as he could, careful not to crush any bodies. Abn turned on a transmitter that emitted a strong, hypnotic wave engineered for the human brain. Then he activated an electronic pain-generating field that overloaded the nervous system. The unconscious bodies on the ground writhed in silent agony. The flick of another switch turned on external speakers with instructions to destroy the human race. The combination of the pain and hypnotic waves engraved the commands into their subconscious. The Xxonox were masters of this type of coercion, tailored to each race they had conquered.

After five minutes of the treatment he turned it off. He grabbed an injector gun loaded with mental tracking devices and went outside. The transponders were a specialty of the Xxonox mind-engineers. They were made out of mental energy and were "glued" to a being's psyche. The trackers were invisible to the host and could not be detected by physical means. It allowed the Xxonox to keep track of their souls even after they died and were reborn.

The muzzle end was shaped like an upside-down colander. He went to each prone body and positioned it over their heads. Abn pulled the trigger when a purple light indicated that it was synchronized. He was almost done when he turned over a body and was surprised to see it was a female of the species. Abn had expected only male humans, but she had responded to his subliminal call. She could be useful but just to make sure he went back into the ship and changed the setting of the pain transmitters from wide angle to a tightly focused beam. He aimed it at her body and dialed the intensity up to maximum. As the pain waves wracked her body he transmitted more commands into her psyche. After he was done, he planted the tracker into her and finished with the rest of the men. He went inside his ship, sent a hypnotic command to forget what had occurred and turned off the sleep ray. Outside, everyone slowly woke up and got on their feet. Still in a daze, they stood where they had been standing before they were rendered unconscious. As one, they opened their eyes and instantly forgot what had just happened and stared in awe at the blue demon before them.

*

Serhann marveled how his dream had come true. He listened in rapture to the words of the being from the stars. It spoke magically, without a mouth or lips to form words.

"Brothers and sister, I come from the dark heavens above to save you. A cataclysm is coming to your world. If you sign a pact with me, you will survive. If you do not, you will perish." It looked around them with its strange large eyes. There was no need for them to speak. Their presence there had already sealed their fate.

"You have been chosen to be the rulers of your world. I am not one of your gods. I am only a messenger. The message I have for you is that death and destruction is the way of my god. Chaos is the meat we eat. Fear, the wine we drink. For each being you convert to this path, you will receive gold, riches and pleasures beyond your wildest dreams. For each person you destroy who will not convert, your riches will increase tenfold." Abn's words reverberated in their skulls as the telepathic relay amplified his every thought.

Serhann's mind was filled with the weight of gold in his pockets and food in his hungry stomach. His loins were aroused as images of countless virgins filled his head. Boys and girls threw themselves at his feet and ravished him.

"Tomorrow when the sun is directly overhead, great invisible fires will envelope the land. You must go deep into this cave." Abn pointed ominously to the cave entrance that was only yards away. "If you do not, you will perish in the light of day and your body and soul will be no more." Abn paused to gauge the reaction of the crowd and took pleasure in their fear and awe.

"Go into the cave, take a small torch and light it at noon. Do not emerge from the cave until it has burnt itself out. When you return outside, you will witness the power of our Lord of Chaos and the wrath he has levied upon the non-believers of your world."

Abn looked at the gathering, wide eyed with the power of his message. Without saying anything further, he turned around and went back into his ship. The spacecraft rose silently until it became lost in the firmament above. Dawn was graying the sky. The men rushed into the cave, babbling about the demon's words with religious fervor.

*

Abn docked his shuttle and went to the control room monitoring station. He checked on the humans and they were all deep inside the cave, talking to each other in hushed tones. Now that this part of his plan was underway, he checked on the progress of the solar flare he had created two days ago. They had launched a magnetic missile into the sun. The bomb created an immense magnetic field that immediately collapsed. On a planet's surface, the magnetic bomb would not do any damage to a pre-electronic civilization. However, on the surface of a star, it created a momentary opening, a transient coronal hole. Out of that artificially created sunspot erupted a massive stream of solar radiation. It was precisely timed so that it would hit the Cyn bases point-blank. It was going to penetrate the atmosphere and irradiate Earth's surface with deadly protons. The storm would kill any living thing exposed to it. The Xxonox fleet had two hours before impact, plenty of time to destroy the Cyn bases and leave the system before the storm overtook them.

Abn ordered the attack on the Cyn bases. The first target was the mountain base in Turkey. The Xxonox battleship positioned itself in orbit over the Cyn base. Once its particle cannon was at full capacity and the Cyn base was in its sights, it discharged its deadly load of heavy iron isotope atoms. The cannon replicated the fury of a supernova and focused it into a narrow beam. The heavy atoms burned through the atmosphere at a fraction of the speed of light. It destroyed half of the base in seconds and left an ionized trail in its wake. The massive weapon took ten seconds to recharge, and then the rest of the base was destroyed.

The Cyn's book that Abn had confiscated told of a stone temple that was built to point humans to the Martian library. Abn went to that site, which was not too far from the destroyed base. When he arrived he recognized the floating metallic balls and vividly painted stone structures from the book's images. He landed by the largest of the stone circles, and went inside. The enclosure had a floating, metallic ball between two of the tallest pillars. He climbed up on it and tried to push the ball but it was held in place by a force field. He went back to his ship, aimed a laser cannon at the base of the pillars and blew it apart. The metallic ball, unsupported, fell to the ground. Abn went over and rolled it up the ramp and into his ship. He repeated that procedure with the other globes until he had all of them. Then he took his ship one thousand feet above the site and blasted the brightly colored stone monuments with fire. The heat melted the surface of the stone and turned the paint to ash. Another ship equipped with mining equipment buried the stone pillars under tons of dirt and sand. Thousands of years later, archaeologist Klaus Schmidt excavated the temple area, which became known as Göbekli Tepe. He excavated the elaborate stone carvings and structures, but Abn's destruction had left them undecipherable.

Abn proceeded to the other Cyn base. As he approached it from the air he saw the pyramid. It was many miles in the distance and dominated the horizon. It was larger than he had expected. He was even more surprised to see a large gold cap wrapped by a copper band at its apex. Abn ordered his ship to the top of the pyramid and attached force grapplers to the precious metal and slowly rose into the air, ripping it from the pyramid. When he was at a safe distance Abn ordered his orbiting battle cruisers to bomb the base and destroy the pyramid. A city rose majestically in the shadow of the pyramid and he ordered its destruction as well. Once he was back aboard his ship, he checked on the progress of the incoming solar storm. The attack had taken longer than expected and the solar flare was almost upon them. He gave the evacuation order and the fleet immediately left the area.

The Xxonox had effectively aborted the birth of human civilization. In 10,000 years they would return to rape the Earth of its resources and decimate the human race.

Chapter Twenty-Five

It took 5,000 years for humanity to get back on its feet. Only a fraction of a percent of the Cyn's influence survived the devastation wrought by the Xxonox. It showed up in Sumeria and sustained Egypt through its golden ages. The Egyptians had records of the Cyn pyramid and duplicated them as best they could with chisels and crude mechanical aids. The ashes of the Cyn's program found root in ancient Greece and fueled the growth of the Roman Empire. However, the human agents of the Xxonox thwarted any chance of a full recovery. Through the ages, the two hundred and twenty-five men and woman indoctrinated by Abn did their job well. Nero and Caligula were the same agents of chaos recruited by Abn thousands of years ago.

Lifetime after lifetime, they pissed on the feeble flame of civilization. Attila the Hun, Pol Pot, Genghis Khan and Hitler were the reincarnated people from the cave. The first American female serial killer Lavinia Fisher and Elizabeth Báthory – the female Dracula, were just a few of the incarnations of Lejla the Unspeakable. She reincarnated as Queen Isabella of Spain and used the inquisition to torture thousands of innocent people. Lejla had many lifetimes where she was under the radar of history. She was a hidden evil influence for countless generations.

Despite the odds and the Xxonox knife sunk deep in the back of humanity, mankind continued to stumble forward. The wars and confusion wrought by the alien cabal kept progress in check and cleared the way for the coming Xxonox invasion.

Chapter Twenty-Six

Abn returned with a pre-invasion force 9,995 years after the Cyn massacre. He had lived thirty-four lifetimes since he was last on Earth. Abn's present body was cloned from cells kept alive for a million and a half years. The Xxonox had perfected asexual reproduction. When their bodies died, their minds and memories remained intact. The deceased, disembodied Xxonox reported to the vat factory and picked up their fully-grown bodies. Only the owner, who was tuned to it, could activate the body's brain channels. With proper care and maintenance a Xxonox's body could last 300 years. It took a lot of time and effort to take over a planet. A ten thousand year plan was not a long time for the Xxonox who lived body after body, for millions of years.

Abn had to refresh his memories from the last time he had visited the Sol system. A lot of events had happened in the last 10,000 years of his life and he had forgotten a few things here and there. He reread his reports from his first visit and the ship's logs. One thing he had not forgotten was how rich he was going to become after securing the planet. Abn went over the data that had been collected over thousands of years from surveillance drones and covert missions. He read in detail the xenobiologist's report on their human experimentation. He reviewed the 3D videos the biologists recorded of the human subjects.

For many thousands of years they abducted humans regularly to test different strains of their biological agents. They researched and probed the human body's weaknesses. The xenobiologists were tasked with finding a way to disseminate the virus quickly to the entire population. They looked for any activity that was universal and could be hijacked for their purposes. Their surveillance revealed that earthlings were obsessed with sex. They set up tests to find out if that activity would be a good candidate. Procreation and sexual emotions were foreign to them, especially in an alien species. They began their experiments with subjects who lived in ancient Mesopotamia.

The biologist's field team abducted a female who was working alone in a field. They needed a male of the species and kidnapped a man who was walking alone in the woods nearby. The humans were conscious when they were brought to the mother ship in orbit. The Xxonox made no attempt to put them to sleep or blanket their minds; they were going to die anyway.

They put the two humans in an observation room with a bed of rough straw in the center. The staff of the xenobiology department sat in a circular theater overlooking the room. The humans stood still, barely breathing. The couple was overwhelmed with fear. They thought that they had been abducted by the Demons of the Underworld and had been taken deep beneath the earth.

Using their telepathic control, the Xxonox transmitted recordings of people copulating into the minds of the man and woman. The human subjects had no idea what to do with the pornography in their heads. They had no sexual attraction for each other. They had a kinship, they were human and the monstrosities around them were definitely not. After two days of strange, sexual images intruding into their minds, they refused to have any sexual intercourse.

The alien biologists decided to take matters into their own hands and took telepathic control of their bodies. They forced them together. The man and woman blindly groped each other like manikins coldly touching each other in a department store basement.

The humans had no idea what was required of them. Their minds were filled with strange, erotic images that would be banned in any culture. They felt their bodies moving and doing things, but without their volition. The male, not being able to help himself, became physically aroused. They looked at each other and saw the fear and confusion in each other's eyes. They were made to copulate over and over again in strange and alien contortions. The man silently begged forgiveness. She knew he was not responsible for his actions and forgave him.

After five days, the Xxonox gave up trying to force the humans to have sex. It was too difficult to get their bodies to copulate and it took too much time. The scientists needed to find a better way to circulate the invasion virus into the human population. They released their mental control of the man and woman who then fell limply to the floor, exhausted from their physical exertions. Short, gray-skinned lab workers came into the room, took the couple and unceremoniously dumped them out of the air lock.

The xenobiologists continued their search for thousands of years. With the explosion of drugs in the twentieth century, they finally found what they were looking for. Drug use would be the perfect vector for propagating the invasion virus. The alien xenobiologists concentrated their abductions on drug addicts. Most of the abductees did not survive the process. The few that did spoke of strange alien abductions and were ignored as crazed, tripping druggies.

The Xxonox discovered that drug use debilitated human bodies and made them unsuitable for slave labor. That created a problem because slaves had to be healthy enough to do the work required of them. For many years they tested different drugs on thousands of human guinea pigs. By process of elimination they found that cocaine was the best carrier for their viral weapon. Now they could work on their distribution plan and submit it to Abn.

They tweaked the mechanics of the virus so that it would fuse with cocaine on contact. Once ingested, the virus hijacked the human brain and the sympathetic nervous system. It compelled the host to live healthier, the opposite of what drugs did. That stage lasted six months, during which time the body became more robust. At the end of the dormant period, the virus killed half of those infected. The dying hosts would then expel the mutated virus as a powder, a chain-reaction that would infect others instantly. The Xxonox scientists predicted that the entire human race would be contaminated within two weeks after the six-month incubation period. The infected survivors would then incubate a tertiary stage of the virus. The new strain would concentrate in the brain's control center and prime it for remote manipulation. It was a brilliant plan and complicated enough to thwart early discovery by human scientists. The xenobiologists submitted their report and recommendations to Abn.

Abn had been studying violent groups around the world, in particular the cartels in South America. He was exploring ways to use them to spread panic during the invasion. The xenobiologists report crystallized a new plan. The new plan was going to use the cartel's drugs to spread the invasion virus. He had the perfect cartel leader in mind, Raul "Cojones" Melendez.

Abn had kept close surveillance on Melendez. He had enjoyed watching Raul kill his fellow human beings over the chemicals he sold. Abn was going to use that human's greed to spread the seeds of destruction. He would need approval for his plan from the representative council member on board his ship before he could act on it. He called for an emergency executive meeting with the council executive, the head of the security forces and the lead biologist.

Abn presented the findings of the xenobiologists on the cocaine drug and the virus. He then went into detail of how he was going to trick the humans by letting them disable his craft and allow them to capture him. Abn had the Security officer explain his role in the plan. A small, undetectable security shuttle would be on station a few miles above Abn's position at all times. It would have a crew of gamma ray snipers. If the humans went outside of Abn's plan, they would be killed instantly. The council member approved the plan immediately and a copy was sent to the Supreme Council of Zutox Prime, the capital planet of the Xxonox Empire. Abn did not waste any time in getting his scheme into action, he waited a long time for this moment.

Chapter Twenty-Seven

Abn floated above the river in the area where his surveillance team had spotted the workers from the Melendez cartel. He flashed his landing lights on and off to attract their attention. Through the jungle, he spotted the group of men loading their drugs into a large metallic vessel in the water. Abn alerted the security detail shadowing him two miles above. The snipers were ready to provide any back up as needed.

Abn readied the explosive device attached to the outside of his shuttle. No man-made weapon could penetrate his ship's hull, which was built to withstand direct meteoroid hits at sub-light speeds. When detonated, the explosive charge would blow off fake metal plates shaped like his hull.

Abn slowly approached the bend in the river. The on-board monitors showed the humans had their weapons drawn and were aware of his presence. Abn turned off the external lights and stealthily crept up on them. His gravity engine had no moving parts and was noiseless. When he rounded the bend Abn was suddenly face-to-face with the Melendez guards. He aimed the craft's powerful landing beacon directly at them and turned them on. The men were blinded and after a momentary pause they fired at his shuttle with bullets and explosive missiles. Abn pressed a button and the outside plates exploded outward with a loud bang. Black smoke filled the air and the shock of the explosion created ripples on the river's surface. Abn banked his craft at a sharp angle and flew downwards into the jungle. Trees snapped like toothpicks against the hardened hull. He purposely crashed-landed hard into the jungle floor. Abn barely felt the crash protected by the inertial force field. He unlocked the hatch, laid face down as if he was injured and waited for the cartel men to "capture" him.

Abn was in telepathic communication with the security

crew hovering unseen a few miles above. They were ready when the cartel men entered the jungle clearing. The shuttle was still smoking from the fake explosion. The cartel men surrounded the ship and flipped it over. They saw Abn laying face down and turned him over. Abn felt their fear and revulsion and he relished it. He continued to lay limp and seemingly unconscious. The guard's leader called Raul "Cojones" Melendez and was told to take Abn to the cartel base. His plan was working out perfectly.

The humans took Abn to the compound in a flimsy aircraft. He continued to lay limp as they carried him into the basement of a building. The snipers covering Abn had a gamma ray scope that could see through walls and they followed Abn closely. This was the most dangerous phase of the operation. Abn was locked in a room with killers, but he was not particularly worried. Though he did not have any weapons, he had the telepathic power to freeze an earthling's mind in an instant. The Xxonox race had perfected the telepathic transmission of fear. Every being in the universe shared that emotion and the Xxonox were masters at manipulating it. He could swamp a human's consciousness with enough fear to immobilize them.

Abn was put in a chair and he kept his eyes closed until he was poked hard in the chest. He sat up suddenly and opened his eyes. The reaction in the room was immediate. The people in the room were taken aback and one of them fired his weapon. A member of the Xxonox security team was pumped-up and ready to kill. When the Raul's guard inadvertently fired his gun, the sniper reacted and jerked his finger. A blast of focused, deadly radiation went into the room and killed a bird that was in a corner of the room. Abn sent a scathing thought to the premature shooter and continued his charade. He read the minds of everyone in the room and used their fear, multiplied with his own mental energy, against them. The men in the room thought he was afraid of them, unaware that he had instilled that emotion into them.

Abn continued playing his charade of the frightened alien,

even when Raul picked up the shears to cut off his finger. He was ready to blast Raul's mind if he tried it. Raul was convinced that he was scared of him. He put away the shears, which spared his life. Raul played perfectly into the web cast by the xenobiologists. Humans are infinitely stupid, greedy and easy to manipulate. This was going to be the easiest pre-invasion I had ever been involved with.

He enjoyed telling the lie about his need for aluminum. Abn's planet was flooded with that worthless metal. Raul's rapaciousness was beyond bounds and he took the entire bait. Raul thought he was making the deal of his life and ran headlong into the trap. The trade agreement was signed, which put Abn one step closer to getting away from Earth. He was tired of his pretense and could not wait until he was back in his orbiting ship.

He felt like a giant among tiny insects and had to be careful not to step on them. Raul's smugness and feeling of superiority irritated Abn. There were many times when he restrained himself from ripping Raul's head from his neck. Abn could have used one of his many juniors to play this part, but he wanted to make sure that nothing went wrong. He maintained his composure and continued his play-acting. Abn's hard work was paying off and the last phase of his plan would soon be over.

The virus had been already been formulated years before, but he acted as if their labs had just made them. After a short period of time, the virus was delivered to Raul. The weapons and gravity engines were next which had cut-off timers secretly installed in them. Abn had convinced Raul to use one of his common transportation vehicles. He did not want humans to have a space-worthy craft and possibly interfere with his operation in orbit. When Abn was finally released from his obligations to Raul, he took the last of the aluminum payment, loaded it into his shuttle and left as fast as he could. Once the ship was far enough away, he dumped the aluminum trash into the sea.

*

The shaman awoke with a start. He was disoriented and tried to get his bearings. The afternoon sun burned his swollen, red eyes. The villagers were going about their business, unaware of the guillotine hanging over the head of humanity. Someone had put a blanket over him while he slept. Everything around him seemed normal. Children were yelling and chasing each other, scattering dogs and chickens in their path. The smell of cooking filled the air mixed with the odor of wood fires. The strains of a popular Cumbia song played festively from a hut. A teenage couple was dancing in a circle to its beats, swinging each other around and laughing.

The shaman felt his age as he slowly sat up. A passing elder asked him if he would like something to eat. He nodded a quiet yes. He looked into the jungle at the edge of the village and expected to see a horde of aliens rush at him. His visions slowly faded, but they left an aftertaste of doom. He tried to shake it off, to no avail. Unseen forces were gathering in the darkness above the noon sky and the end of humanity was near. The shaman spooned up the bowl of mush that the elder had placed in his hands, but he had lost his appetite.

His connection to the alien's memories had ended. He could clearly see the past, but the future was cloudy. An image slammed into his consciousness of a white man at the compound. The stranger was an important player in the upcoming struggle but he was in mortal danger. This was not a memory, it was happening in real time at that very moment.

The shaman abruptly stood up and spilled his bowl into the dirt. With the agility of a young man, he ran the two miles to the compound. He arrived out of breath at the fence surrounding the Melendez estate. He saw the man in his vision surrounded by swirling dust from a helicopter's downwash. The shaman tried to get his attention, but the American boarded the helicopter and took off. The shaman was too late. With a heavy heart he disappeared back into the jungle. It was already too late to change the coming course of events.

Chapter Twenty-Eight

Maryann was working the on-ramp to 205 South, in Portland, Oregon. She was holding up a barely legible and misspelled sign that read, "Layed off work. Aneything Helps. Godbless." The twenty dollars or so she made a day barely paid for her meth habit. Today someone had thrown two twenties at her. She hadn't eaten in two days, with the forty bucks she could get a quarter gram of meth and have enough left over for a Whopper with fries.

She boarded a TriMet bus to North Portland. She wanted to buy her fix and camp out under a highway overpass. She got off the bus and walked until she came to the alley entrance where she usually met her drug connection.

Larmaine "Chompers" Maurice was making a killing selling 'Blue.' The cartel dealer who sold him his first test batch had been right, this shit was more addictive than anything else he'd ever sold. His clientele had tripled in just one week. Larmaine was selling Blue on both sides of the Willamette River and expanding across the Columbia River into Vancouver, Washington. In fact, he was making more money than he could spend. Though he had fifteen dealers selling for him, Larmaine still liked to be on the streets now and then to keep his finger on the pulse of the market.

Larmaine was leaning against a light pole on the corner, when he saw one of his customers walking toward him. It was that crack-head, Maryann.

"Hi Maryann, wassup?" Larmaine called out to her.

"Hey Larmaine I'm doing alright. I just want to buy some crank." Maryann swiveled her bony hips and gave him an alluring eye as she spoke. Larmaine looked her up and down. He liked to get a little something extra from his female clients, but Maryann was too damn skinny and skanky even for him.

"Maryann, I don't sell that crap anymore. I have something even better."

"Fuck no, Larmaine! Come on, man." Her voice was high and whiny. "I need my meth, you know that's the only thing I use."

"You dumb-ass bitch, didn't you hear what I just said? I don't sell that crap no more. You can find someone else to buy your crank from, or try this new shit I got. It's called 'Melendez Blue' and it will really fuck you up. Blue is way better than crystal meth anyway. I'll even give you an extra hit for free. Damn girl! Stop fucking with me. Buy what I have or move the fuck on." Larmaine put his hands on his hips as he impatiently waited for her response.

Maryann didn't have another connection and Larmaine knew it. Reluctantly, she handed over her hard earned cash. Larmaine nodded three times to his partner, who was standing thirty feet away. The runner surreptitiously sauntered into an alley behind him and retrieved three packets from a hidden cache. Then he walked over, handed it to Maryann and continued walking past her.

"Hey Larmaine, can I cook it the way I do crystal and inject it?" Maryann was looking over the small plastic baggie in her hand. It had a sticker of an alien's face on it and a bluish powder was visible inside.

"Nah, just snort it." Larmaine turned his back on her to greet another customer. Maryann took her hits and headed for the nearest Burger King. Once Maryann was settled in and had eaten all of her Whopper and fries, she snorted a pinch of the new drug. Instantly, her mind cleared and she felt better. Maryann took another long snort. Her mind raced with memories of her past. Her life had not always been this bad. She was raised in a supportive family and had carried a 3.0 grade point average at a southeast Portland high school. Everything had changed when Maryann met a girl named Amanda. She was a popular girl who also did double duty as the school's drug dealer. Amanda convinced Maryann to try a little meth just once, but one time was all it took and she was helplessly addicted. Within three months, Maryann had dropped out of school and ran away from home. She had been on the streets and homeless going on three years now. Maryann sat up straighter as she realized she needed to get her shit together. The blue drug was really good and she wanted more of it. Holding up cardboard signs on street corners and on-ramps was not going to cut it anymore.

Six months later, Maryann's life had turned around. She revived her talent for making jewelry out of copper wire and colored beads. She made a living selling them on the street by the Skidmore Fountain, just outside the Saturday Market. She made more money selling her trinkets than she ever did holding up a cardboard sign. She had a good location and the other panhandlers left her alone. She had even made a few friends with the local street people. Maryann had a small dog that was always by her side. She had found it half dead in Laurelhurst Park. Maryann used to sleep there, deep in the bushes where no one could see her. Sometime during a rainy night, the dog had joined her while she was asleep. She woke up to a longhaired, white dog with dark patches, snuggled in her arms. Its hair was matted with cockleburs imbedded deep in its dirty fur. One eye was sunken; its eyelids glued together with dried puss. The dog had come there to die. She shared the scraps of food she had and nursed it back to life. Maryann named the dog Merry, because it had lifted her spirits.

Maryann kept the dog by her blanket when she sold her jewelry and it helped her sales. Merry's one-eyed smile and wagging tail attracted a lot of attention from pedestrians. One of Maryann's customers was a dog breeder and told her that it was a Havanese, a popular breed. One day just for fun, Maryann put an eye patch over Merry's missing eye. The new look doubled Maryann's sales. The MAX train stop was just a few yards away and gave Maryann plenty of customers to sell to. Her life was getting better, she had put on some weight and her skin was rosy.

One morning, Maryann woke up nauseated, but it soon

passed. Later that afternoon, she was sitting on the sidewalk with her wares spread out on a blanket. Merry was asleep cuddled up on her bags, gently snoring. The feeling of nausea came over her again, but stronger this time. Maryann stood up and looked for a place to throw up. She was going to go between some parked cars but only got as far as the fountain. She felt dizzy and sat down on the fountain's ledge. She leaned over and vomited into the water and fainted. As she went down, Maryann's head hit the concrete edge of the fountain hard. She fell unconscious onto the sidewalk. Her eyelids fluttered and her scalp oozed blood. On the base above her limp body was a bumper sticker that read, 'Keep Portland Weird.' A panhandler saw what had happened and rushed over to help. Before he could reach Maryann, her mouth opened wide and she coughed out a blue dust. Her eyes bulged and exploded with the same powder. The MAX train had pulled up and the passengers had a good view of the whole scene. There were sounds of disgust from the riders and before the doors closed a gust of wind blew some of the dust into the train. The conductor, oblivious to what was going on, closed the doors and continued on to the next stop.

Merry sensed something was wrong. She woke up from her dog dreams and did not see her master anywhere. She sat up alertly. Her ears were upright as she sniffed the air. She saw Maryann lying on the ground and ran to her. Merry caught her scent, but it was mixed with something that scared her and raised the hackles on her back. She sat by Maryann's head and gently licked her face as panicked pedestrians yelled to call 911.

Chapter Twenty-Nine

Paul was on a non-stop domestic flight to Washington, D.C. The past couple of hours were a blur. He had only slept a few hours in the past three days. The adrenaline rush of hunting down Raul and finally confronting him, was wearing off. His mind was still numb from learning that aliens were real and contact with them had exposed people to an alien disease. Once in flight, the steady drone of the plane's background noises lulled Paul into a deep slumber.

Paul's sleep was troubled by nightmares. He was chased by a horde of giant cockroaches. The insects' heads were triangular shaped with large, black eyes. He urged his body to move faster, but it felt as if he was running under water. Paul looked frantically behind him; the cockroaches were gaining on him. He felt their feelers on his back. Paul screamed as mandibles closed on his neck and pierced his skin. The cockroach burped a foul stench of rotten eggs as it chewed on him. In the background he heard drumming and chanting. The beat started out faintly, and then became louder as it got closer. Out of the corner of his eye, Paul saw the chanting was coming from an old medicine man. It was the same shaman he had seen in the clearing before he took off in the helicopter. The Indian was waving his staff and pointing at Paul. On the shaman's shoulder perched a gray eagle surrounded by a cloud of hummingbirds. He was trying to warn Paul about something.

"Wake up. Wake up!" The old man yelled at him. Paul felt a roach pulling at his shoulder and another one grabbed his right leg and knocked him down. He lost sight of the shaman as the insects overwhelmed him.

"Wake up! Sir, wake up!" Paul awoke to a flight attendant shaking his shoulder. Her brow creased with worry.

"I'm sorry, but you were having a bad dream and you were

screaming in your sleep." She was apologetic and concerned. Paul looked down the aisle. Some of the passengers had turned around to stare at him.

"Thank you, I'm sorry." He rubbed his face, still feeling groggy. "Can I please have a glass of water?"

Thank God that was just a dream! Paul felt the back of his neck under his collar and he was relieved there were no puncture wounds. The flight attendant returned with his glass of water and he drank it down quickly. He was feeling queasy and hoped he was not getting sick from something he ate in Mexico. Fighting down his nausea, Paul looked through the pouch in front of him, found an airline magazine and started thumbing through it. He was still exhausted, but he was damned if he was going back to sleep anytime soon.

When Paul's plane landed at Washington National Airport, he was met by the Secret Service. The two agents rushed him into a black SUV that was parked on the tarmac. Paul sat in the back seat as they sped through the streets of Washington, D.C., red and blue lights flashing their right of way. The Secret Service agents took him directly to the White House through the security entrance. The President, his staff and Paul's DEA team were waiting for his debriefing in the situation room. While he was en route from Colombia, Paul had sent a synopsis of his interview with Raul to his superior. That information had been sent up-lines to the White House, prompting an emergency briefing. When Paul entered the briefing room, there was a lively discussion going on but everyone stopped talking when Paul walked in. Paul's superior, John Holcomb, came up to him, shook his hand and welcomed him back.

"Paul, I know you've just landed, but we need you to debrief us right away. The virus is spreading and it is out of control. The situation has gotten worse since we received your report," he told Paul in a low voice.

"Mr. President, this is Paul Brittany." John introduced Paul to the other people in the room. Sitting around the large oval table was the President, the Vice President, the Secretary of Defense and the Chairman of the Joint Chiefs of Staff. The head of the Center for Disease Control and Prevention, Dr. Debbie Fergel, PhD. Seated at a separate table were DEA Special Agent Carlos Martinez, Dr. Joy Anderson and DEA Chief John Holcomb. After the introductions were made, Paul walked to the dais at the end of the room.

"Mr. President, the human race is in a lot of trouble." Paul took a deep breath, "In the course of our investigation of the Melendez cartel, we uncovered a plot to use alien technology to distribute their drugs." Paul paused, expecting a snicker or looks of disbelief; there were none. Paul related his investigation and experiences in Mexico and Colombia. He then gave a synopsis of Dr. Joy's research and conclusions as well as Carlos' surveillance report. After Paul was done, John Holcomb stood up and spoke.

"I met with the FBI, CIA and the NSA to share our information and look into any threat to national security. The NSA had been monitoring voice and email communications from the Melendez cartel. They recorded references to drugs modified with an alien virus; we believe this to be credible. One of our team members, Dr. Joy Anderson, had analyzed the drug's components. She forwarded her findings to the CDC and I would like Dr. Fergel to present us with her findings." John took a seat. The room was deathly quiet as the CDC chief approached the dais. Before she began she pulled down a projector screen that was behind her.

"A week before I received the information packet from Dr. Joy Anderson, our office received a report of a body in Baltimore that had exploded and emitted a blue dust. We quarantined the area as best we could and brought the body in to the CDC. During the autopsy, we discovered the virus in the blood of the subject.

"Two days later, we received reports of two people who had been exposed to the blue dust but had not taken the drug. One of them died and exploded within two days. The other infected person appeared to be normal except that her skin was cyanotic. We immediately brought in the dead body and sealed it. We contacted the infected woman and brought her in under quarantine."

"The next day, I received the reports from Dr. Joy Anderson. We confirmed her results. When we studied the blue dust, we found it was made up of a new spore form of the cocaine virus. It was highly contagious." Dr. Fergel paused for a minute, what she had to say next was not going to be easy.

"The infected woman survived and appeared normal except for her bluish skin. The virus has phases, which affects the hosts differently. The first phase made the cocaine super addictive to the user without adversely affecting their body the way meth does. Addicts on 'Blue' became healthier and more productive." Dr. Fergel indicated to her assistant to turn on the projector. On the screen was an electron microscope picture of a deflated primary stage virus. It had burst and released a new, smaller virus.

"This is the image that Dr. Joy Anderson sent me. It shows something we have never seen before, a virus creating a different version of itself. Each strain has a specific purpose and affects specific areas of the brain. This is an alien virus. It did not go through millions of years of evolution on Earth. It must have been manufactured to use humans as hosts."

"In the first stage of infection, the virus concentrates in the hypothalamus, a pleasure center of the brain. After an incubation period of around six months, the virus goes into a second stage with two different outcomes. Half of those addicted to blue die and expel a virulent cloud. The other fifty percent survive, but their skin turns blue and the virus changes its location in the brain." She indicated to her assistant to go to the next slide. In an MRI image labeled "Stage One," the slide showed a blue-tinged hypothalamus. In the next slide, 'Stage Two,' blue spots covered the parietal cortex of the brain.

"This section of the brain controls volition and free will." Dr. Fergel used her laser pointer to indicate it on the MRI slide. "Our lab took a biopsy and found that the virus had grown a synaptic connection to healthy brain cells. This is conjecture, but the alien virus' concentration in this part of the brain indicates this could be a conduit for mind control." Dr. Fergel finished and set her laser pointer down. Everyone was stunned and speechless. The Secretary of Defense finally broke the silence. "Doctor, is there an antidote or a cure?"

"Sir, the virus' DNA is not from this planet." She spoke haltingly, "It has an unknown, fifth nucleotide to the normal A, C, T and G DNA sequence that we designated as 'XX'. It would take years to decipher it before we could even think about a vaccine or a cure." She fought back a tear as she continued.
"At the current expansion rate, the virus will overtake the human race before we can get an antidote tested and mass produced. We tried conventional and unconventional means to break its genetic code, without any luck."

Dr. Fergel nodded to her assistant to play the next series of slides. The first one showed the reported infected cases worldwide in small, red circles. The next slide showed the same map, but the red circles had multiplied into one large, red stain over the entire planet. The slide was labeled 'Projected - Three Week Vector.'

"In three weeks, the virus will have run its course. Humans have no immunity to it and the brains will be compromised in those left alive. The survivors may wish they were dead." She did not mean to end the briefing on a gloomy note, but there was no way around it. She looked around the room to see if there were any further questions; there were none. Dr. Fergel left the small stage and sat down.

An uncomfortable silence filled the room. The aliens had put a lot of thought, planning and effort into the subjugation of mankind. Thoughts of loved ones ravaged by extraterrestrial pathogens dominated the minds of those present. Everyone turned toward the President. He was as worried as they were. Despite his own fears and doubts about the outcome, he had to maintain an aura of control. He was the President and the Commander-in-Chief of the most powerful country in the world. However, he knew his military could not defend against an enemy from space. Despite his feelings he had to continue to be decisive and give hope. The President stood up from his chair and addressed the group.

"In all of the history of civilization, there has never been a threat to humanity such as this. A technologically advanced alien race is attacking us and their ultimate purposes are unknown. It is evident they want to kill as many people as possible and make slaves of any survivors." The President looked around the table defiantly.

"My advisors have cautioned me not to go public with the alien connection; doing so will cause mass hysteria. We are going to do all we can to slow down the spread of the virus. The FDA is making an announcement stating the virus is being spread by cocaine contaminated with a blue, mutated strain of H5N1." The President paused; he could tell by the blank look on their faces they did not know anything about H5N1.

"Doctor Fergel, can you give a brief explanation of H5N1?" Dr. Fergel stood up, "The H5N1 virus is an avian influenza strain that was genetically altered by scientists. It is considered to be the most dangerous virus in the world and it is securely locked up in a facility in Rotterdam, Netherlands. There were some worries that terrorist groups could gain access to it and use it as a bio-weapon." The President thanked her and continued.

"A press release is going out asking anyone who has the tainted cocaine to turn it in. An amnesty is in effect, no questions will be asked and no one will be prosecuted for possession."

"A commando strike team is en route to Colombia to destroy the Melendez base and any of the blue cocaine there. Our military was put on DEFCON 1 today. All military personnel will be in biohazard gear to prevent any further contamination of our troops. I am going to go on the air in an hour and put our country in EMERGCON. This is an emergency condition reserved for an ICBM attack on our soil and has never been assigned. Martial law will go into effect tomorrow morning." The President's voice became firmer as he spoke. Everyone in the room was fixated on his every word.

"This is highly confidential. The CIA's Special Activities Division has ballistic missiles designed to take down enemy satellites. They are being retrofitted with tactical nuclear warheads. NORAD discovered alien ships in orbit and are tracking them. They are invisible to radar but were found by star occlusions. I have been in contact with the U.N. and every country is doing what they can to contain the virus and work out a defense strategy."

"Stay focused on your jobs, people. We will survive this crisis. Thank you." The President pushed his chair back and left followed by his aides. Everyone in the room stood up as the Commander-in-Chief exited. The Dogs of War were about to be unleashed on the alien enemy. The room buzzed with quick conversations. An electric excitement filled the air. Humanity was not going to go down without a fight.

Chapter Thirty

Coalition Battle Commander Cian was in low Earth orbit. His ship was invisible and shielded from electromagnetic detection by the Xxonox. The panoramic view below him reminded Cian of one of the moons of his home planet, Acyan. Cian looked at the floating Earth below him as one would a priceless work of art. Nothing was so glorious as encountering a planet with life after traveling through the trackless voids of space. There were billions of habitable planets throughout the galaxy, but the galaxy was vast and made those planets a rarity. They were a rare treasure, a small fire in the blackness of space. That was one of the benefits of joining the coalition, having neighbors. The cold, impersonal vastness of space was easier to confront when there was a friendly beacon in the wilderness.

It had been over ten thousand years since the Xxonox had backhandedly attacked the Cyn bases on Earth. Unbeknownst to the Xxonox, the Cyn and their coalition of fifty planets, had declared war on them. Their mission; remove the Xxonox from the Earth system. Their goal was to give back to earthlings the knowledge that was stolen from them thousands of years ago. The Cyn military engine was primed and ready to go. The warships under the domes of Venus were on battle readiness. There was one final step needed before Cian could give the order to attack; confirmation that the virus antidote worked. Cian had a few moments before he headed back to Venus. He relaxed, closed his eyes and let his mind wander over the events that led to this moment.

Cian remembered the day when news of the attack had reached his home planet. An emergency meeting was held in the world capital city of Acyan and representatives of all the planets of the coalition were in attendance. After the attack, M'yani had flown from Earth to a base on Venus and then he was put on an interstellar flight back to Acyan. He was present at the council meeting and gave his report. The council reviewed M'yani's testimony and the recordings from the Earth stations. The information and footage of the carnage wrought by the Xxonox shocked the inhabitants of fifty planets. They had never seen such a wrong done to another race.

The coalition council voted unanimously to forcibly remove the Xxonox from the solar system. There wasn't any feeling of revenge or hate against them. The Xxonox were a malignant cancer that had to be excised in order for humans to move forward. The coalition devoted their vast resources to building an immense war machine. Cian Cy-M was voted to be the Coalition Battle Commander and M'yani became his second-in-command. Cian remembered how M'yani had taken the news of the attack hard. He had lobbied strongly to put the Earth in the Planet Advancement Program and it was now his responsibility to get them back on track. The Cyn were committed to other planets that were under their tutelage and needed the coalition's full attention. The earthlings would have to survive until they could return in 10,000 years.

During that time the Cyn invented and perfected space weapons and the tactics to use them. They were concerned about undue suffering among the enemy combatants. The battle had to be swift and precise. To make sure the Xxonox died quickly, they created the Helix-Plasma Cannon. The weapon discharged compressed radiation stored in a magnetic casing. Each cartridge had the cosmic energy of a small solar prominence. The Xxonox ship's outer skin could partially block the radiation beam so coalition scientists created a molecular dissassociator field wrapped around the plasma stream. The dissassociator beam would rip apart the metallic bonds in the ships hull and turn them into monoatomic dust. The exposed Xxonox would then die instantly and painlessly under the concentrated fury of the space cannons.

The Cyn sent undetectable probes to the Earth and Mars to spy on the Xxonox's activities. The Xxonox's home planet was located and monitored by robotic drones. The Cyn's Extraplanetary Corps of Engineers secretly built military bases on Venus. The Xxonox despised Venus-type planets, which were too hot and the atmosphere too heavy for their tastes. This gave the Cyn a planetary base free from Xxonox scrutiny. The extraterrestrial engineers built enormous domes that covered small towns and military bases. The forts had massive air locks that could cycle out an entire fleet of ships in minutes. Thousands of ships and hundreds of bases were hidden under Venus' sulfurous clouds. The coalition created an intelligence corps, which infiltrated the Xxonox's communication network. They had full access to all of the Xxonox's dispatches between Mars, Earth and their home planet. Details of their invasion plans were an open book.

Commander Cian had spent thousands of years perfecting their nascent war machine. Every possible battle scenario was analyzed as they prepared for the campaign. Cian had moved to Venus twenty years ago so he could be at the forefront of the battle. Finally, after almost 10,000 years, the engagement was only days away.

Aside from the military part of the campaign, Cian also had to deal with the Xxonox's virus threat. Before the Earth could be totally freed, the virus had to be neutralized. There were two planetary societies in the coalition that specialized in biotechnology. They used their genetic skills to create better crops and eliminate diseases on the planets that joined the coalition. The Cyn's spy network had stolen a sample of the virus and the bioscientists had deciphered its genetic code. It only took a month to create an antidote. The anti-virus worked on human computer models, but they needed to test it on a live human. Cian had ordered a special mission to find a suitable human subject to test the antidote. They needed to find the longest surviving, infected human. They finally found someone who qualified, Jonas Neumann.

Cian activated the ship's muffled space engines and slipped out of Earth's orbit. The Xxonox ships were on the other side of the planet, unaware of the Cyn in their midst. When he was beyond the moon's orbit he gave full power to his engines and arrived at his Venus base the next day. He waited anxiously for the abduction team to bring in the infected human.

*

It was late at night and no one saw the strange craft that hovered over the roof of the apartment building. The small space ship slowly drifted down the side of the building until it reached Jonas' floor. To verify they had the right human they emitted an analytic beam through the window. The monitor showed the Xxonox virus rampant in his body. The virus was dated and confirmed that Jonas was the human they were looking for. The Cyn's beam had awakened Jonas. He got out of bed and the ship's crew focused a sleep ray on him. A tractor beam gently lifted the unconscious Jonas and floated him through the open window into the ship. They flew undetected by the complacent Xxonox in orbit.

Jonas was unconscious on the entire trip to Venus. When he came to he found himself in a hospital room. He did not know what had happened or how he got there. He wondered if he had passed out from his blue-skin disease and had been taken to a hospital. He closed his eyes and tried to remember what had happened. He recalled the bright light that had awakened him and getting out of bed. There was a blank in his memory between that moment and waking up in this bed.

Jonas opened his eyes, raised himself up on one elbow and looked around the room. He had thought he was in a hospital room, but it was unlike any he had ever seen. There was a table next to his bed with an intricate, delicate machine on it. Strange symbols and balls of light floated over it. He reached out to touch one but his fingers did not feel anything, it was a 3-D projection. The floating text next to the orbs was not in any language or alphabet he knew. Jonas paid closer attention to what was around him. The walls were painted in a color that was off somehow but he could not put a finger on it. The bed he was in was larger than the typical hospital bed. The sheets were thin and metallic and kept him warm. The medical equipment in the room was beyond his comprehension. The closer he scrutinized the room, the odder it became. Jonas came to the conclusion that he must still be still asleep and dreaming a lucid dream.

There was a knock on the door and a doctor in a white coat entered. Jonas unconsciously picked up differences in the man's physical demeanor, which made him feel uneasy.

"Hello Jonas. My name is Cian." The doctor spoke in a friendly manner and Jonas relaxed. A wave of peace fell over him like a soft pillow. Jonas did not wonder how the strange doctor knew his name or that he spoke fluent German. Like any dream, illogic seemed natural. As Cian spoke, odd images entered Jonas' mind that could not be accounted for by his own experiences. When the doctor came closer, Jonas saw that what he thought was a lab coat was actually a metallic one-piece suit.

"Excuse me Cian, but how did I get here? Where am I?" Jonas went along with the dream. He had lucid dreams before, and while in that state the dream was the reality.

"No Jonas, you are not dreaming. I am not of your planet. Earth is under attack by a race of beings known as the Xxonox and we are here to stop them. You are on the planet Venus. We brought you here because we need your help." As Cian spoke, mental images flooded Jonas's mind. Jonas experienced emotions he never had before, as if he was in tune with the alien's soul. Jonas shivered as frightful images of the Xxonox invaded his mind.

Jonas knew that Venus was a hot planet covered by sulfurous clouds and about the same size as the Earth. That was all he remembered from his high school science class. Jonas tried to feel the weight of his body on the bed. Venus had ninety-one percent of Earth's gravity, and he wanted to see whether he could feel any difference. Jonas felt lighter, but he was not sure if it was because of the lesser gravity or from being light-headed.

"How can I help?" Jonas asked. Cian told him this was not a dream but Jonas was not convinced. One does not go to bed, and then wake up on Venus having a casual conversation with a purple-eyed alien.

"Jonas, you were given an alien virus mixed with a drug. Your skin color is a symptom of that virus infection." Cian spoke emphatically in a soft, vibrant voice. "The virus was created by the Xxonox as part of their invasion plan." He hoped this was not going to turn into a nightmare. He vividly remembered his encounter with the drug cartel in Colombia. As horrific as that experience was, he would never have associated it with invading aliens.

"Our scientists found a cure but we need to test it on a live human being. We are asking you to be our test subject. I cannot promise you the serum will be effective, or that you will survive the test." Cian looked directly at Jonas, he had spoken without moving his lips. Cian's intensity, clarity and high purpose left no doubt in Jonas' mind that he was sincere. Indeed, if Cian had said there was a hundred percent chance that he would die, Jonas would have volunteered anyway. If he could save the human race from mass death and alien slavery, he would gladly give up his life. Jonas was religious and had faith that God in all his wisdom and power, had a hand in creating this alien as well. After a while, the strangeness of being in the presence of someone from another planet faded away. Jonas felt comfortable and at ease. If there was a devil, it was in league with the invaders. The age-old battle of good versus evil was being played out in space. Jonas sat on the edge of the bed and stood up.

"Cian, I give you my consent. When can we begin?" Jonas held his head high. His eyes squinted as he prepared himself for whatever was to come. This was not a dream. He did not need to pinch himself. His senses became crystal clear and his mind was fully awakened. His blank memory was filling in. He recalled, from a distance above his body, being hit with a beam that put him to sleep. He saw his body go out the window and into the ship. He sensed the acceleration of the craft as it left Earth. His eyes had been closed but he saw the Earth dwindle in the distance. He had no doubt that he was indeed on Venus.

Cian opened a drawer from a metallic desk nearby and pulled out a small vial. He held it between himself and Jonas.

The glass bottle was filled with a gold powder, it shimmered and flowed as if it were alive. Cian poured the contents into his cupped hand. With a flourish he waved his hand and dispersed the gold powder into the air. The gold cloud hung suspended, expanding and contracting as if it were breathing. Parts of it extruded tendrils as if searching for something. The cloud's fingers pointed at Jonas and then rushed at him.

At first, Jonas was taken aback by the sudden attack, not from fear but from how fast it had moved. The particles settled on him and then painlessly disappeared into his skin. He felt an immediate sense of well being as the golden specks swam through his veins and into every cell of his body. He was being cleansed from the inside out. The particles then came together in his brain and destroyed the alien virus housed there.

The gold particles exited his body through his skin. They hovered in the air then rotated as they looked for another target. Finding none, they settled back in Cian's hand. He gently put them back in the vial and locked the cap. He looked up expectantly at Jonas and asked him, "How do you feel?"

Jonas looked at his hands. The blue tint was gone. The skin was pink and glowed with health. Jonas mentally felt around his body the way someone felt for broken bones after a fall. He felt no trace of the drug-virus that had been a part of his life for so long.

"I feel wonderful. I can feel the virus is out of my system. It worked!" Jonas barely whispered in astonishment.

"Good! That is great news." Cian's sense of relief filled the room. "An anti-virus particle will remain dormant in your body. If you ever get re-infected again, it will multiply instantly and destroy it." Cian returned the vial to the drawer.

"Thank you for your help Jonas. We will take you back to Earth now. Your memories of what occurred here will not be erased or tampered with."

"But...but..." Jonas had so many things he wanted to ask, but Cian abruptly cut him off.

"Jonas, I know you have a lot of questions. We will reveal everything when the time is right. Your people are in great danger and we need to act soon." Cian shook Jonas' hand and left the room. Two Cyn workers came and escorted Jonas to an interplanetary shuttle. This time, he was wide-awake as they traveled from Venus to Earth. He was enraptured, wide-eyed as Venus dwindled in the distance. His home planet slowly grew through the forward port window. He had seen NASA images of the Earth from orbit but nothing compared with the real thing. The blue planet filled his field of view as the shuttle entered Earth's orbit. Jonas was transformed by the experience and returned a different man.

*

Confirmation of the serum's effectiveness completed the last phase of the Cyn's war plans. Hundreds of tons of the antivirus were manufactured. Customized spaceships were built to disperse the dust serum worldwide. An alert went out to the coalition's military to prepare for deployment. Hundreds of war ships exited their domed bases and held station just underneath Venus' clouds. Cian boarded his command ship on Venus with his staff and crew. They went to a staging area on the backside of the moon. Tall, crystal towers emanated a force field that blocked Xxonox sensors and a hundred square mile tarp duplicated the moon's regolith and camouflaged the fleet. There was a remote Xxonox monitoring station on the side of the moon facing the Earth. They were never aware of the Cyn's base on the other side.

It was time to make the Cyn presence known on Earth. The earthlings needed to know of the coming battle and the truth behind it. But Cian knew he could not stand on a street corner and make his announcements. He needed someone who could arrange an audience with the President of the United States. Cian used his thought waves to connect to the massive computer in the ship's data center. He accessed the database of people they had been monitoring who could help in the coming conflict. After he inputted his criteria, a picture of Paul Brittany appeared in his mind. There was a blinking red tab in the left corner of the image. Cian accessed it and a note appeared, 'INFECTED WITH THE XXONOX VIRUS.'

Cian turned off his thought link to the computer. He went to the intercom on his console and called M'yani to his office. Two minutes later, the door to the bridge opened and M'yani rushed in. M'yani had signed up for the coalition military as soon as it was formed. He had a personal interest in the success of the war and had become Cian's closest aide.

Cian informed M'yani of the recent developments. Cian ordered M'yani to contact Paul and get his help to set up a meeting with the American President. Cian showed M'yani the screen shot of Paul. The red light was blinking faster indicating that the death stage of the virus was imminent.

"M'yani, the serum cure is ready. Take a vial and go to Paul right now. Our surveillance tracked him and he is in a bar in Washington, D.C." Cian gave M'yani Paul's coordinates and a bottle of the antivirus.

M'yani rushed to a shuttle and went from the moon to Earth's surface as fast as he could without leaving a telltale plasma trail. He landed on the rooftop of an abandoned building in Georgetown. He exited the craft and remotely stationed it three miles above. M'yani had changed into human clothing. He pulled down his hat and put on sunglasses to disguise his eyes. He hailed a cab and gave the address to Paul's location. The cabbie did not give M'yani a second look and drove him to the tavern, unaware that there was an alien in the backseat.

Chapter Thirty-One

After the briefing, John Holcomb asked Paul to go home and get some rest. Paul told him he had a better idea; he was going to find a bar and have a double rum and coke. Joy overheard him and asked if she could join and then Carlos chimed in that he needed a drink too. They met at a local bar government employees frequented. After one drink, Carlos had to leave. Joy got a call from her mother who was concerned about the announcement of the viral outbreak. Joy went to her hotel to call her back.

Paul was not in any mood to celebrate the coming New Year. He stayed at the bar after the others left, ordered another drink and pondered the day's events. What a way for the human race to get wiped out. Paul felt a pang of regret. If he had busted the Melendez cartel sooner, this never would have happened. Paul stared into his half empty glass and mulled over his career. The country was losing the war on drugs. As soon as he busted one dealer, three more were set free and went back to work. When he plugged one drug tunnel, two more would crop up. Paul shook his head and downed the last of his drink. He glumly ordered another rum and coke. It was surreal, the end of the world was at hand and there he was in a bar full of people who were oblivious to the forces conspiring against them. Some patrons prematurely wore their New Year hats and festively talked about their New Year's resolutions

It had been a while since he talked with his mother and he planned to call her in the morning. He had an estranged brother he should also contact. His brother was an anti-establishment, drug-using hippie who viewed Paul as a pawn of the New World Order. Differences like that were minor when faced with the annihilation of humanity.

Paul took another gulp of his drink and without warning

the room began to spin. A cold sweat enveloped him and he had the urge to vomit. I didn't drink that much. Maybe I'm coming down with the flu? Paul massaged a muscle spasm in the back of his neck and remembered feeling sick on the flight in from Colombia. His abdomen was bloated and painful. He rubbed his stomach but it did not make it feel any better. Paul had to shake off the image of an alien creature bursting out of his belly. The back of his eyes throbbed and added to an intense migraine. It felt like a finger was pushing from behind his eyeballs. Paul rubbed his eyes and had an overwhelming urge to throw up. He put his drink down hard, splashing it onto the bar. He didn't know if he had enough time to make it to the rest room. He was going to make a run for it when there was a light tap on his shoulder. Feeling a little green, Paul covered his mouth and turned around to see who it was.

The man on the stool behind him was smiling. He had on a hat and large dark sunglasses. The stranger's body was large and his muscles looked dense and strong.

"Hello Paul. I represent an extraterrestrial race and we are here to help your planet." The stranger spoke to Paul in a melodic voice with an east coast accent.

"What?" Paul was not sure if he heard the man correctly. He hoped he was not going to throw up on the stranger's lap. He was about to tell the man to fuck off when the stranger took off his sunglasses. His eyes were larger than normal with irises like purple gems. He did not have any hair on his brow. But rather than making him look strange, his features looked natural. For a split second it made Paul wonder, why the hell do humans have eyebrows anyway? And then the realization hit him; oh shit... this is a real alien!

"My name is M'yani. Our civilization is from a star system that is many light years away. We have been involved with your planet for thousands of years. The race that is trying to take over your planet is our enemy as well."

As the alien spoke, a translucent halo appeared around his head. It shimmered at the edge of Paul's visual awareness. Invisible beams of psychic energy pierced Paul's mind. He momentarily forgot his nausea. The alien's eyes were windows to its otherworldly soul. There was a strong sense of familiarity, a déjà vu feeling like he knew this being. He was trained to remember faces and Paul was sure he had never met him before. But the feeling persisted.

"Paul, there isn't much time. I have a lot to explain and we need your help. Will you allow me to connect to your mind and directly transfer information?" This time Paul heard him in his mind and not through his ears. The alien's lips had not moved. Along with the words and images, Paul felt the vastness of the stranger's mind as well as a powerful, vibrant energy.

Paul nearly laughed out loud and looked around; no one had noticed the outer space being sitting at the bar, casually asking Paul to do some kind of Vulcan mind-meld. After all that he had been through in the past week, Paul did not doubt he was face-to-face with a real extraterrestrial. What if this is one of the bad aliens? Paul had a moment of doubt, but he went with his gut feeling.

"Yes," Paul said decisively, "Please, go ahead. I give you my permission." The Cyn looked deep into Paul's eyes and for the next few minutes, Paul's mind was flooded with Earth's secret history and the true story behind the alien invasion.

Chapter Thirty-Two

Alien images and strange feelings pierced the thin membrane of Paul's consciousness. He gasped for air as their minds merged. He replayed the beginning of human civilization through M'yani's eyes. Paul saw the splendor of the Cyn's pyramid built thousands of years before the Egyptians. The tone in the story darkened as he relived the Xxonox attack on the Cyn bases and the solar storm's devastating effects. Paul was overcome with a strong feeling of déjà vu. He remembered now where he had seen M'yani before. Paul had lived during the time when the Cyn were on Earth. His life at that time came into sharp focus. He remembered the name he had then, it was Luap. He was the priest M'yani had befriended.

He saw himself in the robes of the priesthood, dying on the walls of a crater. Before he took his last breath, Luap saw M'yani's ship hovering over him. That was the last time he had seen his alien friend. There was no doubt now that Paul had lived before. The remembrances of that time were more real to him than the reality of the present. His awareness of his past life increased as he accepted the truth of his existence. The events after the Xxonox attacks streamed unimpeded into his mind. Paul's ego went into the background as M'yani's thought images flowed into him. He relived M'yani's memories up to the point when he entered the bar. He saw himself through M'yani's eyes, an alien looking at a human.

Paul was forcibly jerked into the present like a fetus ejected from its womb. The mind connection ended and he was back in present time. When Paul turned around to greet M'yani, like a good cop, he noted what time it was on a clock on the back wall; it was 11:18 p.m. When he looked at it afterwards, the clock's hands were at 11:20 p.m. Only two minutes had passed? But it had felt like centuries! Paul's cheeks were wet. He had been cry-ing when he was reminded of his lifetime as Luap and the losses he experienced then. He got off his seat and hugged M'yani and cried. M'yani held him tight as tears welled up in his large, purple eyes.

Paul's happiness at finding his long lost friend turned into a gut wrenching fear. He was infected. Fuck! It must have happened when Raul's body had burst, some of that shit must have fallen on him. His mood soured. He had forgotten about his symptoms and now they returned worse than ever.

"Paul, you are infected." M'yani had read Paul's thoughts. "The Xxonox virus is active in your system and it is about to go into its spore stage. Our scientists have developed an antidote." M'yani pulled a yellow vial from his pocket. "It has been tested and it will neutralize the virus." Before Paul could respond, M'yani poured the contents of the vial into his hand. The gold dust glowed with its own inner light. The flecks moved like a living entity.

M'yani flung the contents between them. The particles hung suspended in the air and slowly rotated. They turned toward Paul and rushed at him and landed on his skin. Before he could register shock, they burrowed into his body through his pores. Immediately Paul felt a tingling energy course throughout his body. After a few minutes the particles left his body. They hung suspended in the air for a few seconds and then returned to M'yani's hand.

"Paul, you are cured." Relief colored M'yani's words.

Paul's stomach pain was gone. The nausea had disappeared as well as the ache behind his eyes. Oh, My God! I'm going to live. Meeting a long lost alien friend and finding out he was infected and then cured all in a matter of minutes, left him overwhelmed. But this was not the time for celebration.

"M'yani, thank you, I feel better already. I understand Cian wants to meet with the President? I was in a meeting with him earlier today. My boss has a direct line to him, I'll call him and set it up." Paul put his emotions aside and focused on setting up the meeting and called his boss, John Holcomb.

"John, I am in contact with an alien species who are going to help us. They have an antidote for the virus and a space fleet ready to attack the invaders. Their leader wants to talk to the President right away. Can you arrange it?" Paul had to slow down and explain it twice before John believed him.

"Ok, Paul, give me a few minutes." John hung up and called back three minutes later. "Alright, I had to wake up the President but he is ready to talk now, when can your alien contact come down?"

Chapter Thirty-Three

In the situation room at the White House, Paul sat next to Cian and John Holcomb. Everyone from the earlier DEA debriefing was also there, including the President, the Vice President, and men in civilian clothes that Paul didn't recognize. John Holcomb stood up and addressed the President. All the eyes in the room were focused on Cian. It was obvious he was not human but peace and serenity emanated from him and filled the room. There was no fear in the room, just wonderment at seeing a being from another world.

"Mr. President, we were briefed earlier on the alien virus threat and the CDC did not have a solution to contain it. One of my agents, Paul Brittany, was contacted this evening by an alien who wants to help us." John pointed to Cian. There was not any need for him to do so; everyone was already looking at the extraterrestrial.

"His name is Cian Cy-M, he is from the planet Acyan. Their sun is the star Alcyone in the constellation of Taurus. He has shown Paul and I the truth of what had happened in our ancient past and what is happening now." When John met M'yani, he received the history lesson telepathically and knew the truth for himself.

"Mr. President, please allow Cian to speak and judge for yourself." John sat down. The President nodded his permission because he was speechless. Cian stood up and addressed the President and everyone else in the room. He retold the history of the Cyn's interactions with humans and used his telepathy to add depth and truth to his words. Everyone was in shock, but no one questioned his veracity. Cian outlined the role of the Xxonox on Earth and brought the listeners up to the present stage of events.

"Our scientists have developed an anti-virus. It has been

tested and there are no detrimental after-effects." Cian took out a vial from his pocket and emptied the shimmering contents into his hand. He threw the gold powder in the air. An aide ducked under the table in fear while the others sat transfixed. The particles hovered in mid air and then darted suddenly toward the Vice President. He cried out involuntarily and the Secret Service agents in the room leaped forward with their guns drawn.

"Hold it!" The President shouted at them and they froze. The particles landed and then vanished into the Vice President's skin. After a few minutes they left his body, hovered in the air momentarily and returned to Cian's hand. Everyone in the room had been unconsciously holding their breath. When the anti-virus left his body, the Vice President smiled and everyone relaxed.

"I feel great, invigorated. I had no idea that I was infected. I can sense my body is free of the virus." The Vice President was exuberant but inwardly he shuddered at his close call. He had not been feeling well lately and had attributed it to stomach flu.

The President asked, "How much of this anti-virus can you make for us? We need to dispense it as quickly as possible." He had received an update on the alien virus an hour before the meeting. The epidemic had spread faster than the CDC's prediction model.

"We have specially designed robotic ships with dispersal units and enough anti-virus to blanket the planet. The robotic ships will need to fly a few hundred feet above ground level to disperse the serum. They will be visible and will look strange to your people. To avoid alarm, you must inform your entire planet immediately of what I have just told you. Our robotic ships are in orbit now and ready." Cian finished and sat down. Everyone started talking at once. One of the men sitting next to the President was unknown to anyone else in the room. He was from an ultra-secret branch of the National Security Agency. He leaned over and whispered to the President. The President nodded solemnly to him and addressed Cian.

"Mr. Cian, we cannot allow that. We are going to issue a

press release informing the people that this was a genetically altered virus created by a Mid-East terrorist group. We are not going to let the general public know that aliens from space are the cause of the epidemic. It would create worldwide panic. Our military, as well as every nation in the world, are mobilizing to handle the invasion threat. We have tanker planes that we use to drop water and chemicals on forest fires. We can retrofit them to disperse your anti-virus." The President looked uneasily at the NSA agent. His close group of advisors, the Secretary of Defense, and his Joint Chiefs of Staff, had all advised him against telling the public about the alien invasion.

Cian was taken aback. He could not believe what he had just heard. Was the government willing to let people die just because they felt the truth would not be taken well? Cian stood up abruptly. Everyone stopped talking and looked at him. He suddenly seemed bigger and taller than his already large, physical size. All hint of the friendly, serenely peaceful alien was gone as he addressed the President.

"NO!" The intensity in his voice shook the windows. The authority and power of his post as Commander of the fifty star group armada filled the room. Cian was the representative of a million year old, superior civilization. He was about to wage war on an evil invading species intent on taking over this part of the galaxy. Ten thousand years of planning and hard work had gone into this moment in time.

"We do not have time for your political games. The Xxonox will destroy your planet and billions will die. The Xxonox's virus will go beyond the point of no return in a few hours. Tell your people exactly what I have told you. We will begin our robotic dispersal in ten minutes. Is that understood?" Cian's power and intensity had grown to an unbearable crescendo. The President sat back in his chair in awe. The verve and panache with which he had begun his presidency resurfaced. The room was quiet and pulsated with unseen, powerful energies. The President stood up and addressed Cian with stony resolve.

"Cian, please give your robotic ships the order to start the virus dispersals immediately." Then he turned to the Press Secretary, "Jim, get the broadcast room ready, it's time the public knew the truth for once."

Chapter Thirty-Four

To millions of people who heard the shrill sound of the Emergency Broadcast System, it was just another interruption to their radio or TV show. However no matter what anyone was doing, they waited to make sure that it was only a test.

On New Years Eve, every TV and radio station was interrupted by the harsh sound of the emergency alarm. Every smart phone and computer displayed the civil defense banner. A secret National Security Agency program that was to be used only in extreme emergencies, overrode all cell phone and Internet providers.

"This is not a test. Please stay tuned for an important emergency message from the President of the United States."

"Oh shit, this is for real," A college football fan turned to his friend. He had just sat down to watch the college game he had recorded earlier. All across the country eyes and ears were glued to TVs, computers and smart phones. In Times Square, hundreds of thousands of people had gathered to watch the Ball drop for the New Year. Over the last few months, the news agencies had been abuzz with the latest viral outbreak. Every day brought more horror stories of people exploding or turning blue from the infection. Despite the doom and gloom, Times Square was packed full as revelers partied, ready to ring in a new and better year.

Amongst the crowd were the Baktunists, named after a cycle of the Mayan calendar. They were a doomsday group patiently waiting for the end of the world. The Baktunists had been ready for the Mayan doomsday back on December 21 of 2012. When the world continued on without even a minor earthquake, the Baktunists were devastated. They had wanted to be a witness to the End of Days, even if they died in the process.

Their faith was restored when a new Mayan calendar was

discovered in the ancient ruins of Xultun, Guatemala. A Mayan researcher had interpreted the new calendar glyphs to predict that the world would come to an end on December 31 of the current year. The recent virus epidemic was proof that this was the beginning of the end. Baktunist posters had gone up all over New York City proclaiming that this time, the doomsday prediction was for real. The throng in Times Square was there to welcome in the New Year with liquor, kisses and high hopes. The Baktunists were there to bear witness to the end of the world.

At twenty minutes before midnight, the Times Square crowd was very festive, drinking and dancing to the live band on stage. It was thirty-five degrees outside but the Naked Guitar Man was playing in the streets with nothing on but his guitar and a sequined G-string. The New Years ball was brightly lit in anticipation of its drop.

Without warning the lights went out in Times Square. All of the over-sized TV panels had turned off. It was unnatural to see Times Square dark at night. Shrieks and screams punctuated the rising hum of the crowd's shouted questions. The only lights on were the news banner message boards and TV's.

"Stay tuned for an emergency broadcast." The digitized words paraded brightly across the displays and TVs in shop windows. "This is not a test. The President of the United States will make a statement in sixty seconds." The scrolling letters lit the faces of the shocked crowd with an eerie glow. All thoughts of partying were gone. The Baktunists were the only ones smiling; their attitude said it all..."I told you so!"

Everyone wondered what could have shut down Times Square on New Year's Eve. Waves of fear spread like a tsunami around the world. The White House emblem came on the screen and then shifted to the President seated at his desk. A hush fell over the crowd. The only other lights were from the thousands of smart phones recording the event.

"People of the United States and the world. I have some very important news that affects our survival as a species. I had an emergency meeting with the Secretary of the U.N. and this broadcast is being simultaneously translated and transmitted worldwide. New Years Eve is a time of celebration and renewal. But events have been set into motion that does not take into account holidays or celebrations. Our survival is at stake and time is of the essence." The President talked in a calm, authoritative voice, what he was going to say next was going to shake everyone's reality.

"The deadly virus epidemic had our scientists baffled until we found out its true source. The virus was created by a race of outer space aliens. They spread it by using cocaine as a carrier. The aliens want to take over our planet to mine our heavy metals and then destroy the human race. We have no defense against the virus or their superior technology." The President took a breath. The crowd in Times Square was listening intently. A man said out loud, "What the fuck!" Another asked, "When are the lights coming back so we can party on?" Someone else shouted, "I knew disclosure was going to happen this year!" Most people were trying to process a reality that should have been in a science fiction movie.

"I have been contacted by a representative of an advanced, extraterrestrial species who want to help. In a few minutes their ships will be releasing an anti-virus dust. Please, do not be alarmed. They are here to help us. Do not panic when you see strange aircraft overhead. These friendly aliens are called the Cyn and they are going to do battle with the aliens who mean to do us harm. Do not be alarmed at unknown ships in our skies." An image of Cian standing next to the President filled the screen. The picture of a human-like alien eased the tension that had been building up.

"The anti-virus dispersal will start in thirty seconds. I do not have a lot of time to say more, but a website has been created with more information." A banner appeared at the bottom of the screen that displayed the web site's address. The screens of thousands of smart phones lit up like candles at a rock concert as they accessed the web site.

"I am going to give another update from the United Nations

in an hour. The Press Secretary will come on the air to give further details. May God have mercy on us all. Thank you." The President's seal filled the screen with the website address.

The Times Square ball lit up again along with the rest of Times Square. However, the festive mood was gone. Even the die-hard partyers were stunned. After the President's broadcast everyone stood still. Many looked up, searching the night sky for any sign of alien ships. A few had hoped a banner would pop up saying 'April Fools!' But they knew it was not April and this was not a joke. Twenty seconds elapsed and everyone did exactly what the President had asked people not to do; panic. Pandemonium broke loose as everyone tried to rush home. Cell towers were instantly jammed by frantic calls made by millions of people at the same time. All thoughts of bringing in the New Year were gone. At midnight the New Year's ball hung motionless and overlooked a dark and deserted Times Square.

Overhead, the lights of midtown Manhattan reflected off the bottom of low-lying clouds. The tranquil belly of a dark cloud bulged outwards and gave birth to a metallic, black triangular craft the size of Yankee Stadium. The lights of the city reflected off the underside of the huge space ship. The craft floated down soundlessly, until it was lower than the top of the Empire State building. Millions of New Yorkers watched as gigantic bay doors opened underneath it. Intense ultraviolet radiation streamed from the interior of the ship. It was so intense that people could not look directly at it. A golden mass filled the opening, momentarily blocking out the light. Then a blast of golden dust exploded outward and mushroomed out over the city and descended like the ash fallout from a volcano. Despite the President's speech, hundreds of people ran screaming through the streets. It did not matter if they ran or hid. The dust tracked down anyone who was infected and cured them.

Hundreds of tons of Melendez Blue were neutralized in drug houses throughout the city. The same scenario was played out around the world. A Cyn ship blotted out the sky above Paris. Astonished diners at the Eiffel Tower Restaurant were eye level with the low flying spaceship. In England, a spacecraft was just a hundred feet above the London Eye Ferris wheel. A rider jumped to his death into the Thames River as he tried to escape the extraterrestrial dust that suddenly enveloped him. In Detroit, gunfire erupted from rooftops as gangs tried to shoot down the dispersal craft that hovered above the city.

The anti-virus cloud spread out from the cities and into the countryside. When the ships emptied their cargo, they refilled their hold from massive tanks on the backside of the moon. They continued dumping the golden dust upon the peoples of Earth until every infected human was cured.

Chapter Thirty-Five

On the East side of Manhattan, an emergency meeting of the UN was in session. The large TV screens in the front of the auditorium were filled with images of the Cyn robotic ships as they spread their anti-virus. The President of the United States took the podium in front of the stunned UN assembly.

"Ladies and gentlemen of the United Nations, humanity has come to a crossroads. This emergency security meeting was convened because the Earth is under attack by an alien species. They infiltrated our planet with a virus that was circulated with cocaine." He let that sink in for a few moments.

"Our scientists have not been able to synthesize or find an antidote for the enemy virus. The military did not have a defensive plan for an invasion from outer space. This U.N. session was initially going to be convened to work out a way to save what we could of our race." Some of the ambassadors were uncomfortably shifting in their seats. They had secretly hidden their families and top staff in underground 'doomsday' bunkers, leaving the rest of their country to fend for themselves.

"We are going to be addressed by an extraterrestrial who represents an advanced space civilization. They call themselves the Cyn and they are here to help us." There was an audible gasp from the U.N. assembly. A few days ago this would have seemed utterly fantastic, but not today.

"A few hours ago, an agent from the Drug Enforcement Agency was contacted by Cian Cy-M, a representative of the Cyn. Cian came to the White House and informed me of the truth behind the alien attack. The ships that you see on the TV monitors are Cyn ships spreading the anti-virus they created." A collage of major cities worldwide appeared on the main screen showing hundreds of space ships dispensing clouds of golden dust.

"I want to introduce you to Cian Cy-M, of the planet Acyan."
A hush fell upon the assembly.

Cian entered from the right side of the stage and walked across to the podium. The entire assembly stood up to get a better look. Cian was bigger than life as he walked confidently across the stage. At the podium he had to adjust the microphone to accommodate his taller stature. The television cameras in the room were transmitting to every network in the world. Every TV program around the world was preempted to show this being from outer space.

"People of Earth, your world is under attack by a race of beings intent on taking over your planet's natural resources. They are planning on eliminating most of your population and keeping the rest as slaves. When they are done, they will kill the remaining survivors. This has been their operating basis for hundreds of thousands of years. Their virus is the first stage in their invasion." Cian spoke in perfect American English to the English listeners, and the delegates heard Cian in their own language, without interpreters. In just a few words he managed to put everyone at ease. It was easy to forget that he was not of this world.

"We are here to help you. We were here thousands of years ago to give your civilization a boost." Enhanced by his telepathy, Cian related what had happened to the Cyn pyramid and the effects of the induced solar proton event. The Xxonox virus and invasion plans were laid out in grim detail and exposed the full extent of their plan.

"The Xxonox have a small invasion force in orbit around your planet right now. They have monitoring stations on your moon and military bases on Mars. Their main fleet is one day away from entering your solar system. For thousands of years, we have been secretly building a military base on Venus to counter their invasion. In an hour, we will begin our offensive. We will destroy the Xxonox ships in Earth's orbit and on the moon. A battalion of Cyn war ships is already en route to Mars to destroy their bases there. The main part of our fleet will engage the incoming invasion armada before they enter your system."

The entire assembly listened silently and hardly breathed, their paradigm was shifted far beyond their reality.

"The anti-virus will continue its work until all traces of the invading virus are gone. It is then programmed to lie dormant unless the alien virus resurfaces. We could not come forward earlier without alerting the Xxonox prematurely. We did not want their invasion fleet alarmed before they got within range. Our goal is to destroy as much of their military as possible. After we have repelled their attack, I will meet here again with the governments of your world and go over the next step to be taken. I know you have many questions, however I must leave now to supervise our counter-attack. I have a direct link to the President's communication device and I will send updates when I can, thank you."

Cian left the podium and walked off the stage and left a stunned silence in his wake. The heads of state were not used to being told the truth so directly. The President returned to the podium amid a cacophony of shouted questions. He settled in and answered the questions as best as he could while the fate of humanity was being determined in outer space.

Chapter Thirty-Six

Abn was in his command ship in Earth orbit preparing for the final stage of the invasion. He had received an interstellar message from the lead ship of the invasion fleet. They were going to enter the solar system in less than twenty-four hours. At long last all of his pre-invasion work was coming to fruition. The battalion he had hidden underneath Mars' surface was put on readiness alert. Abn had been monitoring the progress of the virus and it had exceeded his expectations. The second stage was working as planned. When the Xxonox fleet entered Jupiter's orbit, Abn would signal the ships on Mars to commence their attack on Earth. He had twenty ships evenly spaced apart in Earth's orbit. Each one was equipped with telepathic transmitters. At Abn's command, the virus would be activated and transform the infected humans into Xxonox slaves.

Abn was at his console when an emergency icon projected into the air above his monitors. He waved his hand over the icon and an urgent message opened up with the heading, 'Unknown ships on the planet's surface.' Attached to the message were overhead video clips of large triangular ships dispersing clouds of yellow dust.

Clearly, they are not human-made craft! Abn went to the Planetary Surveys Unit to find out where the unidentified flying objects had come from. What threat did these ships pose? Everything had been going so well. Thousands of years of planning did not foresee this. The fleet was less than a day away, Abn had to handle this development before they arrived. When he entered the survey control room, Abn felt a palpable tension in the air.

"Where did these ships come from and what are they doing!" Abn shouted his mental command at his staff.

"Sir, we just pulled this from one of their satellite's newsfeed." The operator played the news clip. It showed Cian's U.N. speech, it was being replayed worldwide and had preempted regular programming.

"The Cyn!" For the first time in Abn's million-year existence, he was afraid. He had forgotten about the Cyn after he had routed them from this system. Abn's blue skin paled as he continued watching the hi-jacked newsfeed. The Cyn ships had released an anti-virus! Abn ran full speed back to his command console to activate the enslavement sequence. Abn burst into the control room and knocked over an aide as he sprinted to the console. His frantic demeanor alarmed his juniors. On the console were a series of large buttons to initiate each phase of the pre-invasion sequence. The telepathic transmitter initiator button was primed and ready to go. Abn's hand was raised to push down on the button hard when a strident siren cut the air like broken glass. It was the anti-collision alarm used to avoid space debris.

At the same time another alarm went off and a map of the solar system appeared in the air above the console. Hundreds of unidentified flying objects were approaching them at a high rate of speed from Venus. Another 3D map popped up from the anti-collision sensors, it showed missiles coming directly at his ships from the backside of the moon. Abn's hand was still moving toward the telepathy relay. It shifted in midair and landed instead on the general quarters alarm.

Multiple reports came in from his ships in orbit asking for orders. Before Abn could respond, he saw silent explosions outside his viewports. The kinetic weapons were destroying his ships. He activated the telepathic link to the ship's navigation system. At the speed of thought, he wrenched his spacecraft away from Earth's orbit. Five missiles flew through the point in space he had just vacated. They exploded with the force of atomic bombs as they smashed unimpeded into Earth's atmosphere. One by one the frantic calls from the other ships went silent as they were blasted into expanding balls of hot plasma.

Abn made a sharp turn and fired all of his engines, propelling his ship at hundreds of miles a second. The G-forces taxed the ship's anti-acceleration field, throwing anyone who was standing to the floor. Three more missiles had locked on to Abn's ship, but they fell behind as he increased the ship's speed. Abn's blue skin drew taut and his large eyes sank deep into their sockets as the ship accelerated. The sudden, immense G-forces threatened to break the ship apart. The anti-acceleration field held as the craft raced to the edge of the solar system. Abn plotted a course to intersect the path of the incoming invasion fleet. He had to warn them of this new development.

Chapter Thirty-Seven

After his address to the U.N., Cian went to his space shuttle parked on the helipad. As he walked down the sidewalk surrounded by the Secret Service, Cian heard a roaring sound. On the other side of the street, stretching for miles in both directions, hundreds of thousands of people had gathered to see Cian. Their clapping and roars of approval were thunderous. The life of the planet was hanging in the balance and there was the extraterrestrial savior walking down the street. Everyone had been following the televised U.N. address. People had traveled from New Jersey and all over New York City to cheer him on. Flags waved wildly, representing every country of the world. There were hastily made signs thanking him and a few asking for his hand in marriage. An isolated group of skeptics were waving signs claiming that aliens did not exist. Another group waved banners stating that Cian and the Xxonox were fakes, a ruse created by the men in black who were in league with the Illuminati.

Cian stopped walking and stood still. He felt the energy of the hopeful crowd, lifted his hand and waved. The people's cheers grew even louder. Cian reached his ship and after a few minutes the ship rose silently and powerfully up into the sky. Everyone followed its path until it disappeared from sight. Cian docked with his command ship on the other side of the planet. His military contingent was on the far side of the moon, which shielded them from the Xxonox ships in orbit. When he arrived, he settled into his commander's chair, his second-in-command M'yani was by his side. Cian nodded to him and M'yani gave the order to the fleet on Venus to commence the attack.

The Cyn's war plan had multiple battlefronts. The bulk of the Cyn's forces went to head off the invasion force before they entered the solar system. They were going to engage the Xxonox inside the Oort cloud. After thousands of years analyzing battle simulations, the Cyn had determined that a fight in that open area would ensure the total destruction of the Xxonox invasion force.

A fleet went to Mars to destroy the Xxonox that were based there. After Mars was secured, the ships would then spread out into the asteroid belt. It would create a perimeter to intercept any enemy ships that managed to get through the Oort cloud. Cian's contingent would attack the Xxonox that were stationed on the moon and in Earth's orbit. They would also act as a final, defensive front if any enemy ships got past Mars' defensive line.

*

The attack on the moon caught the Xxonox by surprise. Simultaneously, the Cyn attacked the moon bases with high energy-lasers and the Xxonox ships in Earth's orbit with missiles. The kinetic bombs were hollow spheres of fractured osmium that surrounded a warhead that was made to expand on impact like a dumdum bullet. They were fired from the Cyn's attack ships at ten percent the speed of light. The kinetic energy from the impact was equivalent to a megaton nuclear explosion. The Cyn used the slower missiles because they would disintegrate in the atmosphere if they missed their targets.

The Cyn's first volley blasted all but one of the Xxonox's orbiting ships. They sent missiles after the surviving ship but it sped off and avoided destruction. The Cyn did not give chase. Their job now was to form a cordon around the Earth and protect it from any Xxonox ships that might get through the outer defensive lines. They tracked the escaping ship's path; it was headed out to meet the incoming Xxonox invasion group. A dispatch was sent to the Cyn Oort cloud contingent with the description and trajectory of the escaping enemy ship.

The exploding Xxonox spacecraft turned night into day and outshone the sun on the daylight side of the planet. Immense sonic booms shook the earth as the explosion fronts smashed into the upper atmosphere.

The Cyn's Mars attack force arrived at Mars' orbit. They

knew the exact location of all of the invasion bases. The Xxonox had originally built domed structures on the surface of Mars. However, over the years, humans had begun putting satellites into Mars' orbit. At first, the Xxonox damaged or eliminated the intruding probes and satellites. But the human's technology kept advancing to a point where destroying them would have raised suspicions. The Xxonox space fleet went underground into buried lava tubes beneath the flanks of Martian volcanoes. Their main base was underneath the eastern flank of Olympus Mons. The Xxonox entered and left their lava tunnels via skylight openings in the lava tube ceilings. The skylight caverns created a ready-made entryway to hundreds of miles of underground tunnels.

When the Cyn forces entered Mars orbit they split and attacked Phobos and the Martian bases simultaneously. The Xxonox military had gone on full alert after they received the alarm from Abn. As the Cyn forces approached, dark delta shaped ships exited the caves like bats out of a Martian hell.

The Cyn's plasma cannon had a narrow kill zone. Too far away and the disassociator beam became dispersed, too close and the beam was too narrow. The Cyn attack ships were flying below the orbit of Phobos, two thousand miles above the surface of Mars. They were too close for the cannon and used their kinetic bombs instead. The muzzle velocity was so high that a special ablative shield was needed so they would not disintegrate in the thin atmosphere. The kinetic energy and explosions from the missiles shattered the Xxonox ships. The enemy craft were easy to pick off as they exited the tunnels.

The Xxonox had not expected an attack on their Martian bases. They had not worried about an attack from Earthlings. The humans could barely send unmanned probes to Mars; much less mount an interplanetary attack. The tunnels gave them cover but they were also a tactical mistake with their limited number of exits. The Cyn knew this and above each tunnel opening, they stationed a detachment of Cyn ships. Each ship fired their missiles at the rate of ten rounds per second. Whatever the Cyn did, they did it in abundance, even when it came to killing. The enemy ships were blasted out of the air like flies caught in a rocket's exhaust. Missiles that missed their target impacted the Martian surface with the force of small nuclear bombs. Mushroom clouds of red Martian dust were flung high into the atmosphere. A planet-wide Martian dust storm created by the battle was visible from Earth.

Xxonox ships were trapped in the tunnels. The openings were blocked by tons of destroyed spacecraft. This was the moment the Cyn armada was waiting for. Heavy cruisers came to the front lines. The nose of the ships peeled back and revealed bunker-busting bombs. The warhead's payload created a chain reaction at the quantum level. The effect was catastrophic and yet produced no radioactive fallout. The cruisers fired their weapons and massive explosions rocked the Martian surface. What were once Martian Xxonox bases became smoldering craters and collapsed lava tunnels.

The same tactics were used on the Phobos base. The first target was a large monolithic structure that was used to access the interior. The Cyn then attacked the openings in Stickney Crater, on the backside of Phobos. After they shot down any ships that tried to escape, the cruisers fired a Quantum bomb the size of a house and guided it through an opening, deep into the hollow interior. The explosion lifted the entire surface of Phobos a hundred feet. When gravity brought everything back down, it collapsed the entire moon inward and filled the void that was once its center. All that was left of Phobos was a jumbled mass of rock that was half its original size and perfectly round. All of the massive crystals that had taken millions of years to form were smashed and compacted into the center of Phobos. Phobos became the only moon in the universe with a solid core of opal and olivine crystals.

Everything inside Phobos was utterly destroyed. The few remaining ships that had escaped the initial onslaught were shot down. Mars was now secured. The Cyn fleet then created a defensive line between Mars and the incoming enemy armada.

The main Cyn force headed out toward the edge of the Oort cloud. The Xxonox had received the warning from Abn and were ready to do battle by the time they entered the Sol system. They were not expecting an attack this far out. The Xxonox invasion fleet was composed of two groups. The heavily armed ships were in front. Trailing behind them a parsec away was the logistic supply convoy. At the rear of the convoy was the mother ship with the Supreme Commander of Zutox and his executive staff. The Xxonox had not expected to fight a space-worthy opponent. Earth by now should have been a chaotic mess and in its last death throes. Most of the population would have died and the survivors placed under mind-control. The invading alien army had expected to walk in and take over without any resistance. Survivors would have lived with the horror of their bodies controlled by aliens and watch helplessly as their planet was raped and pillaged. That was the scenario the Xxonox invading forces had expected. But they had not prepared for this contingency.

The Xxonox fleet began braking maneuvers at the outer perimeter of the Oort cloud. Their space ships had traveled faster than light in the vast emptiness between stars. As they approached the solar system, they slowed down. The Oort cloud's outer envelope of gas, rarefied as it was, would have disintegrated the ship's hulls at full speed. The invasion fleet transitioned from super-light to sub-light speed. This was the attack window the Cyn had calculated. The Cyn's armada approached the invasion fleet head on. The Cyn's ships spread out from their tight flying formation into an umbrella-like configuration with arms stretched out from the center. From a distance, it looked like an octopus had opened up and extended its tentacles. This arrangement was optimal for the forces they were about to unleash. The speed of the incoming enemy ships and the Cyn's outward speed were calculated to within a few centimeters per second.

The plasma weapons were targeted and locked in. Dozens of the cannons were aimed at each Xxonox ship. As one, the Cyn's ships released the magnetic caps and thousands of rounds were fired. The surrounding space crackled with the fury that was unleashed. The solar proton event the Xxonox had let loose on Earth thousands of years ago was a pale candle in comparison. Spiraling slightly ahead of the plasma, were the disassociator beams. The enemy did not know what hit them. They were at their battle stations and before they knew it, they were an expanding cloud of organic particles. The battle was over that quickly.

The Cyn did not want a protracted battle. After ten thousand years of planning, they achieved their goal. The Xxonox commanders in the rear saw what happened and turned around while they were still out of range. The Cyn did not pursue them since their objective had been achieved, the end of the invasion. The Cyn turned their armada around and headed back to Venus. They left behind an ever-expanding cloud of dust that had once been the mighty Xxonox fleet. After millions of years, the Xxonoxian debris cloud coalesced into a comet. For millions of years it orbited the solar system until the sun swallowed it.

*

Abn had witnessed the destruction of the invasion force. His ship was alone in space with a deadly enemy on his heels. Abn's home planet was too far away to reach with the interplanetary drive in his command craft. He had no choice but to continue on his trajectory. A proximity sensor popped up over his console. The Cyn fleet was returning and he was right in their path. He braced himself and waited for his annihilation. However, his ship continued on past them without being attacked. He relaxed and started planning for his survival. The best he could do was to continue toward his home planet and hope that a rescue ship would find him before his life support systems failed.

After a few hours in deep space, Abn received a faint Xxonox "friend or foe" identification signal. He jumped to his screens, it was the invasion command ship headed back to Zutox. Abn increased his speed and got close enough to establish contact. They acknowledged his signal and slowed down to let him catch up. With a sigh of relief he docked with the mother ship. He was safe at last.

Abn was in his quarters inputting his de-briefing into the ship's computer when there was a knock on his door. He opened it to find five security guards flanking the captain of the ship. The captain pulled out an order from his pouch.

"Abn Su, by the order of the Supreme Council of Xxonox Prime, you are hereby relieved of your command." On that note, the security guards roughly bound Abn with aluminum handcuffs. Abn was too stunned to resist.

"You have failed to secure the Earth planet and allowed the destruction of our invasion fleet. For these crimes, your body will be destroyed and you are hereby sentenced to xOmah." It was the severest punishment an Xxonoxian could get and it was rarely used. When their bodies died, they would leave the dead flesh behind and report to their birth vats. They animated the vat-grown body that had been assigned to them and were "born." In xOmah, the assigned body was destroyed and the soul was banned from ever being reborn.

Abn mentally screamed with waves of fear and propitiation. He pleaded with them, but to no avail. The heavily armed security guards took Abn to the air lock and brusquely threw him inside. He tried to escape but a guard punched him so hard he fell on his back. The inner door locked and then the outer doors opened, whooshing Abn outside the ship. His horror was frozen on his face as his eyes exploded outward into the vacuum of space. Abn left the frozen carcass that used to be his body and watched the mother ship continue on without him. He was alone, an alien ghost doomed to haunt interstellar space.

*

The Supreme Council representative on board the mother ship had watched Abn's demise in space on his main screen. He wanted to confirm that Abn's body was dead before he signed off on his death certificate. He replayed the last moments of Abn's passing before he changed the channel on his screen. There was an incoming message from Zutox Prime waiting in his inbox. He had informed his superiors of the destruction of their fleet and Abn's utter failure. He opened his message box and a series of orders hung in the air before him. As he read the orders, a compliance icon popped up. He mentally toggled the 'read and understood' 3-D switch to 'Yes' for each one. Instead of heading to Zutox prime he was ordered to report to the planet Boole. It was the last planet the Xxonox had invaded. It had more mineral wealth than all of their other conquests combined, but it was too far away to manage profitably and was left dormant. The planet Boole was given a new purpose; it was going to be transformed into a planet-sized military base.

The last message was a Prime Executive Directive, war had been declared on the Cyn and the Earth system. The Xxonox had never been defeated before or failed to conquer a planet. Their focus changed from planetary conquests to revenge. The Supreme Council canceled the two planets on their invasion schedule. The Xxonox were going to use all of their resources toward one goal: destroy the Cyn and the Earth in 1,200 years.

Chapter Thirty-Eight

Cian was in his orbiting command ship monitoring the battle. After the Earth orbit offensive was completed, he received the report of a ship that had escaped. He ordered them to let it go since it was headed out of the solar system. Cian and M'yani received second by second updates as the battle for Mars and the Oort zone unfolded. Cian kept the President of the United States informed verbally. At the same time Cian was in telepathic contact with his staff. The Cyn's computers were used for menial tasks like storing large amount of numbers and data. The Cyn's mental capabilities far surpassed any modern, human computer. Their supreme analyzing ability came from their mind's ability to function unattached to their bodies. They retained memories of thousands of past lives in unlimited memory banks. As a group, their combined intellect, when joined telepathically, created a living super computer.

The Cyn military command constructed a real-time mental globe of the battle. In it, every ship in the conflict friend or foe was kept track of. Communications and orders were given telepathically, without the lag time of radio waves. The Cyn's battle group was composed of five thousand men and women from the fifty planets of the coalition and they worked as a cohesive unit. The Xxonox had been successful when they used superior weapons and covert tactics on under-developed planets. But when faced with a highly intelligent race that was not afraid to use force, they utterly failed.

The war was a success. The Xxonox presence in the solar system was eliminated. Their rear support group had turned around and was headed back to Zutox. The Cyn combatants had not suffered any casualties. There was no collateral damage on Earth despite the horrific battle in low earth orbit. It was estimated that eight hundred thousand Xxonox had died in that conflict. After making sure that there were no further threats, Cian ordered the fleet back to Venus. The success of the battle was relayed worldwide.

*

All around the world, from the slums of Calcutta to the condos in Boston, east to west and north to south, the golden anti-virus cloud had done its work. Like a voracious swarm of locusts, it eliminated every alien virus on the planet. As an added bonus, the anti-virus cured drug addicts from the physical addiction to any drug. It offered a chance for millions who wanted to be drug free but were slaves to their body's dependence.

News of the destruction of the invasion force was met with worldwide jubilation. The crowd around the U.N. had grown. Everyone wanted to see the alien who had saved the human race. Some broke down and cried in the streets. There was excitement and renewed hope for the future. There were a few who did not care about current events. They looted unguarded shops and ransacked cars that were hastily left unlocked in the streets around the U.N., they did not care that the question of life on other planets had been answered.

Cian's ship landed at the helipad amidst a sea of people. When he exited the ship, cheers from the crowd buffeted him. The skies overhead were clogged with news and police helicopters. F.D.R. Drive was a parking lot as frustrated drivers abandoned their cars and walked to the U.N. The East River was a solid mass of boats. The N.Y.C. Harbor Patrol and the Coast Guard tried in vain to clear a path for river traffic, to no avail. The entire world was hungry for news of the battle out in space. Anyone who owned a telescope was an instant celebrity. The Mars orbiting satellites took pictures of the aftermath of the battle and NASA's website crashed from the online demand. Every news outlet around the world reported stories of people cured of the Xxonox virus.

There were so many people crowded around the U.N. that the Secret Service could not walk or drive Cian there. They had to use a military helicopter to transport him from the helipad to the roof of the U.N. Cian once again walked across to the podium of the U.N. General Assembly. This time, he was met with thunderous applause and a standing ovation. After five minutes everyone settled down enough for Cian to address them.

"People of Earth, the Xxonox bases in your star system have been destroyed." Cian was interrupted by another standing ovation.

"We returned to finish what we started over 10,000 years ago. Our goal was to nudge your civilization into becoming a society that could traverse the stars. We were making progress when the Xxonox destroyed the work we started. They booby-trapped your upward climb from barbarism, but they were not able to stop your progress. A lot of work needs to be done to repair the damage they caused." The delegates were listening raptly and did not interrupt him.

"It takes thousands of years to build the social and technological infrastructure to colonize space. The path to the stars must be earned. This is a great responsibility and is not to be taken lightly. Our coalition of fifty stars is peaceful and freely trade with each other and we want your planet to join us. The war with the Xxonox was our first conflict and hopefully our last. You have a chance to finish what we started, but first you must undo the damage the Xxonox have done. We had a monument on Mars that had the blueprints for advancing your technology. It was destroyed thousands of years ago but we are building another repository. It will have detailed instructions on how to build an alternative energy source to replace your use of fossil fuel. You will need to send a manned mission to Mars to retrieve that information. I will leave the coordinates for that site before I depart." A low murmur steadily became louder.

"Our job here is done for now. We are going to go back to our star system soon, but we will continue to stay in contact. Our coalition has done all we can do for now, it is up to you to do the rest. When you are ready, we will return. Thank you."

Cian ended his speech and walked off amid a crowd of Secret Service agents. The room erupted into pandemonium as delegates stood up and everyone started talking at once. The Secretary-General of the U.N. took the podium.

"Everyone please sit down. I know this is all very abrupt and you have a lot of questions. The Cyn has assigned an ambassador to the U.N.; she will handle any queries you have. Please be seated." The Secretary-General repeated his demand for order. Events had moved too fast and it was too much to take in all at once. The room suddenly quieted and everyone took their seat as a female Cyn stepped onto the stage. No one had really thought about it, but they had assumed that all Cyn were male like Cian. The tall, stately female Cyn slowly walked across the room to the podium. She was six feet, five inches tall and carried her heavier weight well. She weighed two hundred and six pounds, her bones were denser and her muscle structure more compact to withstand the heavier gravity of her planet. But when she turned her large, purple eyes on the audience there was no doubt that she was definitely a woman. She had a bounce to her step as she stepped up to the podium and adjusted the microphone.

"Hello. My name is Cy'ja. I have been assigned as the Cyn ambassador to your planet. I am here to answer all of your questions." Cy'ja's voice was melodic and higher pitched than Cian's. A flurry of hands went up and the air was filled with the cacophony of hundreds of different languages. Cian was just about to leave the assembly room. He turned around and saw Cy'ja addressing the assembly. He got into the elevator and rode it up to the roof helipad level. Cian had requested a private meeting with the President after the U.N. speech and Secret Service agents were escorting him to the White House.

*

Cian was rushed to the President's Marine One helicopter. The blades were already spinning and it took off as soon as he was inside. Along with two armed Apache helicopters, it flew at its top speed to the White House.

When it landed on the White House lawn, armed agents escorted Cian through a heavily guarded door. He was taken to a high-level security room where the President was already waiting. When Cian entered, the President motioned the guard to close the door. A vibration shook the floor as a bulletproof panel slid into place behind the door.

The President motioned Cian to a comfortable sofa in the corner of the room and sat across from him.

"Cian, I want to thank you again on behalf of the human race for your help." The President reached out and shook Cian's hand. He tried to hide his surprise at how warm and human-like Cian's hands felt.

"Mr. President, we were unprepared for the Xxonox when they attacked us. In all of the millions of years of our civilization, we had never come across a destructive species like the Xxonox. Our council chose your planet because your race has the potential to evolve and then join our coalition. We could not allow the Xxonox to destroy that future." Cian bent his head closer. "I wanted to talk to you privately because the war is not over yet. We won the battle in space and against their virus, but there is one more situation to handle. We have identified two hundred and twenty four humans who are agents of the Xxonox. They were implanted with commands to create dissent and chaos. This has been going on for ten thousand years and they are still active."

"What?" The President frowned. "How can they still be alive after 10,000 years?"

"There is a part of every living entity that continues to live on after the body dies. Eons ago we learned to control that process and keep our memories intact when we shift to a new body." Cian explained, but the President still looked dubious.

"Cian, I am a religious person. In my faith we believe that when we die we go to heaven or hell. I don't know about reincarnation. However, a few weeks ago, I didn't think there was any intelligent life out in the universe. That ignorance almost cost us our lives and I don't want to make that mistake again." He spread his hands, " I'll trust what you tell me, even if I don't understand it."

"Thank you, Mr. President. In this last mission, we can advise but we cannot be directly involved. If you allow them to continue in your society they will find a way to destroy it. They are enemies of humanity. They have transponders and they can still be contacted and manipulated by the Xxonox."

"Tell me where they are, Cian." The President's expression grew grim. "We have highly trained soldiers who can take them quickly and quietly." He reached for the red phone on the desk to the side of him to call in the Secretary of Defense. Cian softly touched the President's hand and stopped him.

"Mr. President, you cannot kill them. What I mean is, you can kill their bodies but you can't kill the beings inside. Killing them is only a temporary solution, they would simply reincarnate and continue on with their mission." The President pulled his hand away from the phone and leaned back, his frown deepening.

"We learned about this Xxonox cabal many years ago. After a lot of study we worked out a solution to that problem. Our scientists developed an extractor ray. The beam is tuned to the Xxonox tracker's wavelength and pulls the being out of its body. They will then be sealed into special containers. After you have collected all of them, they will be buried in a cave in a secret location on Venus. Their Xxonox imprint will fade away after 8,000 years. At that time they will be released and can be educated back into society."

The President was taken aback. Aliens invading the Earth were easier to believe in than reincarnation.

"What happens to the bodies after their souls are extracted?" He shook his head in disbelief.

"Their bodies will continue to function. They will be able to walk, talk, and eat but without the being which had been animating it." Cian felt the President's inner turmoil.

"Mr. President, I understand these concepts are new to you. If the future of your race were not in question, I would not have brought this subject up. Our space society does not interfere with the political, religious, or moral beliefs of any planetary culture. To help you understand further, I want to show you something." Cian took out a small, metallic tablet and laid it flat on the coffee table between them. He pressed a button on the side and a high-definition, 3-D image appeared in the air above it. Cian touched a 3-D button on the floating screen and an image of an Al-Qaeda leader appeared.

"This image was taken yesterday." Cian indicated the 3-D picture. Superimposed around the man's head were bright red points in the shape of a pyramid.

"These markers indicate exactly where in the brain the Xxonox imprint is located." Cian touched another button image and brushed his fingers across the screen. The man's picture flickered and kaleidoscoped into a cascade of different faces.

"Those are his past lives." Cian moved his hand left to right and made the images scroll until he stopped on one frame. He tapped a blinking green symbol, which opened a column of lists in an alien language.

"This is written in Cyn, it is a synopsis of this man's crimes during that lifetime." Cian translated some of the items on the list until the President turned pale at its brutishness.

"This being lived 165 lifetimes since his first contact with the Xxonox. What I have read is only a small sample of his atrocities." Cian tapped another floating icon and the 3-D screen collapsed back into the tablet.

"Cian, I must tell you the idea of living lifetime after lifetime scares me and goes against everything I believe in. Regardless of how I feel, I do not want any vestige of the Xxonox left around. I will do everything in my power to root them out." After the meeting, the President arranged an emergency session with the Joint Chiefs of Staff.

Chapter Thirty-Nine

Deep in the bowels of the Pentagon, men from SEAL Team Six, the 1st Special Forces Operational Detachment-Delta, were getting briefed on a bizarre mission. On the table in front of the Operations Chief lay twenty odd-looking guns. Boxes of metallic canisters the size of beer cans were on a separate table. Along with the SEAL team there was a DEA special operations group headed up by DEA special agent, Carlos Martinez.

"Gentlemen, we are tasked with eliminating the last of the Xxonox influence on our race." The Chief went on to briefly explain what Abn had done to the group of men so many thousands of years ago and the damages since then.

"I know this sounds fantastic and to be honest with you, I found it hard to believe myself." He gestured to a large pile of folders. "These are the dossiers of the 224 human Xxonox agents, along with an outline of their crimes. I can tell you this, they have been responsible for the deaths of millions of people." He pulled down a screen behind him. On it was a map with 224 locations marked worldwide.

"We are going to send out twenty search and snatch teams. Each group will be assigned to an area. Some of the targets are civilians. Others we would love to double-tap and kill right there. But under no circumstances are you to kill them. They need to be alive to hold the being in place so we can extract them. Avoid collateral damage, but if anyone interferes, you have the authorization to use deadly force as necessary to carry out the mission. The filled canisters are A-1 top priority and must be protected and transported to your coded coordinates. From there they will be taken care of by the Cyn." The Chief picked up one of the guns on the table along with a gadget similar to a TV's remote control.

"This is a detector that picks up the signal from the Xxonox implanted tracker. The arrow on the screen indicates distance and direction to the target. The Cyn calibrate each one to a particular target." He put down the detector. This looks like a gun but it doesn't shoot anything, it does the opposite – it pulls things in." He went to the table with the canisters, lifted one up and smartly snapped it into a bracket above the pistol.

"The red light on the left side of the pistol grip indicates the extractor is primed and ready to go. An LED light in front of the muzzle will blink yellow when the target is within range, which is about fifty feet. When the target is extracted all the lights will turn blue. When that occurs, pull the trigger again and it seals the canister. We have a simulation room set up so you can practice and get a feel for it."

"Any questions?" A SEAL operative in the back raised his hand and the Chief beckoned him to speak.

"Sir, what happens if we accidently kill them before they are extracted?"

"From what I've been told, when the body dies the person's soul leaves and moves away quickly. The extractor gun only works if the being is in physical contact with its brain. We have no way to trap it once free of the body. It can then plug into any baby at birth and start his criminal life all over again. In other words, don't fuck up and kill them first." That brought a chuckle from the men. There were no further questions.

The Chief called out the twenty groups and their team leaders and gave them their list of targets. Carlos was in charge of the DEA group. His experience in the field in Latin America, and his initial investigation of the Xxonox, gave him the honor of heading up that section. Carlos' team was tasked with five targets in Mexico and South America. Once operational procedures were completed, each group went about securing their targets.

*

Deep in the jungles of Mexico, Carlos' camouflaged team melted into the trees and broad leaves around them. The man they were after was Manuel 'Diablo' Torres Munoz, the head of Los Zetas. They used the Xxonox tracker as a GPS signal and found him in an uncharted jungle in a makeshift camp. It was 2:30 a.m. and the Los Zeta soldiers were either asleep or passed out drunk. His team slipped quietly into their camp. A cartel man got up to take a piss. As he was unzipping his pants he looked up and saw five men with weapons trained on him just two feet away. Despite the cluster of red laser lights on his chest, he grabbed for his weapon. The plan had called for no shooting unless it was absolutely necessary. A Special Ops team member went for the cartel guard with his combat knife. He aimed for the throat to stifle any screams, but the man got out a yell before the blade severed his windpipe. The commotion awoke the Los Zetas soldiers. They were in a stupor, but they were trained killers and went for their weapons. A brief firefight broke the silence of the sleeping jungle. When the skirmish was over, ten Los Zetas men were dead and only one of Carlos' men was wounded.

The Zeta chief had been naked in bed with a woman when the gunfire broke out. Before he could reach his weapon, two of Carlos' men jumped him and held him down. The woman he was with was given clothes and escorted out of the room. The prisoner cursed and yelled loudly for his men. The silence told him his men were already dead. Carlos entered the room and aimed his extractor at the man. The trigger sight was blinking hard and the weapon was primed.

That was the first time Carlos had used the gun on a live person, he did not know what to expect. He pressed the trigger and involuntarily braced for the recoil. The Zeta chief stopped cursing, his mouth went slack and he became eerily quiet. His expressionless face was devoid of personality, his body relaxed and he stopped resisting. The men who had been holding him released their grip. The Zeta man sat on his bed listlessly. The canister's light was a steady bright blue, indicating that it was filled. They had extracted and contained the first Xxonox operative on their list.

The sound of an approaching helicopter echoed through the jungle. Carlos had called it in to extract the wounded soldier. They hurriedly searched the room and took the Zeta's smart phones and laptops. After the wounded agent was evacuated, Carlos and the rest of his men went back into the jungle and rendezvoused with a river extraction team.

The chief's body, devoid of the spirit of Manuel "Diablo" Torres Munoz which had animated it, was an empty shell. It sat still and quiet and stared blankly out into the jungle.

*

The extraction teams traveled worldwide collecting the rest of the Xxonox saboteurs. They were extracted from areas in South Africa, Mexico, and China. The most challenging one was the president of North Korea, but that target was extracted without incident.

One team was ordered to do an extraction on a public figure that was also a secret member of the Federal Reserve Bank. He was involved with the Bilderberg Group and another clandestine cabal, which secretly manipulated governments around the world. His public persona was pristine but his dossier listed financial crimes that had taken down governments around the world. His past lives listed him as a Rothschild in the 1800's as well as the financial advisor to Genghis Khan. He was secretly involved in destabilizing the Euro at the time of his extraction. He used money the way terrorists used bombs.

Target number two was a difficult mission for Carlos because the extraction involved a one-year-old baby. The baby's parents were a poor peasant couple that lived outside of Cali, Colombia. When Carlos had first seen the target in the dossier, he wasn't sure if he could follow through with it. He changed his mind after he read the description of who was in the baby's body; it was Raul "Cojones" Melendez.

The file had a list of all Raul's past lives starting from his life as Serhann. The list of his crimes in his former lifetimes was horrifying to read. But nothing could top Raul's role in almost destroying the human race. When Carlos looked again at the picture, he saw Raul in the baby's eyes and resolved to carry out the mission. He was also consoled by the fact that the baby would not physically die. An info sheet explained that after Raul's death, his soul left his body and he went looking for an uninhabited newborn's body, but he could not find one. In desperation he settled on the peasant's infant. The baby already had a soul in it, but Raul swamped and overwhelmed the being and took over the tiny body. Raul hoped to live in hiding until his stolen body was old enough so that he could rebuild his empire.

*

Carlo's men approached the house stealthily. It was a late night raid and the village was asleep. They snaked a hose into the hut while the parents were sleeping and filled the room with a narcotic gas to keep them from waking up during the operation. The extraction team entered the house quietly; the only sounds were the frogs in the jungle and the parent's snores.

The baby was lying on a pallet beside the parent's bed, quietly asleep. The men surrounded the makeshift crib as Carlos inserted a canister into his extractor gun. Sensing danger, the baby suddenly opened his bloodshot eyes. He looked up at the men surrounding his crib and there was a light of recognition in his eyes. The baby began to scream. Before his cries could wake up the village, Carlos pulled the trigger. Instantly the baby quieted and his body completely relaxed. The child was asleep and unharmed. Carlos was relieved, he would have felt sick if he had to harm a young child.

The extraction team quietly filed out of the room and dispersed into the jungle. At the doorway, Carlos took one last look at the crib. The baby had awakened. His eyes were wide open; he looked directly at Carlos as if to say 'thank you.'

The infant let out a little laugh and began playing with his toes. The original soul of the baby had returned and he was happy to have regained his small body. Carlos smiled and felt much better. He had saved this family from raising a devil and had given them back their real child. The team quietly left the village unseen and unheard.

*

The peasant man and his wife awoke later than usual with

a slight headache. The wife bent over the bed and picked up an awake and lively baby. He had been colicky and cranky the last couple of months and it had taken a toll on the family. An unseen, dark presence had settled like a dark cloud over the baby. The couple had wanted to take the child to a shaman but the closest one was too far to walk and they couldn't afford transportation. The infant locked eyes with his mother, drooled happily and said *"mami."* The mother sensed that the darkness over her child had lifted and her precious bebé was back. She rose out of bed and danced around the room swinging the laughing baby around. The dad looked on with a sigh of relief. He got out of bed and joined them.

*

After all two hundred and twenty four beings had been extracted, the canisters were turned over to the Cyn. They took the disembodied prisoners to Venus and buried them deep in a cave. The entrance was then buried with tons of hot Venusian boulders and sulfur-laden regolith.

Inside the canister labeled X13, the being known as Raul was conscious. He was aware that he was without his body. It was his soul that was incarcerated. Outside the portal of his cell he could see the inside of a cave. The other two hundred and twenty three prisons were set in niches in the cave wall. He had been put asleep during transport and he had no idea where he was. It was oppressively hot and a flatulent odor leaked into his canister. The air outside was heavy and thick as hot molasses. Try as he might, he could not escape his jail. This was now his new home.

Time crawled to a standstill. There was no way to mark time as seconds stretched into hours and hours into days. Raul had 8,000 years until his sentence was up. His soul was incarcerated for what would feel to him like eternity. With that realization, he quietly went mad.

Chapter Forty

A year after the war between the Cyn and the Xxonox, the Earth was going through a transition. Nations had joined together to form a new world government and wrote up the Constitution of Earth. It let countries keep their identities, local laws and culture. They were united in the progress of mankind. A space program was created which harkened back to the heady days of the Apollo Space Program. The world combined its resources to send a ten man, international mission to Mars within two years.

The survivors who had been addicted to Melendez Blue were cured of any addiction to any drug, a side effect of the Cyn's counter-virus. Drug cartels around the world collapsed due to lack of demand, which was the only way drug trafficking could ever have been stopped. The poppy farmers of Afghanistan found better profit growing food. In Colombia, coffee beans replaced coca leaves as a cash crop.

Muslims and Jews, Catholics and Christians came together at an international conference. Each religion re-interpreted their holy works to include aliens in God's plan. This took the wind out of most terrorist Islamic groups and started humanity on the road to religious peace in the Middle East and around the world. Hard-core extremist groups died out, ostracized by their own countrymen. There was excitement worldwide and hope for the future. Slowly but surely, the tide began to turn for the human race.

*

Carlos was enjoying the weekend at home enjoying a beer when he received a call from Paul.

"Hey Carlos, how's it going?" The double click on his phone's receiver told him this was a secured, encrypted call.

"I am doing alright, things have been quiet around the office. Not much going on, same shit, different day. How are things with you and Joy?" Paul and Joy had married three months earlier and Carlos had been the best man.

"Everything is going great. I've been out of town a lot so I wanted to get her a small dog to keep her company. A few weeks ago, I was at a conference at the DEA office in Portland. I had some time on my hands and decided to go to the Oregon Humane Society and look at rescue dogs. I was just window-shopping, but the cutest dog caught my attention. It only had one eye and an oversized eye-patch on the other. As soon as it saw me it jumped up, wagged its tail and I swear it smiled at me. The nametag on its cage said its name was Merry. Anyway, I brought the dog back with me and Joy loved it. And this is the weirdest thing, a month after that, Joy became pregnant!"

"Wow that's great, Paul. Hey, if it's a boy you better have his middle name be Carlos and if it's a girl, shit, still name her Carlos." He laughed.

"If it's a boy, you got it. If it's a girl, you are shit out of luck. Joy already picked out a name, Maryann." Carlos chuckled and then Paul became serious. "The reason I called is because we uncovered a plot to assassinate Ambassador Cy'ja and I need your help." Paul's tone turned serious. Carlos shifted mental gears.

"I'm all ears." Carlos' previous frivolity was gone.

"Do you remember Manuel "Diablo" Torres Munoz?" Paul asked.

"Sure, he was the Zeta guy we extracted and turned over to the Cyn."

"Your extraction team brought back his computer hard drives and USB sticks and we turned them over to the CIA. They uncovered a plot to assassinate Cy'ja using Zeta hit men. And this part is what really concerned us, they were hired to do so by Al Qaeda."

"Holy shit!" Carlos sat up straight.

"Holy shit is right. The CIA followed up on some leads gleaned from the Zeta's data files and found that the Al Qaeda group was just the tip of an iceberg for a radical political party in Iran."

Carlos was silent for a few moments. "Why would Iran be interested in having Cy'ja killed?"

"When Cian gave his talk to the U.N. he mentioned there was technology in the Mars repository to free us from our dependence on oil. Evidently, this ruffled the feathers of some Middle East oil groups. Oil stocks have plummeted hard. I guess they figured if Cy'ja was killed then the Cyn would retract their offer to help us. To keep the world addicted to oil, they're willing to throw away humanity's future. Don't ya love it?" Paul could barely restrain his anger.

"OK, Paul I'm in. What do you need me to do?" Carlos straightened up in his chair.

"Thanks, Carlos. Cy'ja is scheduled to go to Mexico City next week. I would like you to be in charge of her security detail. Can you report to the Cyn Consulate tomorrow morning? I can schedule you for a meeting with Ambassador Cy'ja at 9:00 am."

"Yes sir, that's fine. I will be there." Carlos hung up. It was great to get back in the field. He was even more excited to meet Ambassador Cy'ja. He had been in the U.N. hall when Cian introduced her and he had immediately liked her.

The next day, Carlos found a parking spot near McPherson Park and walked the ten blocks to the Cyn Consulate in Washington, D.C. He could have parked in their secure garage, but it was a nice day and he wanted some time to settle himself before his meeting. On the way, he stopped by a Starbucks and ordered his favorite, Cinnamon Dolce Latte. He arrived and checked in at the front desk. A Marine embassy guard escorted him to the Ambassador's office. When he walked in, Ambassador Cy'ja stood up from her desk, walked over to him and shook his hand.

"Hello, Officer Martinez, I'm happy to meet you." Her melodic voice left Carlos at a loss for words. In her presence, he could feel the warmth of her soul and her large eyes drew him in. Carlos felt like a teenager. He had not expected to have such a reaction to her. He was speechless and embarrassed that he still held her hand after the handshake.

"Oh sorry, Ambassador Cy'ja, pardon my manners. I am happy to meet you." He finally got the words out, stumbling over them.

"It is okay, Carlos." Cy'ja gave him a large smile. "Please have a seat." She indicated the plush sofa in the office and sat next to him, and simply looked at him. At first, Carlos was uncomfortable under her stare but then he relaxed. He felt as if he had known her for a long time.

"Officer Martinez, I understand there is a plot against my life and that you are in charge of my safety?"

"Yes Ma'am, but please, call me Carlos." He winked and then nearly blushed. He could not believe he had just flirted with an alien woman who represented an advanced, intergalactic civilization. He cleared his throat.

"I have the full resources of our country on this. There is no need to worry. The assassination network has already been neutralized. We are just taking a few extra precautions. You will be safe." As he said this, Carlos twitched his nose and smiled to put her at ease. The smell of cinnamon from his coffee wafted over to her. To his horror, tears suddenly welled up in her eyes.

"I'm so sorry, did I say something wrong?" He started to get to his feet, but she put out her hand to stop him.

"Carlos, we have met before." Cy'ja's voice was tremulous and laced with deep emotion. Carlos silently shook his head. He would certainly have remembered if he had met her in person before today.

"It was many thousands of years ago. At that time, you were known as Closar." Cy'ja reached into a pocket and took out necklaces of purple and blue precious stones. "These were our gems. I have kept them for over ten thousand years in the hope that we would meet again." Carlos looked at the stones in her hands and a flood of memories rushed through him.

He raised his head and looked deep into her eyes. Cy'ja opened her mind to his and Carlos relived those days in prehistoric Turkey and the love they had shared. He felt a deep sadness as he recalled his death on the banks of the river. He had died with the regret that he did not get a chance to say good-bye to Cy'ja and tell her how much he loved her. Snippets of other past lives rose to the surface of his mind. Carlos realized that he had been looking for Cy'ja lifetime after lifetime, until his quest drowned in the sea of time.

"Cy'ja I love you, I have always loved you. My body was buried in that lifetime, but not my love." Carlos leaned over and kissed her. Their lips touched and ten thousand years of being apart was forgotten. Cy'ja pulled away from their kiss and looked into his eyes.

"We will never be apart again, Carlos," Cy'ja whispered. She went to her desk and pushed her secretary's call button.

"Patricia, please cancel the rest of my appointments for today." Cy'ja turned off the overhead lights and sat back down on the couch. She opened her hand with the pendants. One had a dazzling blue sapphire attached to it and the other a purple amethyst gem. She slipped the sapphire pendant over Carlos' head and then turned around so that he could fasten the clasp of her necklace. They kissed again and time stood still for them as they filled the empty bucket of their last ten thousand years.

Chapter Forty-One

Deep in the jungle outside of what was left of the Melendez compound, the shaman held an audience with his tribe. It was high noon. The sun boiled the damp jungle floor and sent steamy tendrils into the still air. The shaman was standing on a small hill, his people spread out below him. The heat was forgotten as his words flowed over the throng like a cool breeze.

"Last night, I had a vision. The people of the white light destroyed the snakes and scorpions at the bottom of the pit. The pestilence that was knocking on our door has been swallowed up by the gold dust from the heavens. The world outside of our little village has changed for the better. The hidden evil has been removed and the path to our destiny is now clear." On cue, an eagle flew through the sky above the village. As the villagers watched, the eagle spiraled into the sun until it disappeared. The villagers saw that as a good omen. They dispersed amid excited small talk and laughter. No one had seen the sickly crow on the branch of a dead tree at the jungle's edge. It cawed twelve times, once for every hundred years before the world would end. When it croaked out its last cry, it fell lifeless to the ground below.

The shaman was alone when he sensed a presence behind him. He turned around and saw his spirit guide in its blue hummingbird form. It had lost its avatar body in the battle with the alien demon and had created another one. The tiny bird darted around his head, its wings a blur. It gently settled on his shoulder and displayed its contentment with soft, clicking sounds. The shaman looked into the sky in the direction of the constellation Taurus and bowed his head.

"*Gracias.*" He said under his breath and slowly walked to his hut and to a new future.

Epilogue

Laurie Patra's jog along Clearwater Beach drew stares. Her bleached blond hair flowed behind her like the mane of a lion. The women looked at her with envy and men stared at her as she passed them. They looked lustily at the way her thong disappeared between her bouncing tight cheeks. Her athletic, tanned legs caused a beach volleyball player to lose his concentration and a spiked ball six-packed him in his face. Laurie was peripherally aware of the looks she was getting. Behind her sunglasses her blue eyes were cold and uncaring. She reached her multimillion dollar condo at the end of the strip, barely out of breath after her eight mile run. The security sensors recognized her and the doors opened automatically. If anyone else had tried to gain entry they would have been met with a soporific gas that would have rendered them unconscious. Last year she caught a trespasser that way. He was never seen or heard from again. His body lay at the bottom of the Gulf of Mexico, minus his penis.

Laurie removed her skimpy bikini and her wig before she got into the shower. She eyed her lithe body in the full-length mirror. The platinum cap on her shaved head was a stark contrast to her darkly tanned olive skin. After her shower she remained naked and sat on the leather couch and turned on the TV. She poured a large glass of Shiraz wine and turned the channel to CNN Earth. Most of the news was about the Cyn and the manned mission to Mars to retrieve the technological treasures stored there.

"Damn the Cyn!" Laurie said under her breath and spat out an ancient curse. If the beachgoers could have seen her then, her baleful eyes and the black aura that surrounded her would have overshadowed the beauty of her body. Unconsciously she rubbed her metallic skullcap. It was smooth except for the Velcro along its edges that held her wig. Titanium bolts screwed into her skull kept it firmly attached to her scalp. She had it specially made to shield the emanations of the Xxonox tracker implanted in her soul. She could recall clearly that fateful day over 10,000 years ago, when she was Lejla the Unspeakable. That was the night she became a disciple of the Xxonox along with the other two hundred and twenty four brethren from the cave. She had been psychically connected to them and had winced as they were extracted, captured and then imprisoned on Venus. Her clairvoyant powers had foreseen Cian's plan to use the Xxonox transponders to find and capture them.

Her skullcap was a theta-wavelength Faraday cage that blocked any emissions from her implant. The Cyn did not know of her existence and she had escaped their purge. It was safe now; Cian no longer monitored that frequency. However, she played it safe and kept the cap on except for short periods of time. Laurie took a sip of wine and undid the platinum latches and removed the cap. It came off with a wet, sucking sound.

The skin underneath was wrinkled and white as a sheet of paper. Her hair had been cut and made into a wig and her hair follicles destroyed with electrolysis. As soon as she removed the helmet she received a telepathic message. It was a communication from her contact in the Supreme Council on Zutox Prime. She poured some more wine and smiled. The Xxonox retribution was coming.

The End

Afterword

The idea for my story came to me while I was watching an episode about 'Cocaine Subs' on the National Geographic channel. The next morning and for the next six weeks, I wrote nonstop. When I was done I had a rough draft of my story that I had my friends and family read. How my test readers were able to read through my incomplete sentences, misaligned tenses and chopped up grammar is beyond me. However, the positive feedback from them was encouraging. My test reader's questions about the plot and the characters helped me to expand on both. I realized that those six weeks of frenzied writing had only produced an outline of my novel. I spent the next year and a half fleshing out the novel and adding additional characters that insisted on being part of the story.

A book cannot be written in a vacuum. I had a lot of help from my test readers who were kind enough to let me use them as guinea pigs. They managed to navigate through my rough drafts and gave me insights into my own work. I had a lot of editing help and suggestions and in particular I want to thank Patricia Felton, Jim Niece and Debbie Gelfer for their invaluable help and support and everyone who gave me their input. I want to also acknowledge my editor Mary Rosenblum for helping me straighten out the spaghetti mess of some of my story plots.

Biography

Efrain Palermo was born in Brooklyn, New York on April 26, 1954 to Puerto Rican parents. He has always been fascinated by space and science from an early age and has pursued those interests throughout his life. When the Mars rover missions began their study of Mars, he became interested in the images stored in NASA's archives and discovered a correlation between the dark streaks of Mars and water on its surface. He co-authored a paper on the seeps of Mars and presented it to a Mars Society Convention held at Stanford University in 2001. He also hosts the 'The Mars Anomaly Podcast' and popularized an unknown formation he discovered on Mars' moon Phobos that became known as the Monolith of Phobos.

Efrain Palermo lives in Portland, Oregon. This is his first novel and will be followed by the second book in the series, 'Tides of Retribution.' For more information please visit the website at www.palermoproject.com. The author can be e-mailed at: alien-cartel@palermoproject.com.

Made in the USA
San Bernardino, CA
31 January 2015